THE
DEFECTIONS

THE DEFECTIONS

HANNAH MICHELL

First published in Great Britain in 2014 by

Quercus Editions Ltd
55 Baker Street
7th Floor, South Block
London W1U 8EW

A CIP catalogue record for this book is available
from the British Library

HB ISBN 978 1 78206 255 4
TPB ISBN 978 1 78206 256 1
EBOOK ISBN 978 1 78206 257 8

For my mothers

I suppose animals kept in cages, and so scantily fed as to be always upon the verge of famine, await their food as I awaited a letter. Oh! – to speak truth, and drop that tone of a false calm which long to sustain, outwears nature's endurance – I underwent in those seven weeks bitter fears and pains, strange inward trials, miserable defections of hope, intolerable encroachments of despair. This last came so near me sometimes that her breath went right through me. I used to feel it like a baleful air or sigh, penetrate deep, and make motion pause at my heart, or proceed only under unspeakable oppression. The letter – the well-beloved letter – would not come; and it was all of sweetness in life I had to look for.

Charlotte Brontë, *Villette*

1979

Mia was born the night the President was shot. It was the night of betrayals, her stepmother was accustomed to saying, and strange things had happened all over the city of Seoul, as though the day had signed its name in red ink. The President was shot by his own right-hand man, the Director of Intelligence. It had been the end of a long dictatorship, but that was never the point.

'What happened to the President, it's like what your father did to me,' her stepmother said, pausing as she ran a blade across the chestnut shell in her fingers.

Her stepmother spoke of this betrayal sitting cross-legged on the hardwood floors, peeling persimmons or preparing root vegetables. Mia watched as the knife's edge sank into her stepmother's thumb but no blood seeped out. Later Mia mimicked the very same motion alone in the kitchen, to the detriment of her fingers, and came to believe her stepmother possessed powers of black magic.

Her stepmother would blink hard when describing Mia's delivery – of how she was passed from doctor to nurse – as though the story's passage hurt her throat. Mia was a tiny thing, pink and raw. They examined the flatness of her nose, the thin, narrow lines of her sunken eyes. These things they had come to expect from a newborn.

'But it was your green eyes,' she would add. 'It was a reminder of the line crossed. Borders disobeyed.'

Bad luck befell everyone present in the delivery room at the time of her birth. The attending nurse lost her only son during a routine military exercise. The doctor contracted a rare heart disease from a patient. Her Appa had a stroke that left him paralysed and unable to speak. And Mia's mother disappeared.

Or so the story went.

This was the version of her arrival to the world that she was spoon-fed when she first came to live with her stepmother at the age of five. Over the years, other variations of that fateful night in 1979 were told. Her stepmother preached about her charity in bringing Mia home – a baby left in a sack of pebbles by the Han River, the Christian life they led in taking in a child turned away from the orphanage. In other versions, she was described as a disposable rag doll of yellow hair and grey eyes, left at the bottom of Hooker Hill.

During these stories her Appa, who had not spoken for as long as Mia could remember, sat on the stone step leading to the courtyard, while his wife salted and rubbed chilli flakes into the cabbage to prepare the *kimchi*. He would gaze for hours at the dying Ginkgo tree in the garden. Mia knew he was listening from the way he turned scraps of newspaper between the fingers of his good hand, crumpling them at certain parts of her stepmother's stories and then smoothing them out again over his knee at others. When they were alone, he would try to speak to her and nothing but a raspy croak would come out of his throat. He ripped out colorful propaganda campaigns from old magazines and put them in Mia's hands. In his later years, when he found solace in painting, he would produce ghostly figurines moving across vast landscapes.

But this never gave Mia any clues about her mother, who was never mentioned in the house, and, out of sympathy for her father, she had refused to speak until her uncle had coaxed her out of her silence. She clutched at snippets of memory – the whiff of nutmeg in her mother's hair, her heavy sighs when she held Mia to her chest – small fragile memories which Mia pitted against the lies she was told. She became deft at sticking herself to walls, eavesdropping on her stepmother and uncle as they talked about her father's condition. If there was one thing she learned, it was that truth was changeable, and Mia could not pierce their stories in quite the same way that she pierced the sliding rice-paper doors of her stepmother's room.

2008

Summer

Mia sat by the window with her back turned to the reports she had brought home from the Embassy, work she knew she would be hard pressed to finish before the end of the week. She could hear the neighbour's dog moving about in the yard, his metal lead dragging across the gravel. He was prone to long fits of barking which almost everyone had learned to ignore. The approaching monsoon announced itself in the thickness of her damp T-shirt. She lit a cigarette and switched on the small fan by her desk; exhaled through the mosquito net covering her window.

Always there was this reluctance to begin her work. A fear that she would get it wrong. Every translation was a test. Proof that she too could be one of them. She absent-mindedly circled the word 'Yongguk'. England, she wrote. Literal translation: 'Great Nation'. Country of tea, gentlemen with top hats, Big Ben, 'Dah-ling' and 'Dear' and English women at Embassy parties who turned their backs to her when she approached them.

This anxiety for perfection had been heightened by the arrival of the new political counsellor, Thomas Dalton-Ellis, who replaced old Willis after he had retired early some months before, on account of his emphysema. Dalton-Ellis was taller and younger than any of his predecessors, often came to the office without a tie and with his shirt sleeves rolled back. An Embassy darling, it was rumoured that diplomacy had trickled down through several generations of his family. In contrast to the American soldiers, whose bodies Mia had come to know so well, Thomas seemed long-limbed and lanky, but since his arrival, there had been a noticeable increase in the attendance of Embassy wives at official events. Dresses became more extravagant. His presence provoked an aspiration of some sort in everyone. Mia thought of Mrs Christie who had fluttered from one person to the next at the Ambassador's birthday drinks, touching her husband's guests on the arm with practised affect. Mia had watched her, mimicking the movement of her lips, practising her enunciation, trying to feel the crisp 'T's on the tip of her teeth, just as she heard them on the BBC. Mrs Christie had spoken at length with Thomas, gazing up at him in a sparkling way that she had held back from the other guests. Mrs Christie had laughed at something Thomas said and her body shook. Then she had checked herself, and smoothed the back of her hair, the nape of her neck.

Thomas's arrival had resurrected an old uneasiness, a self-consciousness in Mia. A sense that she teetered on a tightrope, on the verge of being banished from a world that could be her birthright. Suddenly precision in her work became of the utmost importance. She took another drag of her cigarette and wrote: 'The Korean chamber of commerce and industry, the largest and most influential business federation in Korea, representing...' and stopped. Her translations occasionally provoked a twitch on the side of Thomas's mouth. He would make an offhand comment about Americanisms, and then her tea-stained reports would appear at the bottom of his wastebasket. When she tried to confront him her tongue swelled to twice its size. He was never direct. There was something in his restraint that she wanted to unravel. His eyes and mouth were in constant opposition. His mischievous lips were perpetually on the verge of either a pout or a lopsided ironic smile. She could never tell whether he was joking or serious.

Through the thin, yellowing floors she could hear her stepmother,

Kyung-ha, moving around in the kitchen downstairs. She extinguished the cigarette in her fingers and resented the adolescent impulse to do so. She was an adult of almost thirty, but the unearthly pitch of Kyung-ha's voice still had the power to freeze her blood.

She returned her attention to the translations. Was there an entire world held back behind the stiff upper lip of the English? Did they feel the same emotions as the Koreans? Was it merely that they lacked the words to express them? There were endless adjectives for sadness in Korean. She imagined her English translations of these words as thieves with holes at the bottom of their already undersized sacks. Mia tapped her pen against her desk. Did this make Koreans more articulate or more emotional? Her stepmother never held back in expressing herself. The sting of her stepmother's hand on her face could bring her back to focus.

The dog across the road began to bark again. She wished it could be put out of its misery. She lit another cigarette. Relief seemed more important than any consequent retribution. After all, there was little Mia could do to inspire her stepmother to hit her these days. And strangely, she felt this as a growing lack of interest. After Mia's hospitalization, her stepmother had grown distant. The reason for the absence of beatings did not seem to be Mia's vulnerability. In fact, her stepmother had hardly acknowledged that she had almost died. She had begun her translations in hospital. In converting one word to another, all was not lost. Meanings could be salvaged and carried across borders.

What about words like *jeong*? How could she explain that? Affection, she wrote. She scratched at the word with the pencil. Affection had a ring of choice about the matter. Affection alone would not cover it. *Jeong* was more a-deep-attachment-rooted-in-shared-history-regardless-of-whether-you-like-it-or-not.

★

13

Mia stopped writing at the sound of her uncle Han-su's voice from the kitchen below. There was something heavy and urgent in the way he spoke. Over the years, she had grown accustomed to the visits where her uncle would announce a political arrest or the interrogation of one of his students at the school he ran for North Korean defectors. Since they had stopped speaking, Mia had tried to acquire a deafness to the turn in his voice, but the anguish in it today was hard to ignore. She had once adored him after all.

'*Aigoo*, you can't carry that burden as your own. You gave him every opportunity. You gave him an education, you helped him get on his feet,' she said.

The unfamiliar consolation in her stepmother's voice was particularly alarming. She was not normally like that with her brother-in-law. Mia rose from her chair and drew closer to the edge of the room, where the floorboards were thinner. She picked at the linoleum in the corner and rolled it back, exposing a narrow crack through to the kitchen. She saw her uncle wipe his face with a handkerchief.

'It wasn't enough,' he was saying. 'They say Myung-chul was hanging from the shower railing for hours before he was found. Think of his parents. Still in the North. Imagining that their son is alive and well. That hope alone must keep them alive. And they don't even know . . .'

'You have to think of all the kids who are in a better place because of your school.'

She let go and the linoleum rolled itself flat with a slap. She had heard enough. Over the years she had been tormented by these stories of her uncle's students. Those who had broken free and risked their lives: ripping their hands on barbed wire, swimming through frozen rivers, past snipers and brokers and people who would trade them for a copper pipe or scrap metal. They survived to kiss the gravel of their dream land. And yet they suffered, still. She had concealed her fear of these stories from her uncle. He didn't know why she had refused to work with him and had been outraged when she had announced that she wanted to work at the British Embassy. He had spent his whole life resisting government bodies, participating in movements against the dictatorship. There had been almost a decade when he had had no permanent address and had survived on the charity of friends who had concealed him in their homes. The idea that his own niece, whom he had come to see as a daughter, would work for a government institution was taken as a personal affront.

She retreated down the ladder outside of the washroom and crossed the courtyard, past the blue gate leading to the street, to her father's room, kicking off her shoes as she slid open the door.

Her Appa was leaning over a painting in the corner of the room. He gave her a crooked smile. His low table was cluttered with opened paint pots and dirty brushes of different sizes.

'What is this?'

He was painting what looked like a skeleton walking across a desert plain.

'Well, that's pretty creepy.'

Her father's face seemed to fall a little with disappointment. He groaned in reply.

'I wish I knew what was going on in your head.'

He smelled gingery, the tips of his fingers stained with paint. The rush of affection she felt for him was always accompanied by fear of his frailty. She examined the yellow pallor of his skin, the soft whistle of his nostrils when he exhaled. Yet for all the anxiety she felt in his presence, there was something comforting about her father's silence.

When she was younger, her ears had been filled with the cacophony of her stepmother's contradictory stories. Kyung-ha rarely told the same story twice and had a selective deafness to her questions. She spoke of girls who were sold by their mothers. Of girls whose spirits left their bodies and inhabited foxes who would live for a thousand years. Or fireflies that clung to *dokkaebi* she had seen in the mountains as a child. Sometimes she would talk about the city that had been wiped out by the dictator in a single day, but when Mia asked her about this, she would say that to be interested in politics was a dangerous thing. Kyung-ha did not comment on her brother-in-law's activities. As Mia grew older she realized the absence of intimacy in these stories. Her stepmother never spoke of her own childhood. Or of Mia as a child. Or what had happened to her father. And he would never be able to fill the holes left in these plots of her life.

'I wish you could tell me more about my mother,' she said to her Appa. She stroked the top of his head as though he were a pet. 'How did you manage? How did you explain words like *jeong*?'

The morning her brother-in-law, Han-su, arrived on her doorstep unannounced, Kyung-ha had had a premonition of death while she was slicing a lotus root in her kitchen.

She was preparing a side dish for lunch, something simple to eat in the stifling heat, when she saw a glimmer of movement in the living room and was faced with the image of her dead son, Jong-ho. She dropped her knife onto the cutting board. Over the years she had often sensed her son's presence, but had rarely seen him. She followed him as he passed through the living room, descended into the courtyard and unlatched the rusting blue gate, where Han-su stood sweating in a thick black suit.

Kyung-ha blinked several times, unsure of what she'd seen, her body as cold as stone, unsure of what she was inviting in as Han-su crossed the threshhold into the house.

He stood in the kitchen, holding a cup of barley water in his hands for several moments before saying, 'I lost a boy.'

'He might come back,' she said, though she had an inkling of what he meant.

'No,' he said, shaking his head. 'It's my fault. I pushed him too hard.'

'*Aigoo*, you can't carry that burden as your own. You gave him every opportunity. You gave him an education, you helped him get on his feet.'

'It wasn't enough,' he said. His hand shook slightly as he wiped his face with a handkerchief. 'I don't understand. He wasn't...broken. They say Myung-chul was hanging from the shower railing for hours before he was found. Think of his parents. Still in the North. Imagining that their son is alive and well. That hope alone must keep them alive. And they don't even know . . .'

'You have to think of all the kids who are in a better place because of your school,' she said, but she had to turn away. Not because she knew the boy, but because she knew there was nothing for grief but time. With time there was forgetting and even then, the grief did not fade, but hid in strange corners, ready to be uncovered at unexpected moments – at the appearance of the first autumn sunlight, under the relief of the shade of a tree. They sat for a while in silence, listening to the occasional studio laughter that came from the TV in Jun-su's room, the groaning of wood in the heat upstairs.

'It's not your fault,' she said, but the words lacked conviction. She had not been able to absolve herself of guilt when it had been her son.

She sensed that her brother-in-law was about to ask for something. It was rare for him to pay her a visit unannounced. To confide in her. His presence solicited a deep-rooted sense of guilt. Han-su's work made her own at the church look like a hobby. After years of hiding he had returned from his missions in China and had started a school for North Korean teenagers who had defected across the border. He had held his first classes in his own single-room apartment and then had managed to build a school through charitable donations. She looked after a cripple and her wayward stepdaughter, but he looked after so many more at his school. The children were often troubled and struggled to adapt. They often disappeared. Some left for Scandinavia, she had even heard of others who had gone back to the North. But suicide was a rare occurrence.

'I have to ask you for a favour,' he said finally. His hand trembled as he reached for the drink in front of him. His eyes shifted uneasily. 'It's a lot, I know you have more than you can carry already.'

Kyung-ha said nothing, afraid of encouraging him.

'There's a boy, Hyun-min. He lived with Myung-chul. Take him for me. He's eighteen. I'm worried about him. I don't want him to be alone.'

'You think this is a house of charity?' she snapped. 'We don't have anywhere for him to stay.'

'Give him a futon. He can sleep in the living room.' He sighed. 'I would take him but the others might ask questions about why he's special. I can't take them all.'

He looked at her as though she were a saint. That was the lie between them. This man who had dedicated his life to broken children saw her taking care of his brother and thought they were the same. She knew she couldn't say no. And it felt like another challenge. Another burden to atone for her sins. She had taken Jun-su back despite his many women. Taken his child. But it wasn't enough. She still lived with that haunting spirit, the guilt that crouched on her sleeping shadow every night. She didn't want to get involved in these politics. After everything that had happened after Jun-su's arrest, she had vowed to steer clear of it all.

'I know things are tight with money. I can help. Not much. But just so you don't have to dig too deep in your pockets to feed him.'

A reminder. Of how long she had been in Han-su's debt. Over the decades he had often helped her by handing over envelopes of money.

She glanced at the envelope he stretched out to her.

'Hyun-min was the one who found Myung-chul hanging. Think about it. As if it wasn't enough already. To find your roommate, your friend, like that. What that would do to a boy,' Han-su said. 'He won't say it, but I know it's shaken him up. It will only be for a short while. Till he finds his feet.'

Kyung-ha stared into her palm. The Lord giveth and the Lord taketh. She thought of the parable of the Prodigal Son and agreed to take the boy.

Later that evening, Kyung-ha filled a bucket with water from the taps and prepared her husband's bath. The sorrow that coursed through her blood, the persistent ache in her gut – the *han* – it was her inheritance; she had been born to a nation of people who were destined for hardship and sorrow, who toiled for others until their backs broke. They were not like Westerners, who flitted from one choice to another based on what they desired most in the moment. Squatting on the cold tiles of the toilet, she undressed her husband and dipped her hand into the bucket to check the temperature. The paralysis was not so severe that he could not bathe himself, and touching him was not without discomfort, but she bathed him every day nonetheless. Pinprick-like pains travelled inside her veins as she washed him. The water was a little too warm, but she dipped the ladle into the bucket and poured the water over his head. He let out a cry of protest but she had already begun scrubbing his thin, patchy hair with shampoo, gently at first, and then vigorously. She remembered the morning's sermon. It had begun with the passage from Matthew. 'If ye forgive men their trespasses . . .' She eased the pressure of her hands and instead stroked the oily soap over his bony chest. How many women had touched him there? Their eyes met. Though his left eyelid drooped, his good eye was startlingly lucid. Kyung-ha looked away for a moment before turning back and scrubbing him hard, leaving red marks on his skin. Outside a vendor was calling for unwanted cats and dogs on the streets. A mother chided a child. The evening chill was beginning to set in.

She poured water over her husband's shoulders. 'All that talk and here we are, old man.' She paused as she refilled the bucket, then poured the water over his shoulders and turned him around. They had known each other all of their lives. They had grown up in the same village and had swum in the lake by the rice paddies on their way home from school. In the summer, they sat outside their houses sharing watermelons while batting away mosquitoes and spotting fireflies before being called inside by their parents. He knew everything there was to know about fireflies, about anything. He read all the time. Everyone knew that he was bright. When he left to attend Seoul National University, she thought she would never see him again. Kyung-ha held the ladle in her hand for a moment, lost in the memory.

Her mother had passed away a year later. People had begun leaving the countryside and when a neighbour told her she would find work in a factory in Seoul, she packed her belongings, hoping that she might see Jun-su again.

Seoul was not at all what she had expected. The city seemed to expand forever. She had been overwhelmed by the noise and lights, the dusty streets cluttered with signs and advertisements, the sight of the roads filled with cars and buses. In her village they had been lucky if they saw a truck once a month.

She could not say how much time had passed when she saw him among a crowd of students outside the university gates. She had blinked several times; her eyesight could not be trusted after the many hours she spent under the harsh lights of the factory. And he had changed. He was paler. His clothes were neat. He led her to the darkened cafes where students whispered about democracy and Marxism during the curfew. She had been ashamed that she knew so little about such things. He had become a fantastic speaker. He could make her believe she wasn't breathing when she was. But the same old awkward silences came between them as they went to the local bakery. They had exchanged stilted conversation over a slice of Castella cake. She had mistaken his sudden shyness for something else. Now she saw that she had been handed a lifetime of servitude in exchange for confectionery and a glass of milk.

She wondered what might have happened if she had never seen him again. If she had pushed away that plate. If she hadn't followed him to those darkened alleys. If she hadn't made the phone call that changed their lives for decades to come.

'I forgive you,' she said, but she left him shivering on the cold tiled floor.

Mia woke the morning after her uncle's visit to the smell of her stepmother's cooking, heavy and putrid. Her skin and hair smelled sour, as though she were covered in a thin film of garlic. She scrubbed herself hard with the cheap cucumber-scented soap her stepmother bought at the market. Embassy wives never smelled of anything but floral detergent and musky perfumes. After her shower, Mia stood over the sink, examining the scars across her ribs. They looked raw, as though they were new. The heat made everything swell and her fattened fingers were unsteady as she tried to button her shirt.

'Mee-ah-ya!' Her stepmother called out to her from the kitchen.

Her stepmother wore a white T-shirt tucked into flower-patterned trousers she wore high around her waist. Her dyed black hair had been permed into stubborn curls.

'Chop this,' her stepmother said, handing her an onion, without looking at her.

'I'm going to be late,' Mia said, putting the onion on the counter. She was rarely given work in the kitchen. Or if she was, it was only so that she could be corrected. It was an exercise of her stepmother's power. A wielding of wills. To deny her stepmother the opportunity was to tempt her over the edge, to beckon the palm of her hand to her cheek. It would have meant a sharp relief to the anxiety that had been building inside her since the day before. But there seemed to be little Mia could do to inspire her stepmother to hit her these days. There had been a time when there was hardly an excuse needed. The blur of Mia out of the corner of her eye had once been enough.

'And when you're done, clear out your room. Your uncle's bringing a boy here.'

'What do you mean he's bringing a boy here?'

'You can sleep in my room or in the living room.'

'What for?'

She saw the tensing of her stepmother's jaw.

'One of your uncle's students needs a place to stay. His roommate has had an accident,' she said.

Mia remembered the conversation she had overheard the day before, but still didn't understand. 'Why—'

Kyung-ha put down her knife and erupted. 'Why must you question everything? Just accept things as they are. Do I question why you landed on my doorstep? No. I took you in. No questions. That is just the Lord's way.'

'What about my job? You can't just bring him here without asking me. I work at an embassy—'

'Don't talk to me like I'm an idiot. It's as stubborn as the blood in your veins, this idea of living only for yourself. You don't understand the idea of sacrifice for others. The boy needs a place to go. His roommate hanged himself and the boy was the one who found him. You think he'd want to stay in an apartment like that? Don't you care about anyone else?'

'You don't think that it might be a problem with the job that I have for a defector to be living with us? You don't think it's bad enough, with this family's history . . .'

Her stepmother stared at her pointedly. For a moment Mia thought she might strike her, but she did not.

'If I lose my job, who's going to pay for Appa's medical bills?'

'What are you implying about your uncle? You think he would bring trouble to this house?'

There was no point in continuing the argument.

'I'm not giving up my room. Put him in the living room,' Mia said.

As she walked down the narrow, uneven slope towards the main road, careful to avoid the potholes and loose bits of brick on the path, Mia tried to pinpoint the growing sense of unease that was gathering in the pit of her stomach. It was an unusually crisp morning for June, the sky a shock of blue. At the end of the alley, she looked down at the green flat-roofed houses below. The mountain views were wasted on a city so densely packed. Mia paused a moment to survey it. If it weren't for the high rises, she thought, the city could be mistaken for the wreckage left by a tornado. She wondered whether the architects who built the city were acquainted with shapes and colours other than squares and red brick.

She had seen an aerial photograph of London once and had been struck by how organized the buildings seemed. Mia imagined each building had been constructed with aesthetics in mind. Seoul had been constructed in a hurry – a jungle of competing neon signs, cars lined bumper to bumper along the 88 Highway at dawn and dusk. She looked at the slow creeping of the slums towards the rise of the skyscrapers downtown. It was a city that forever reinvented itself. Entire street corners disappeared overnight, skyscrapers were erected, places where her hair had been patted by pitying neighbours had gone to concrete slaughter.

She walked down the back street, past the edge of the market, where a man sold shiny black office shoes for the price of a handshake. Another vendor sold socks from the back of his blue van. Older men and women pushed as they queued for the bus. The passengers stared at Mia. She was used to the questions in their eyes, their attempts to unearth the roots of her existence. To them her mixed blood told the story of a trespassing. A half-ling. They would see Korean features on her face as they entered the tunnel, and then find themselves sitting beside a foreigner as they emerged on the other side of it. As a child, school children had pointed at the 'American child'. A creature of terror. They had run away in horror. There had been little point in trying to call out to explain that she was in fact, half English. She had even less of an idea of what English meant as opposed to American than they did. That morning she felt particularly irritated by the prejudice given away by their glances and she knew it had to do with her uncle and the defector who had hanged himself. The defector would also have been the subject of merciless scrutiny, his accent betraying him right away.

She tried not to think about what the Embassy would have to say about her living with a defector. Reporting the change in her living arrangements would be the right thing to do. There would be interviews. It had not been expressly stated, but her uncle's work with the defectors' school had held up the paperwork of her job offer for several weeks. Though there was nothing illegal in what he did, his history of participation in activism had him blacklisted by South Korean security agencies. In the end the Embassy determined that it mattered little to them, but if it hadn't been for the near-fatal accident of another candidate for the position, Mia wouldn't have been offered the job.

The bus stood at a standstill. The man standing beside her began to mutter and curse at the traffic.

'Stupid protestors,' he muttered. 'Some of us have jobs to go to.'

Mia looked out of the window. Outside people had already begun gathering around City Hall. Every night that month, more and more people had gathered in protest against the newly elected President's announcement that they would resume importing beef from the

US. There had been a five-year ban after BSE had been found in the imports. People had begun calling for the President to resign, that he was selling the country to the US. Mia had been assigned a translation of the newspaper reports and a brief summary of the situation so that Thomas could write an assessment of whether a change in policy was warranted.

'Open the door,' the man shouted. 'It's going to be faster to walk through this shit.'

The bus driver opened the door and Mia squeezed out of the bus. Commuters moved in a monochrome wave towards the city. At the red light, office workers stood shifting their weight like anxious cattle.

Setting her bag at her desk, Mia ventured down the airless corridor past Thomas's office. He never came in before half past nine. Sunlight stretched across his desk. His office was clean, neat. There were a few rice-paper maps of Korea hanging from the walls, a gift left for him by his predecessor. He had not been in the posting long enough to acquire clutter. There were no photographs of him and his wife.

She had no idea when she had acquired the habit, the need to be at her desk to watch him come in. She admired his assuredness; there was a security about the world he inhabited. By comparison her world felt tenuous. She felt she had to prove her competence to him. Her eyes flickered over the partition every time she heard the lift doors open.

'Morning.'

'Go away, Charles, I have work to do,' she said, trying to look behind the man who had walked out of the lift.

'It's so charming how grumpy you are in the mornings.' He paused, waiting for a reaction. 'I've got a question for you.'

Mia dropped her pen and glared at him. He leaned against the partition, and rested his chin on his hand. The hairs on his arms were thick. He had recently cut his silvery brown hair, though it was combed back as usual. His thick horn-rimmed glasses made him look comical. Charles had the manner of a man who had joined the Foreign Service with the enthusiasm of a boy stealing away on a cargo ship. His seniority in the service came as a surprise to almost anyone who met him. He had an informality that disarmed everyone and never seemed to do any work. He spent all his spare time travelling to remote corners of the country, wasting Monday mornings by boring Embassy employees with stories of his conquests and odd relics – imitation Koryo ceramic pots and Buddhist paintings – that he had discovered on the road.

'So I'm with this lady,' he looked at her, eyebrows raised, 'a friend of sorts, I suppose you could say. I'm afraid she must have been upset with me. She kept repeating this word. *Beechutsuh*? Whatever does it mean?'

Mia rolled her eyes, bored of this game he insisted on playing with her. Charles knew more Korean than most of the diplomats at the office. He was always making sure she knew he thought of her as a local girl. 'It means you're pathetic and you should find better uses for your time.'

'Really?' He leaned back, looking pleased with himself. 'It means all that? How fantastically efficient. I really should take up those Korean lessons again.'

'Why don't you?'

'But then I wouldn't have the pleasure of speaking to you.'

'I'm busy so . . .' she gave him her best smile. 'Go away.'

'What are you working on? Not related to the Bateman visit, is it?'

She had forgotten about the Minister's visit. Thomas would not be in the office for most of the week.

'Nope. Not me.'

'So you'll be around for lunch?'

27

'Maybe,' she said.

Charles tapped at the partition. 'Good, I'll come your way lunchtime. And you can tell me what it means?'

She gave him a blank look.

'*Beechutsuh.*'

'It means you're a crap boyfriend.'

He laughed and began to walk away. 'You've got corn stuck in your teeth. You Koreans will eat anything for breakfast,' he said, shaking his head.

The lift doors opened and Thomas appeared in the corridor. His hair was wild and curled at the ends. His mouth was thin, his upper lip almost invisible. The stubble on his face, engineered. David, the registry clerk, stopped him to ask a question. Thomas's eyes were heavy with thought and as he spoke, his gaze moved slowly across the room, as though he were assessing who was watching their conversation. He selected his words carefully. David nodded as Thomas replied. Mia loved the way he spoke, the way his voice slid over the curve of every syllable, every letter. No hint of shyness hidden, no slurring in a tumble of words, he was a man who needed no external assurances.

Yet when his eyes met hers over the partition every morning she found him searching for something.

That evening, Charles caught up with her as she passed through the Embassy gates.

'You shouldn't be walking out alone in this,' Charles said.

'You mean the protests? This is about as peaceful as they get, anyway, as far as protests in this country go,' she said, thinking of the stories her uncle had told her of the student demonstrations of the seventies and eighties.

'We all know you're trouble,' he grinned. 'You're bound to find a way of getting yourself arrested.'

'I don't know what you're talking about,' she said, thinking of her situation at home. It was probably nothing. He would stay a few days and then disappear.

They walked through the brightly lit streets, into the crowds. The candlelight vigil had grown. The atmosphere was almost festive. Traffic had been diverted around the centre of the city and people walked freely on the roads. A man shouted into a megaphone to the crowds. An elderly woman offered her a candle. She accepted it and then turned to find that Charles was no longer beside her.

She looked beyond the crowd. Large media vans had taken up permanent spots alongside the riot-police buses.

'Up here.'

Mia raised her hand against the glare of the street lamps. Charles waved from the roof of the subway entrance where several photographers had gathered to get a different angle on their shots.

'Come and see this. I'll help you.'

He gave her his hand and pulled her up.

'This is unbelievable.'

'Incredible, isn't it?' Charles said. 'I'd say there are a hundred thousand people out here tonight.'

A group of policemen rushed through the crowds. Orange candlelight dotted the sea of black heads stretching out in every direction as far as Mia could see.

'You Koreans are passionate about your food, aren't you? What's the chance of them importing infected beef? What's the big fuss anyway? Let them eat pork instead.' He took a few photographs of the families sitting by the roadside.

'It's not just about beef, Charles. They think the President has caved to the Americans. It's about democracy and who gets to make the decisions. The FTA agreement is—'

'I was joking.' Charles lowered his camera. 'It's quite festive, actually. Shame about the riot police.'

'They're harmless. Most of them are teenagers. I heard they were recruited overnight from the countryside.' Mia scanned the crowd. Her eyes met those of a policeman speaking into a walkie-talkie. He held her gaze for several long moments. The sense of unease she had been feeling all day returned. 'I should get out of here. I have to write this brief by tomorrow morning.'

They squeezed through the crowds. Charles ducked as a placard swung in his direction.

Charles smiled and shook his head. 'The English are apathetic. They'd complain and moan but it'd never come to this, I'll tell you that. It's this hot-bloodedness that I love. Why don't we find somewhere to eat? All this talk of beef and I'm starved.' He rubbed his hands together. 'How about some chicken feet?'

She scowled. It was always like this with Charles. He was always trying to prove that he was not afraid of local culture. It was almost as though he wanted to be Korean. She didn't understand why he would want to be anything other than an Englishman. 'I should go. I've got work to do.'

'Don't be such an old maid. I'll help. I found a great restaurant that does that chicken hotpot I love. You'll have that, won't you? What was that called again?'

'*Samgyetang*,' she said.

'That's the one.'

Mia looked over his shoulder. Crowds had gathered around the subway exits. 'I can't stay long.'

They settled in a quiet corner of the restaurant. Charles sat by the window looking out over the busy, neon-lit street. Red-faced businessmen toasted each other several times over the hiss of raw meat laid on the grill. Charles ordered a bottle of soju. Under the yellow light, he looked tired, his face sallow, a trace of green around his eyes.

'So my time is up,' he said, pouring them a shot.

'What?' Mia avoided meeting his eye. He confided in her more often than she liked. She played with the pickled cucumber on her plate with her chopsticks.

'I'm being shipped back to London. I've spent enough time abroad apparently. They think they're being kind.'

'Why don't you want to go back?' She couldn't understand his fascination for all things Korean.

'Haven't been back in eight years. Funny how time flies.'

'Don't you miss it?'

He reached for Mia's cigarettes and lit one. 'First cigarette in years. Think I'll take it up again.' He let out a dry cough. 'Don't miss it, no. What is there to miss? It's horrible. Damp. Miserable. And that's just the people.'

Mia took a cigarette herself and rested her chin on the palm of her hand. 'I've always wanted to go. I find it all so fascinating. . .' She thought of Thomas. 'The English people I've met are so witty, so razor sharp, so knowledgeable.'

Charles brightened. 'I had no idea you thought so highly of me.'

Mia narrowed her eyes. She rarely thought of Charles as English. He had been in Seoul longer than any of the others and was one of the few people at work she could actually speak to. With all the other diplomats, she felt the syllables she spoke wedge themselves in her throat. 'Not you.'

'You have such sweet ideas about the English.' He leaned against the window and, looking up at the ceiling, sighed nosily. 'I don't see myself leaving. I'm considering resignation.' He poured himself a shot, swung it back and said, 'Never thought I'd grow to love the taste of this stuff. But now I'm a regular Korean *ajutshi*. It's just so wonderfully balanced. This sense of society being ordered so that everyone knows exactly where they are, based on how old they are—'

'You're drunk.'

'Don't interrupt. See, I think you Koreans are so clever. You've constructed this way of placing everyone socially so everyone knows exactly where they stand. I'm talking about these words like *komo* – it's so specific to have a word that means aunt, sister of one's father, don't you think? Don't get me started on honorifics. In England it's a disaster to be old. Here, life gets better with age. You get more respect.'

Mia said nothing for a moment. It was pointless to argue with him. She wouldn't try to explain that therein lay the trap. He glamorized it because he knew he could leave any time.

He shook his head and grinned. Small pieces of red pepper were stuck to his gums. 'Maybe we should get married. You could support me with your job at the Embassy and then when our fabulously Korean children arrive, I could be an English teacher. We could live in Kangnam, near your parents and once a year we could holiday on Jeju Island.'

Mia stubbed her cigarette out, hard. 'Maybe you should stop being such a creep.'

He pretended to be hurt and then a look of sincerity came over his face. 'You know I've always had a soft spot for you.'

Mia crumpled the paper chopstick wrapping in her hand. She had not touched her soju. 'I thought you were going to help me write this report. Fat lot of help you are.'

Charles took another shot and grimaced. 'Who's it for?'

'Thomas.'

He shrugged. 'I wouldn't worry about Thomas Dalton-Ellis too much. There are more important people you should be trying to impress.'

'That's your contribution to my report?'

'I wouldn't waste your time. He won't read it anyway. You're better off keeping it short, rattle off some recommendations of people he should speak to. You know, journalists, activists and so on.'

'Why don't you like him?'

'I don't dislike him.'

'Come on.' She gave him a look.

'He's a drunkard. I can't take him seriously. You know,' he leaned in conspiratorially, 'rumour has it that he was so wasted that he took a piss in the Ambassador's library during an official function in his last posting. He's an Embassy darling because his father's an old hand, has a bit of clout in Whitehall or some nonsense. I've heard that the Ambassador has him on a tight leash.'

She found this hard to believe. Thomas always appeared so perfectly composed.

'Now you know,' he said. 'So don't worry about it and stay for another drink.'

'I should go.'

'Don't be like that.'

'I need to get home.'

He scratched at the dark hairs on his arm, making no effort to move. 'I suppose I should go too.'

Outside, the streets had emptied. The riot police were sitting down to eat their meals from metal trays, others were sleeping inside the bus. She felt a chill in the air. Inexplicably, Mia had the curious feeling of being watched. Her uncle's request of her stepmother had put her in a strange mood. She glanced over at Charles who was walking a few steps ahead. For a fleeting moment she considered lightening the anxiety she had been feeling all day. She had never before wanted his reassurance and could only imagine how flippantly he would react to the news of the imminent arrival of a defector in her home. He was not one to take such things seriously. He would only view her confidence as encouragement. She unfolded a scarf and threw it over her shoulders. A woman with a hymn book in her hands was singing, nearby a sleeping child was resting her head on her mother's shoulder. Groups of students walked together, occasionally stopping to take photos of each other.

Mia walked a little faster. 'I'm taking the bus.'

'In that case, we'll have to say goodnight here.'

He leaned to kiss her goodnight and she flinched. It was instinct. She did not like people touching her. He lingered as though he intended to kiss her lips. The smell of soju on his breath turned her stomach.

Mia took a step back and pushed him away. 'Try that again and I'll punch you.'

'Always the lady. That's what I love about you.'

Mia turned from him and began to walk away. She refused to be one of his local collectibles.

The book slipped from her fingers. Her thoughts, elsewhere. Lately this continued to happen, her mind drawn to Thomas like elastic, snapping her to him the harder she tried to think of something else. She didn't understand the nature of these thoughts, the pull of them. Mia slid her back further down the wall, her chin sank to her neck as she pushed the pillow against her knees and gnawed on the inside of her mouth. She tipped the lampshade and illuminated the book in her lap, as though this would keep her from reading the same line over and over, her attention fragmented by the murmur of a neighbour's television, her father groaning downstairs. She was drawn to Thomas's silent pauses, the way he seemed to measure his words, drain them of emotion. When he spoke he was calm, collected. But she often caught him brooding, saw him standing in his office, looking out onto the Embassy gardens.

Mia got to her feet and propped her elbows against the window-sill. The summer air was warm and moist against her face. Outside, most of the street was asleep; husbands and wives lay against one another in the heat. Were Thomas and Felicity also lying in the same bed, forsaking their sheets, their skin sticking to the other's limbs as they slept?

Mia opened her desk drawer. Inside it were odd pages of reports that she had taken from Thomas's desk; scraps of words and turns of phrases she found impressive. She pulled out the notebook she had taken from his study. Thomas's handwriting was neat and lean.

Was it Owen or Sassoon? In the poem about watching those who are sleeping and being reminded of the dead? I see Felicity as she is sleeping and I recall it.

There was no date on the page, but it had been written at least six months before, at the beginning of the posting when she had been called to his home. It was winter, election season, and Mia was working late to prepare translations of crucial press pieces which would help to inform the Ambassador about what the election might mean for diplomatic relations. The phone in Thomas's office had been ringing all evening. When she couldn't ignore it any longer, she had picked up the call.

'I can't seem to get in touch with my husband. Is there anyone there who could get me some help?'

It had not occurred to her until that moment that he might have a wife. That he loved somebody. 'Mrs Dalton-Ellis?'

'Felicity, please.'

'Are you okay?'

'We've got some sort of leak. There's water everywhere. I was hoping someone from the Embassy could help me ring someone.'

Mia had said she would get in touch with some plumbers but had paused as she took down the address. An opportunity to get a glimpse of his home was irresistible.

Their house was large and grey with splintering wooden window-frames. Mia had expected something luxurious, modern. Felicity greeted her at the door wearing a green wraparound dress and holding a pair of matching green shoes in her hands. Mia had read about the colour auburn, but had never seen it until she had seen Felicity's shoulder-length hair. She was slim, her skin like pale-coloured glass. A soft scatter of freckles across her nose. A large smile that transformed her face. Perfectly shaped, maroon lacquered nails.

Beside her Mia became acutely aware of her own filth. The stretch of her scars. The stench of local food which clung to her ill-fitting black coat.

'I do hope you don't mind doing this. I can't seem to get a hold of our landlord. I didn't know what to do. With the colder weather coming, I'm afraid all this is going to freeze over. God knows where Tom is. Don't worry about taking them off. We could really do with a pair of Wellies here. We never really adopted the shoes-off policy in this house, I'm afraid, I hate the sensation of things sticking to my feet, it gets me absolutely paranoid. Come in, come in. I'm sorry you had to come all this way in the rain,' Felicity said.

They entered the house. Felicity tiptoed delicately around the leak that was slowly spreading in the hallway. Her legs were slim and she had a long neck. The posture of a ballerina. The knowing grace of royalty. She danced through the living room to avoid the spillage. Past a white leather sofa, an antique chest of drawers. Past a Hindu god whose head propped up a lampshade, a porcelain Chinaman with sticks holding buckets of trinkets.

The plumbers came shortly after and shut off the water supply, spending half an hour investigating the source of the problem. Felicity had taken a phone call as they explained to Mia that a section of pipe had corroded and would need to be replaced. They left and Mia had waited in the hall, unsure whether she should stay.

A light was on in an adjacent room. Stepping into it, she had felt an odd thrill when she realized that it was Thomas's study; the room smelled of him. She walked over to the bookcase, not quite sure what she was looking for. She pulled out a clothbound copy of a book about the Azande, flipped through its yellow pages and then replaced it. His oak desk was an antique. Perhaps it was something he had dragged it from posting to posting. It was cluttered with papers and stacks of books. Felicity's voice went quiet for a moment and Mia slipped back into the hall.

Felicity's steps had creaked on the floorboards upstairs, her voice a soft murmur. Mia ventured further into the study. Embassy documents and reports from Amnesty International were stacked in piles on the floor. She picked up a small leather notebook and thumbed through it. It was filled with Thomas's scrawling notes. She flipped a few more pages.

I extricate myself. I try to be detached and I find myself hollow . . .

Mia turned the page to read on but heard Felicity's steps on the stairs. Slipping the notebook into her bag, she rushed to the hall and stood awkwardly waiting outside the study, scratching at the stain on her shirt, unravelling a thread from the hem of her sleeve.

'I should go,' she said as Felicity approached, her heart hurling itself against her chest. 'The plumbers said they'd be back tomorrow.'

'Stay. I'd be riddled with guilt if I sent you out into the cold like this. I hadn't planned on going out. It's a rare treat when one can have an evening in. Well, it would have been if it weren't for this business with the water pipe. You must think I'm a terrible bore. I'm sorry, I get carried away.' Felicity ran a hand through her hair and seemed lost in thought for a moment. 'Where were we? Did you say you'd like a cup of tea?' She ushered Mia into the kitchen.

'I should get going—'

'I insist. I've managed to get some wonderful scones from the bakery at the Hyatt this morning.'

The phone rang in the other room.

'That might be Tom.' Felicity left the kitchen.

Mia had waited for Felicity to come back, looking at the bare surfaces of the room. The faint smell of foreign antiseptic made her want to sneeze. She slipped from the stool to her feet, the urge to pry too tempting. Everything was too neat, the cutlery too orderly and aligned in the drawers. She found a tin of tea with a picture of a picnic which reminded her of a Renoir painting she had seen at the National Museum of Art. Mia had thought about slipping the tin in her bag when Felicity re-entered the room.

'False alarm. I've just taken on a new job and it's a bit hectic. I don't know if I'll have time for this house. We refused to live in the high rises. Those apartments are grotesque, don't you think? One needs a bit of green in a city like this. But I hear that the service is much better in those apartments. Now with going back to work, I won't have time to be waiting for the servicemen.'

'What do you do?'

'Sorry?' Felicity hesitated as she stirred the tea. 'I don't suppose Thomas has mentioned it. Of course he hasn't.' The spoon scraped the bottom of the mug: the only other sounds were the hum of the heater, the heavy rain on the roof of the veranda. Then Felicity seemed to remember that Mia was there and the storm receded from her face.

'I'm going to be writing for *The Herald*,' she said, at last.

They moved from the kitchen to the living room and finally Mia managed to make her excuses and leave. At the bus stop, she held the length of the umbrella in her armpit as she searched for Thomas's notebook in the bottom of her bag. Most of it was filled with notes on meetings, memos about administrative tasks. Some of the pages had been ripped out. Then, there it was.

Is the nation still great? We, who have no role models, no spirit . . .
We're cursed by our perspective, we who have more information

within our grasp than our forefathers who marched into the trenches, who were able to subscribe to those grand narratives of nation.

And I begin to wonder about the other grand narratives we tell ourselves, the fiction we construct to keep us where we are — that vows should last forever, when nothing else in life reveals such permanence.

The next page was blank.

His words had made Mia consider her own reflection for the first time in years. When she got home, she had turned off the lamp and opened the wardrobe to see her silver outline in the darkness. Scars stretched from under her breasts, across her ribs. Her knees were scarred too but that had been the children from the neighbourhood. They had let her ride the bike down a slope and she had not realized that the brakes had been cut until it was too late. She examined her wide shoulders, her hands which seemed too large against her small face and small breasts. Then it had begun to grow, the inexplicable need to know him.

The Ambassador was looking at him expectantly. Thomas realized he was waiting for an answer.

'Sorry?'

'I said, when do you think this report on the protests will be ready?'

'By the end of next week.'

The Ambassador continued to stare at him. He wanted more. He leaned back in his chair. 'How are things?'

Thomas cleared his throat and wiped a thin film of sweat from his upper lip with his hand. The Ambassador had small, mole-like eyes with large folds of skin which hung along his eyelashes, giving him the appearance of perpetual sleepiness. His lips were strangely rectangular and when he spoke he revealed only his two front teeth, in a manner which often seemed like disdain, but rarely was. He was sitting now with his hands gathered over his protruding waist, and had taken on an increasingly familiar tone, the manner of a physician or psychiatrist who wanted a piece of Thomas's inner life. It made him want to reply petulantly. 'Fine, of course.'

The Ambassador drew back in his chair, as though considering something. 'You know. It's all right to say that you're unhappy here.'

'I'm not sure I know what you mean.'

'There will always be some postings that are more exciting than others.'

'I appreciate you saying so—'

'It's all right to say that. In the right company, of course.'

For the first time he felt a little anxious. Was he letting things slip? He had always been assured of his discreetness. He was in control of his habit. He studied the Ambassador's face for clues that he might suspect him.

'Have I been inappropriate in some way?'

The Ambassador stood up and picked up a piece of paper from his desk. 'I've had a telegram from London about your application for another posting.'

'I see.'

'Would you still say you're not unhappy?'

The question felt unreasonable. Was it an obligation to be perpetually happy in one's occupation?

'I have my reservations about Seoul,' he said.

'I think your posting here is generous. Given what happened in Phnom Penh. Many would consider it a step up. I am having a hard time understanding why you'd ask for a transfer.'

He hesitated. He could not find the words to explain it either. 'It's just that after Phnom Penh . . .' he began, unsure of where he was going.

'At the risk of sounding terribly managerial, I won't tolerate any more mistakes. Whitehall has decided not to consider the transfer. You need to make the best of this posting and show us you're back on track. Am I being clear?'

'Of course, I understand.'

'I know it's difficult. God knows, it's not easy with so many functions. The Koreans will drink you under the table if you give them the chance. I just hope the nasty business is behind us. I hate to see a bright young thing's career blighted by an unfortunate weakness.'

He wasn't sure whether the Ambassador was referring to the incident in the library or what had happened with Felicity.

The Ambassador gave him a stern look and then seemed to decide to soften his approach. 'You'd be surprised how much it's wasted perfectly talented young men. It's unfortunately too common in the service. Do you understand?'

He did.

'Good. Well I think we're all right then.'

Thomas stood up and walked back to his office. The poisonous grip on his head was receding; his mind was beginning to clear. It was midweek; a two-day reprieve approached. Sweat clung to his shirt. The air conditioners did nothing more than circulate the stench of rotting creatures through the office. The humidity was relentless. He picked up his pace down the grey carpets, thinking he might have another stab at breaking the seal on the windows in his office.

Peter stopped as they passed each other in the corridor. 'Just the man I was after. Can I count on you to join us this afternoon?'

Thomas tried to remember what Peter was referring to.

'The trade talks?' he asked.

Peter nodded. 'You don't mind, do you? With this American beef debacle, they want a hell of a lot more from our end. Do you think we could offer them anything? I suggested that perhaps we could give them visa waivers, you know, that kind of thing? You've seen my brief?'

He vaguely recalled seeing the second draft. He had had a few drinks at the bar and had stumbled back to the office under the pretense of doing some more work. He thought of the pile of untouched papers on his desk and nodded.

'Was there anything after the second draft?' Thomas scratched the back of his head and tried to look concerned.

'No, I don't think so.'

42

Thomas checked his watch. An hour was sufficient for a quick mock-up of ideas.

'I haven't sent anything to Nigel, I just scribbled a few things down. It's all terribly provisional.' He hoped that sounded convincing. He tried to clear his head of the fog that continued to cling to the edges of his mind.

'That's all right. So long as I can get a copy of your notes?'

'I'll ask Mrs Moon to send you one. There aren't any specifics, you understand, just a clause saying that we may review our current visa and immigration policy.'

Peter looked relieved. 'Excellent. Listen, it's probably best to leave Whitehall out of this for the time being. Let's see what they come back with first.'

'Of course.'

Thomas wiped the sweat from his forehead and turned the corner into his office, closing the door behind him. He was grateful, at least, that he had this quiet retreat. It was an improvement on the days when he would sweat out his hangovers while trying to ignore the rattle of Bremerton's voice over the excruciating flapping of the desk fan.

He took out a small bottle he kept in the bottom drawer of his desk and took a sip. Just to take the edge off. His tongue felt thick in the heat. These days he could hardly taste it.

Thomas sat down to do the notes for Peter. The heaviness in his chest threatened to descend on him again. These days he felt that the less he tried, the more he was rewarded. It was sufficient to be a shell, an empty presence. It was a far cry from the world he had witnessed as a child. He remembered his first visit to Cairo. It had been the only time his father, a diplomat who was usually reserved and distant, had taken an interest in showing Thomas something. They had walked through the souks together, past the saffron market, and the carpets of sedated snakes. Thomas recalled the excitement of new sensations, the sand in his mouth and nose, the shock of spice in his food. The calls to prayer at dawn.

Thomas went to his window and stared at the line of smog, the colour of nicotine, on the horizon. Beyond the Embassy gardens, he could see over the stone walls of Deoksugung Palace and into the large gravel grounds, the black tiled roofs with ornately painted undersides. Here, at least, was a touch of culture. The drink was working. The headache had almost completely disappeared and it was in these moments, before the despair of sobriety took hold, that he allowed himself to uncover the source of his sadness. Everything about his new posting seemed familiar. The skyscrapers, the shops, the traffic. Another Asian city. Where was the Orient? Developing nations were all beginning to look the same. Only the Embassy gardens offered relief from the tyranny of concrete and glass, a rare green space in a city full of grey.

As he stood looking over into the palace, he tried to imagine the King as he sat beyond the paper doors, receiving foreign diplomats. He often daydreamed of the times of his forefathers and what it must have been like to discover places anew. He imagined discovering India, South America, seeing the natives in all their nakedness. It was what he imagined he was discovering in Cambodia – raw culture, untouched by external forces, the purity of tradition. The grittiness of it all.

He sat at his desk and began to scrawl a few notes.

Mia knocked on the door.

'Here's the press summary you asked for.' She went to put a document on his growing pile of papers, looking from the document in her hand to him and then away, a small tooth appearing at the corner of her mouth as she bit her lip. Her eyes lingered on him like a child looking for reassurance. She rarely looked him in the eye when she spoke.

'Fabulous. Thank you,' he said. 'Mia, I was just going through this report.'

'Was there a problem?' Her face suddenly rippled with concern.

'Now I'm afraid I'm going to have to admit my own ignorance. How would you translate this word? It's continually popping up in various discussions.'

She came to him. He leaned into the smell of green tea and salt on her skin, his eyebrows furrowed in mock scrutiny of a finer detail. He could feel a fever rising from the base of his neck.

'Immigration.'

'Right. Of course. Thank you.'

She gave him a smile and threw a look over her shoulder as she walked out of his office. The second she turned the corner, he pressed his eyelids with his palms. His behaviour was despicable – that was as far as he would allow himself to articulate whatever was rising from his chest. It would remain locked in a compartment within himself. To articulate it would be to welcome it to where reason dwelled. He would not make pathetic rationalizations.

He tried to ignore the temptations of the bottle in his bottom drawer and began to type, rehashing previous offers of visa waivers that he had put together for other meetings. As an undergraduate at Cambridge, he had often feigned that he had done no work at all, when in fact he had stayed awake into the early hours of the morning, occasionally disturbed by the sounds of drunk students in the quad, working to ensure that he was on top of his game. He had gone to parties and left on the pretence of going to some other social arrangement and then returned to his room to read. Now he was doing the reverse – doing as little work as possible and coasting along the surface of things. It was easier not to care. He would not repeat the mistakes he made in Phnom Penh.

He drafted some notes for Peter and sent them to Mrs Moon and then frittered away the rest of his afternoon reading the *Economist* and the *New Yorker*. The trade talk meeting went uneventfully and the day sped towards closure. For what? Another notch to scratch on the wall. One more day closer to a new posting.

Thomas's steps grew heavy as he reached home. The bamboo leaves by the front door had browned and dark brown buds had begun to emerge from the stems. Something was burning inside the house. The thick charcoal scent of it gave him a dull headache as he opened the door. Felicity's voice rang out, distorted by the damp walls. The stench grew stronger as he walked past her study on his way to the kitchen. She was on the phone, nodding repeatedly.

'You're right, of course you're right,' she was saying, nodding furiously, fingering the wood of the bookshelf, as though trying to reassure it.

Thomas stared at the ceiling as he leaned against the door, listening to her speak. She was talking to her father, who she consulted whenever she felt frustrated with the state of her career. In the early days of their marriage, he had often found himself jumpy and nervous at the sound of his father-in-law's voice in their room as it was broadcast over the BBC World Service.

He caught her eye through a sliver of space left by the half-closed door, and mouthed to her, 'What is that smell?'

She gave him a look and shut the door.

It turned out to be an angry mass of burned meat. He opened the oven door and shut it immediately, thrusting his face in his elbow to shield his face from the ensuing smoke. The smell of burnt plastic began to circulate as the smoke dissipated and he groped for the window, nauseated. As he shifted the stubborn wooden frame of the window, it splintered and the glass came loose and shattered onto the ground outside.

'Damn.' He stood with his head out of the window for a moment, surveying the damage. Their home, their restoration project, was crumbling around them. They had rejected living in the coveted high rises on the south side of the river. They had wanted authenticity. Something with history. They had pestered an estate agent to show them unusual properties they could rent. Eventually they had come across an old Japanese house that had been built during the colonial era. It was owned by an eighty-year-old woman who was having trouble selling the property and had decided to let it out instead.

'What's going on here?' Felicity said, batting a folded newspaper in front of her face.

'No, don't do that…' he began as Felicity opened the oven door.

Felicity coughed and fanned the smoke from her face. Thomas watched her, unimpressed. It was one of the greatest of surprises of her character that Felicity, whose every action was that of acute and precise calculation, was completely talentless in the kitchen. Her precision in every other area of her life was her insurance that she would never be vulnerable to anyone. She made up for her perceived plainness with her pristine presentation. For many years, she had worn her hair in a bob after she discovered that it would soften the point of her sharp chin. Even when she planned not to leave the house she was on the verge of wearing a suit.

'I must have lost track of the time. I'm sorry— what's that?' She surveyed the shattered window. 'So that's gone as well, has it?' she said. 'I'll ring Mrs Moon tomorrow.'

'This is unbearable.' Thomas shook his head.

'We'll have the workmen come by in the morning.'

Thomas took the blackened tray out of the oven. 'What was it?'

'Lamb,' Felicity said with a wince.

Their reconciliatory meal. It had started as a joke and they had had lamb for dinner on countless occasions after Phnom Penhh. Then they had grown tired of these forced attempts and had begun to avoid each other. Now she had resurrected it, he realized that she

47

was about to apologize for something. Or more accurately, she was on a warpath, about to stretch the periphery of their already gaping wound.

Felicity was poking the thick body of meat with a fork. 'I'm not sure we should eat this.'

'Of course we're not going to eat it.'

'If we cut around the edges it'll be fine.'

Thomas pulled out a block of cheese from the fridge, shaking his head.

'It's fine. Don't fill yourself up with—'

'I'd rather not eat that. I hardly have an appetite in this heat,' he said, getting up from the window.

'Suit yourself.' Felicity opened the bin and dumped the meat in. He could see that she was trying hard not to let him see how much it upset her. Dusting her hands, she disappeared.

Thomas took a plate to the dining room and sat at the large mahogany table, nibbling on the cheese. Outside in the garden the grass looked yellow. He heard Felicity angrily throwing the pans and plates into the sink. He ignored this. She would come to him eventually. How strange, he thought, to know someone so well, to find them predictable, and yet to feel so distant from them. How hard it was to restore one's good opinion once it had been lost. Perhaps marriage implicitly led to a series of betrayals. The familiar route of these thoughts bored him. In the beginning of their relationship they had felt compelled to spend their evenings together – discussing the events of the day, watching television or even reading in the same room and reading passages aloud to each other. But after Phnom Penh they had begun to gravitate towards opposite ends of the house in the evenings, their conversations culled of the things that mattered.

★

Later, Felicity came and sat down beside him, as though nothing had happened.

'So,' Felicity said, reaching for a sliver of cheese. 'How was your day?' she asked in her most civil voice.

Thomas buttered a biscuit. 'It was all right, I suppose. Nigel—'

'I saw Giles this afternoon.'

'Giles? Where did you bump into him?'

'I went to see him actually.'

He put down his knife.

'He suggested that I might do a bit of work for him and I think it's a rather good idea.'

'I see.' Thomas stiffened. The scent of her French almond oil was overbearing. 'I suppose that's why you rang your father?' Thomas undid the top button of his shirt. 'What did the old man have to say about that?'

'You're cross, I can understand. But let me explain—'

'We're going to have this conversation, are we? Fine,' he said, dabbing at the sides of his mouth with his napkin before throwing it on the table. He didn't even feel guilty in saying it. 'I won't have you jeopardizing my career again.'

'Don't be so dramatic, Tom. It won't be like that. They'll be soft feature pieces, lifestyle nonsense. I won't get into anything substantial, no politics.'

They had been here before. She had said the same thing when she had begun writing for *The Herald* six months ago and had broken a similar promise then.

'I've never heard anything so pathetic. You must think I'm a complete idiot.'

'Tom. Please listen. I might go mad. I need something to do. You know what my work means to me. How many times do I have to apologize?'

He stood up, intent on leaving the room with grace. Instead he threw the plate at the wall.

There were times when he couldn't believe how fresh the anger was, how little it had subsided.

That night, the fever returned. The dormant disease had wakened. He would rouse from frustrated dreams, furious, expecting to be seeped in irrevocable evidence of the disease, only to find himself dry. Yet the signs were all there – the shivering in the night, his ravenous eyes which feasted on bare flesh during the day – the patrilineal curse seeped out of his pores and crawled on his skin, flaunting its inevitability under his watchful scrutiny. His grandfather – Sir Theodore Ellis, who had made a fortune in South Africa just after the second Boer War – had the worst case of the disease in generations. As he lay dying on the stairwell of a brothel, he had handed over his fortune to a prostitute whose name no one could remember afterwards, leaving his wife and son destitute.

Thomas stood under a cold shower to cool the fever, then wearily crept to his study where he allowed himself the consolation of a clove cigarette. He licked the sweetness left on his lips by the filter. Delightfully decadent. He thought of the rotating ceiling fan in his bedroom in Phnom Penh, the vision of Chantou through the mosquito net. When Felicity had betrayed him he had been tempted. He shuddered and took another drag on the cigarette. He would enjoy life's finer vices. He pushed thoughts of Chantou out of his mind. He would not succumb to the disease. He thought of the sight of her breasts as she washed her hair, unaware that he was watching her. A pulse shot through his penis. Wearily, he put out the cigarette, loosened his bathrobe, lowered his briefs, and tugging on the curse, inoculated himself.

He settled into his armchair with a dusty copy of Evans-Pritchard's *Witchcraft, Oracles and Magic among the Azande*. As he read, he marvelled that only half a century ago there were undiscovered lands – places and people in the deepest heart of Africa as yet unstudied, yet unconquered. He finished off the glass, feeling the gravity of unpleasant thoughts pulling at him. He poured himself another glass. Those thoughts that had driven him to drink in Phnom Penh had returned. The inevitability of how his life would play out. As a boy he had been full of hope for an expedition that would take him somewhere completely foreign. Now he felt the despair of a man who felt he'd seen everything there is to see.

Kyung-ha opened her eyes to darkness. A heavy resistance against her exhalations. She had the sensation of her breath being sucked out from her lungs. She lay waiting for the spell to pass. A shaman had once uttered words she had never forgotten. She tried to dismiss them as words uttered by an old woman who wanted her to pay for a *ghut*. Yet it was in those moments when she felt the burning as she inhaled, that she wondered if there might be some truth to what the shaman had said. This was no disease. This was the weight of her son's spirit crushing her body.

Kyung-ha walked up the stairs and pushed open the girl's door, shaking her awake in the darkness. She did not want to be alone in the kitchen with those whispering thoughts.

'What? It's Saturday,' The girl said, checking her watch. 'It's not even six.' She lay back down again.

'The boy's coming today. We have to prepare a meal for him. Make him feel welcome.'

The girl threw the blanket over her head. 'I'll buy something later.'

'You think you can fix everything with money? It should be a homemade meal.'

The girl's careless, imprecise movements in the kitchen were a welcome distraction. There was an absence of thought, the girl was forever elsewhere, never present. Kyung-ha set her to work on chopping vegetables and then snatched the chopping board from under the girl's knife, muttering that at that standard, she would do better to do it herself.

She had purchased the very best vegetables and expensive beef ribs. Usually their dinner tables were spare, with a plate of *kimchi* and rice. Seaweed had disappeared as a side dish after prices rose. But today she mixed sugar with soy sauce and ginger and massaged it into the beef ribs.

'How long is he going to stay?'

'I said, slice them finely. Look at this. It's not some kind of garlic variety show.' Kyung-ha said, turning the edge of the cubed garlic pieces on the cutting board.

'Why are you putting on such a show? Beef ribs? Have you heard what they're saying on the news?'

She said nothing. The girl was ignorant. What did she know about anything? Everything about her was awkward – her large fingers and oddly coloured hair. The stubborn traces of whiteness in the girl were infuriating. As a child, Kyung-ha had set her to work outside, to get her to catch some sun, but only to adverse effect – she would return with her hair a shade lighter, her complexion white and the green in her eyes more emerald. It was as though her mother's Western values were a pigment in the girl's skin, a permanent fixture in its luminousness. The girl was selfish and cold, a demon sent by the Lord as a test of her patience and goodwill. She wondered about the Englishwoman, the girl's mother. What was she bound to, if anything? Westerners seemed to float through life tending to their own cares and wishes. She saw this streak in Mia, the recklessness, the obliviousness to everybody else. So long as it felt good, it was okay, that seemed to be the logic. And there was no way that the girl had known how hard it had been to feed her sometimes, how tight money had been just to get a few scraps on the table.

But today Kyung-ha was relieved to be irritated by the girl, this other test given to her by the Lord. 'In the past, a girl like you would have been sold by her own mother. Money would have been more useful.'

The girl set down her knife.

'How long is he staying?'

'I don't know, as long as he needs to,' she said.

She heard the creak of the gate and wiped her hands on her apron. 'They're here,' she said.

The girl disappeared upstairs, but Kyung-ha did not have the energy to chide her for avoiding her uncle. She walked through the living room and out to the courtyard to greet them but her steps slowed to a halt as she saw the spectre standing before her.

Jong-ho. Her son. He crossed the courtyard, dragging his slippers over the gravel, though she had always told him not to. He looked up, squinting in the sunlight and then turned to look over his shoulder as Han-su walked in behind him.

'Here, Hyun-min, *insa* and say hello.'

She heard nothing. Her heart, a dull thud in her ears. Han-su saw him too. Then with the rushing sound of his voice she realized. The boy was a perfect copy of him. He looked younger than eighteen. He wore a baggy orange T-shirt over blue jeans. He blew away the hair that fell into his eyes just as Jong-ho used to do. He had been the spitting image of Jun-su as a young man.

She stood transfixed at the sight of him. He had Jong-ho's eyes. She could almost hear his laugh – it had been louder than the curfew sirens that had rung out at night. The memories like beads, one linked to another, spilled out. She tried to stop all the associated images, because she could not think of this without seeing his hand drop from beneath the white sheet. The spectre returned with an accusatory finger. She screwed her eyes shut to suffocate the thought. But it was too late.

Her head was filled with the cries of a hundred cicadas.

Mia hung back as her uncle brought the defector into the courtyard. All morning she had been accosted by Kyung-ha, being told what to do, and then being told she was doing it wrong.

She looked back at the feast her stepmother had so painstakingly set up in the living room. Small plates filled with lotus flower roots, bellflower roots and persimmons covered the table. Chinese dates had been placed on the left of the table, the persimmons on the far right. Rice cakes were placed at the end of the fruit row. There was something eerie in the arrangement. It was only as Mia walked by it, that she realized what it was: the table looked like an ancestral offering, a meal for the dead.

Mia watched him at the dinner table, assessing the meal as though it involved some calculation. His head was too big for his body; he had a square jaw and a rounded chin. Her uncle had once told her that's what happened when children grew up starving. Here he was, one of his charitable projects. The dinner table was dazzling with colour. Growing up, she had thought that colourful dinner tables were the inventions of television dramas. She did not imagine that people really ate like that every day. It seemed strange that they would put on a feast for a defector, who was unlikely to have seen such elaborate dinner tables himself. Mia wondered what her stepmother was trying to prove. She was watching Hyun-min intently as he picked up his spoon and tentatively put some soup in his mouth.

He put down his spoon.

'Don't you like it?' Kyung-ha asked. Her tone was unfamiliar.

'It's not that.'

'Have another spoonful.' Her voice was uncharacteristically quiet. Tender. 'Is it too salty? Or too spicy?' She looked disappointed with herself. 'I should have thought of that.'

He neither denied or confirmed this. When he spoke it was with a stiff formality, rounded sentences, a manner of speaking that no one in the South ever used anymore. In this way, Mia thought, he kept them at bay. They would never see him at ease or unguarded.

'I can't eat very much,' he said.

Mia looked across the table, each side dish worth an hour's labour. They would last for only a few days before they would go sour. When she was a teenager, her stepmother had stopped her eating if she ate more than a few bites, saying that she should not eat any more to avoid erupting into the salacious curves of white women.

'I understand.' Kyung-ha put down her spoon.

Mia continued to eat. If the rest of them weren't eating, someone would have to stop the food from going to waste. Kyung-ha shot her a look.

'We should all eat a little less,' her stepmother said.

Her stepmother began to clear the food while Mia was still eating. She expected a snide comment about her weight, about the curves of sin that would emerge from her body. But her stepmother said nothing.

She was not looking at Mia.

Mia watched Thomas frown as he read her report on the FTA agreement. Streaks of light fell onto his dark hair. Were those words in his notebook just idle thoughts? There was nothing about his manner that suggested things had changed with his wife. Conscious that she was standing before his desk like a guilty schoolgirl, Mia walked over to the window and peered between the blinds. A gardener leaned over the flowerbeds in the Ambassador's residence. It was rumoured that the Ambassador's wife had sneaked in a few seeds past customs so she could emulate the garden she had in England. The sky was grey and heavy with the imminent monsoon.

'I think it's going to rain. I hope you brought an umbrella with you today.'

He looked up momentarily and dropped his eyes to the floor, as if drawn to a private thought. Everything she said sounded too cheerful, childish. She couldn't invoke the casual manner she adopted in bars. Normally, as soon as she crossed the Embassy threshhold, paralysis took hold of her tongue. Unless she was in a meeting where she was expected to do simultaneous interpretation, her own words filled her mouth but were unable to leave it. More often than not she opted for silence. Now, she wished she had not said anything at all.

'All this over the lifting of the beef import ban?' He dropped the report on his desk and leaned back in his chair. 'I can't say I understand it.'

'The people are worried about BSE. They're worried that with the lift of the import ban, contaminated beef will be sold in every restaurant and—'

'Yes, I gather that from the report.' He squeezed his eyes shut and ran his hand over his hair, as though he was trying to soothe a headache. There was something intimate about the look. A crack in his composure. It was the way he might look at the end of an evening, his tie loose around his neck, standing in the shadow of the doorway of a bedroom. Mia had to look away, afraid that he might see the thought on her face.

'It's more than that. The people are restless – they're unhappy with the way the present government are pressuring the labour market, the sense that . . .' She stopped. She tried to think of what an Embassy wife might say. 'Koreans . . .' she began. 'They overcomplicate everything,' she finally offered.

Thomas smiled faintly. 'Is that right? Well, I'm fortunate to have you to decipher these things for me.'

There was no use in trying to resist the spread of warmth across her cheeks.

Thomas flicked through the pages of the report. 'Are you really suggesting that we're on the brink of a dictatorship?'

She cleared her throat. 'The President is ambitious. He's over-promised on where the economy is going. He wants the growth rate of the seventies. That's how the media are presenting the situation anyway: they're drawing parallels to the Park regime.'

'The media have their own agenda. Journalists are a fearful lot.' He said the last part with a sigh.

Mia wondered whether that was a dig at his own wife. He had never thanked her or mentioned her visiting his home. She wondered if they had just stopped talking.

'What do you think?'

Mia shifted uncomfortably on her feet. 'I think they have a point. There are members of charities and owners of small businesses who have been threatened because they turned up at the protests. Amnesty International has reported that charities have been threatened with the withdrawal of government funding if members turn up to these events—'

'Leave Amnesty out of this.'

Mia stepped back, surprised by his tone. 'I'm sorry—'

'Do you think there are implications on policy here?'

'Well, not right at this point—'

'Just cut it for now then. Let's keep political sensibilities out of the official reports.' He caught the look on her face and seemed to soften. 'We can't have revolutionaries in the service.'

The cuff of his shirt was wrinkled, his hair unkempt. He had the look of a man who had hardly slept. She searched him for more evidence of disarray, a sign perhaps, that his marriage was crumbling.

He tugged at his collar. 'It's so airless in here. It's impossible to think.'

'Do you want me call someone about the air conditioning?'

'No. That's all right. I'll step out in a minute. It's my wife's birthday, I thought I'd take her out to lunch.' He stood up. 'We're finished here, I presume?'

'Yes, counsellor.' Mia turned to walk out of the room before he could see the look on her face. As soon as she turned into the corridor, she screwed up the report in her hand. This self-consciousness had to stop. Whatever animal was itching inside her to get out in his presence would have to be starved.

She didn't understand it. The twist of her tongue in his company. The fear that he would look up and see mediocrity. Later, when the office floor had emptied, she went back to his office and rummaged through the bottom of his wastebasket looking for the red-ink-stained reports. His wounding cut marks across her sentences. There were other notes: details of the next trade minister's visit; an assessment of the implications of the most recent meeting between the President and Prime Minister Taro Aso. She had hoped for more. Hunted for those grand sentences. *That theatre of politics.* Or describing the peninsula as *exhibiting a complex panorama of conflict.* But in the absence of those, she stuffed his notes into her bag. She would master his language. The way he spoke with such assuredness. There was never a moment of doubt, never any hesitation as he searched for the right word. Every night, she was drawn back to the remains, the scraps of his scrawling handwriting. For those abandoned words. His beautiful turns of phrase.

Back at home, Mia pulled out her drawer and removed the clip of Thomas's notes that she had collected over several months. She sat with these fragments of paper spread before her, imagining him sitting at his desk, his eyebrows drawn together in concentration. She had underlined her favourite phrases. There was a passion in his work, she was sure of that.

She began to write the report that he would submit to the Ambassador. Using the words that he had discarded. It was less forgery than imitation. A kind of flattery, done with no purpose other than to perfect what had become an art to her.

In the five months since the landslide election, the President's popularity has plummeted. His promises of economic growth have not been met. Protesters have argued that the beef import deal is a humiliating concession negotiated by the President to appease Washington.

Some believe that these protests could lead to a political changeover in government, with protesters lobbying for the President and his cabinet to resign. There are also heightened concerns as members from unions and charities have been threatened by the government for participating in these protests. The protest last week, with almost a million participants, was held on the same date as the anniversary of the massive street protests in 1987 which brought an end to the dictatorial regime of President Chun Doo-hwan. This is no coincidence. Protesters believe that the President has already put in place draconian measures which echo the country's authoritarian past.

Mia stopped typing and crossed out the last line of the document, dissatisfied with everything she had written. Compared to Thomas's work, it was plain, artless.

She rose from her desk, wanting to abandon the task. The failure of it made her conscious of where she was. Her cell-like room. She tried to imagine Thomas standing beside her. Saw the room through his eyes: the peeling wallpaper where the wall met the ceiling, the crooked wooden chair with flaking paint.

She felt the itch she had not felt in a long time.

The pull of bad, old habits.

Nashville was exactly as Mia remembered it. The same flicker of red neon in the cursive 'i' and the same faded red leather seats smelling of the open grill. As she walked in, she saw the night's imminent disappointments: the Korean girls who would drink too much and fall asleep on the GIs, the man with the paunch sitting alone in the corner who kept trying to catch her eye. She sat at the end of the bar and ordered a beer. A group had just settled at a table nearby. One or two of them were far too young. They were giddy, had probably only recently enlisted in the army.

'Hey, darlin', what're you drinkin' there?' A man approached her at the bar. Mia thought he looked fifty, but he was dressed young for his age in a tight white T-shirt and jeans. As he leaned in to hear her reply, she saw the leather of his skin drooping over his eyes, the close shave of his greying hair. He wasn't the antidote she needed.

'I'm waiting for someone.'

He didn't seem to hear this over the music. 'Can I buy you a drink?'

'No, thanks.' She got to her feet and nodded in the direction of a group of guys sitting near the TV showing the baseball game. They laughed and as they leaned back in their seats, she saw what she was looking for. His short hair accentuated his big, protruding ears. He was quieter than the others and twisted the beer bottle on the table.

He glanced at it before taking a swig. She knew it when she saw it. She had cradled homesickness like that dozens of times. She caught his eye. He whispered to one of his friends and then, moments later, appeared beside her.

'Hi, I'm Adam.'

'Hi,' she said.

He eyed the neckline of her dress.

'Do you want a drink?'

He raised his eyebrows and grinned. 'I'll have a beer.'

'I got stood up by a friend,' she said.

'That's too bad. You can join us if you want.'

She smiled. 'What are you guys up to tonight?'

'Just seeing where the night takes us,' he replied.

'Me too.'

They knocked their bottles together. His story trickled out of him easily enough. Once she had been nourished by their desire, lived a hundred lives through their stories, discovered a hundred new homes, her knees weak at the melodic rise and fall of the Southern drawl. But as Adam leaned forward, his lips on her neck, she thought of predators who hunt but, on tasting blood, abandon their kill.

The US army base at Yongsan had recently become more fortified than it had been when Mia was a teenager. Years before it had been easy to get on base. It was just a case of slipping through the turnstiles when the guard's back was turned. Now there were strict controls and security checks at the gate. The guard held her gaze as he asked for ID when Adam signed her in. Mia knew what he was thinking and held back the urge to smash the glass between them. Beyond the security gates the base was like a small town in the Midwest of America. A pickup truck drove past them as they crossed the street. They went through residential streets with long driveways and neat gardens, just as Mia had seen them on old TV shows like *My So-Called Life* and *The Wonder Years* on AFKN. Once she had been excited by the PX store stacked with candy corn and Dreyer's Rocky Road ice-cream. Now all she could see was the barbed wire on the horizon.

Geckos was the kind of bar that Thomas had once abhorred. It was the same predictable, incestuous hub of expats he could have found at any posting. He had once been frustrated with the insular way the expats avoided the locals. When he had first joined the service, he had thrown himself into familiarizing himself with the resident culture as much as possible, reading volumes of ethnographies and histories of the places he was going to. He avoided the expats, had tried to befriend as many locals as he could. He swallowed foreign syllables and tried to hold them in his mouth, determined to awaken unused muscles in his throat as he learned new languages.

That had been before.

Jim, an English journalist Thomas had known in Phnom Penh, waved to him from the corner of the bar. He was skeletal but had a head full of thick grey hair and sat with hordes of journalists who each had the wandering expression that Thomas had come to know so well. It was the look that Felicity often assumed – nodding attentively while listening to snippets of other conversations. Whether what was being said was of substance or not did not really matter, sometimes she was merely looking for a hook to begin a conversation.

Luckily Walker and Stanton, the American diplomats he had met through the bar circuit, were also having a drink there. They had been known to dispense useful information.

'If it isn't our English gent. How's it hanging, Tom?' Walker put one hand on his shoulder and proffered his other.

'Rather badly.'

'Nothing a drink can't fix, am I right? What can we order you?'

'Hennessy, I should think.'

'Stanton here was just saying that the Finance Minister drinks that stuff by the bottle.'

'Nah, he dilutes it with beer,' Stanton quipped.

'I gather mixing brandy with beer is rather common in this country.' He had heard extraordinary stories of decadence with brandy and women in karaoke bars.

Walker gave him a look of disdain. 'But we're talking Hennessy here, Tom. We almost died of thirst for that stuff in Africa. The guy has clearly got no class.'

They spoke about the minister for several more moments. Thomas was mindful of taking only a few sips. The bars were where most of the real work was done. He was a vulture, picking up vital scraps of information after the hard work of the kill had been done. It was his strategy for keeping afloat until he could figure out exactly what he was doing. Why he had lost his way.

'How is your office coping with these protests?' Thomas asked.

Walker shrugged. 'As far as we're concerned the ink has dried on that deal, my friend, there's nothing that's going to undo it now. People are getting all hot about the beef imports but there's more to this free-trade deal than a few burgers. Know what I mean?'

'So you don't think the President will resign?'

Walker laughed. 'Doubt it. It doesn't matter if a million people turn up at these protests. He's not going to cave, he's got too much riding on this.'

'Of course,' Thomas said, taking a large gulp of his whisky. He locked eyes with Jim across the bar. The man seemed determined to talk to him. There would be no avoiding it. Thomas did not want to be around Walker and Stanton when it happened. 'Excuse me, gentlemen.'

'Thomas,' Jim greeted him. 'Feels like we're running into each other quite often these days. How is life treating you?'

'Reasonably well. Yourself?'

'Managed to get a contract with an Australian newspaper so that's given me a bit of stability. You know what it's like. Of course you do. How is your lovely wife? Must say, I really thought she did a fantastic job on that article about the evictions. She must've made a packet. Who is she working for now?'

Thomas's lip curled at this. 'No one.'

Jim's eyebrows furrowed. A tiny bit of foam from the beer had settled itself on his upper lip. He looked surprised. 'I would have thought she'd be drowning in offers for work. After that splash . . .'

There was no point in explaining to Jim that the article had almost cost both their marriage and his career.

'You'll have to ask her about it,' Thomas said, finishing off the remainder of his whisky and ordering another.

Before he learnt to dissolve his anxiety in whisky, Thomas had thrown himself into local life in Phnom Penh as much as he had in Bogota before that. When he wasn't working late in the office, he met Felicity with the local journalists she had befriended writing for *The Phnom Penh Post*. On weekends, they travelled to Battambang, Koh Kong and Siem Reap, triumphant in learning snippets of local history missing from English history books, told to them by locals in Khmer.

It had been a time of light-hearted exploration. They had been so besotted with the foreignness of it all that they had taken the poverty they saw around them for granted. It was only when they became involved with a young activist called Laura Savatt, working for Amnesty International, that what they saw before them began to be defined in terms of human rights. She spoke of forced, spontaneous evictions of the poor. They were driven out in government trucks to clean up the cities. Laura had taken him and Felicity through the mud to where the people had been relocated. Despite the rain the stench of human waste had been unbearable. Those who had found themselves evicted had set up plastic sheets and cardboard with bamboo sticks to shield themselves from the monsoon.

Laura had reported more disturbing facts. A pregnant woman had been stunned with an electric baton. Three men had been detained for resistance.

He had written urgent telegrams reporting the situation but had had no response from Whitehall. He had been in Phnom Penh for a year and though human rights had been on the agenda, it was one which frequently appeared low down on his list of priorities. Yet once he saw the villagers fighting off the rain in their makeshift homes he had become determined to do something.

He had thrown himself into the work, eschewing all his other responsibilities. He let the administration slip. The Ambassador had warned him not to get involved with the evictions; that it was beyond his remit. Thomas had become more careful after that, forgoing sleep so that he could find someone who might be willing to testify for the detained men. It had taken him beyond the crumbling colonial quarters and into the backstreets, filled with single-storey buildings, their rusted metal shop fronts and flaking paint stained with rain and looking like tired hopes. He had barely been able to get one or two words out of anyone. Instead they had looked back at him with a great silence, one that, for generations, they had learned would keep them safe. He had sweated it out in the dark, back rooms of village shops, trying to find anyone who would talk about forced evictions.

After a month, a witness came forward who was willing to testify for one of the detained men. He had met with Laura and Felicity for a drink in the evening and toasted justice.

To this day he believed that there would have been justice for those men.

If Felicity hadn't run the story.

It had become a front-cover piece in the *New York Times* and she had then been interviewed by the BBC. Suddenly she had offers for work all the time. It had been a triumph for her career.

But the detainees disappeared without a trace. The man who was willing to testify also went missing.

The final straw had come when the Ambassador queried Felicity's reference to a confidential detail about the Embassy's stance towards the local Cambodian government. He suspected Thomas of disclosing sensitive Embassy information to her. She had sworn that it was a coincidence and that she had found the details of the story through her own research. Even today, he didn't know if he believed her. She had always been ambitious. That's what he had once loved about her.

He could measure the size of the rift between them in units of whisky. At first it had just been a glass on the way home. Their arguments had become circular: his career or hers. Then it had become an additional glass on the drive home to warm him up before dinner. Then a glass at lunch.

When he had almost been sacked for being drunk at an official function at the Ambassador's residence, he had maliciously told her it was because of the article. She had given in. She still didn't know the true extent of his drinking.

Even on nights like this, when he locked himself in the toilet of the bar, trying to stop his head from spinning, he knew how to get himself back in order so that she didn't know how bad it was or how often it happened.

Thomas sat with his trousers around his ankles and tried to recall what Walker and Stanton had said. He had misplaced his notebook and wrote on a napkin instead. The pen slipped and stained his white shirt. He cursed, trying to focus on the blurry napkin in his hand. The Minister of Finance. Hennessy, he had written. It was these little details, he knew, which would give the appearance of intimacy with the Minister. He would slip them into conversation with the Ambassador. He had become cynical, he knew, but acting on this cynicism seemed to work.

He stood up in the cubicle and hopped against the toilet door to regain his balance. The vinegary scent of the toilets turned his stomach. Nausea rippled through him. He held his tie against his stomach and retched into the toilet bowl.

Wiping his mouth, he left the men's toilets. The bar had emptied. Walker and Stanton had gone. It was after midnight and Felicity would be asleep. When he came home late, it was always in display of how hard he was working. Thomas fell down the steps of the garden patio of the bar and found himself in an alley. It took him a few moments before he realized where he was. He stumbled towards the main street of Itaewon in search of his car.

A woman called out to him from a doorway. Through his blurred vision he saw that she was wearing a tight-fitting red dress.

'If you could point me in the direction of the Hamilton Hotel, I'd be grateful.'

'What you looking for, honey? You don't go so far to get what you want.'

'Well,' he said with a laugh, though he was unsure of what was funny himself, 'unless you have my car, you're gravely mistaken.'

'I give you a ride, honey.'

Thomas started to say something and then changed his mind. The prostitute gave him a look of impatience. Drawing closer to her in the darkness he saw that there were many layers of make up on her face. Despite this, she wasn't altogether unattractive. Briefly he considered stepping into the doorway and stopping thinking altogether. Would it alleviate the numbness? It would not be a small price to pay to find out, though it would keep him out of greater trouble. He would resurface hollow, he knew that.

'I'll shop around, thanks,' he said.

She stepped past him, apparently already searching for other customers. He stumbled down the sparsely lit alleyway. He was sure that to continue down it was to be exposed to any number of imaginable temptations.

After several wrong turns he found himself on the main street. Relieved to have found it, he stepped inside a convenience shop and bought himself a bottle of water. It was starting to get very humid. He wiped his head with sleeve and sat on the pavement, drinking. Young Korean girls walked past, hanging on the arms of off-duty soldiers, men in tight white T-shirts and baggy trousers which were on the verge of falling off their non-existent backsides.

When he found his car, he sat inside it for several moments before starting the engine. His head spun when he closed his eyes but he set off anyway, driving up the winding steep hills, passing large gated properties.

The road became increasingly difficult to see. He blinked several times to clear his vision. He signalled left as he passed the Hyatt Hotel. There were hardly any cars out on the winding road ahead, or were there? He shifted a little, his damp shirt clinging to his chest. What he had taken for brake lights ahead turned out to be cats' eyes. The traffic lights pulsed both green and red simultaneously.

He thought about pulling over but continued on. If he parked and fell asleep on the roadside, he knew he would oversleep. He would be late for work. The Ambassador had warned him.

The streets blurred around him. The brake did nothing to stop the spinning. He hit his head hard against the steering wheel. Somewhere nearby he heard the shriek of metal followed by a crunch. An odd silence followed. He was no longer in motion. A knot formed in the pit of his stomach, bile on a slow climb in his throat. He tried to open the car door. It was jammed. His mind felt thick with shock, it was as though he had stepped outside of his body as he pushed frantically against the door. He felt a warm trickle on his cheek. He wiped at his face. His palm came away covered in blood.

They lay on the damp single bed, listening to the chatter of voices in the corridors. Mia rolled onto her stomach and turned the knob of the radio.

'I love this song,' she said, forcing herself to be more cheerful than she felt. She had long outgrown these habits. 'Do you have any more cigarettes? I'm all out.'

'Check the drawer.'

Mia opened the drawer and saw a packet of Lucky Strike tucked under a copy of the Bible. 'You're kidding, right?'

'No, ma'am.'

Kyung-ha would approve of this, at least, she thought. 'Do you ever read it?'

'Sure I do. We're technically at war here. Anything could happen. North Koreans have got a bad case of the crazies. Got to make your peace with God when you can.'

Mia felt the thin pages between her fingers and then put her chin on her fists.

He was studying her. 'What's your deal, anyway?'

Mia shrugged. 'How do you mean?'

'Are you going to tell me about it?'

'About what?'

'This.' He pulled back the sheet and touched the raised scar on her collarbone. 'Was it a guy?'

Mia hesitated. She rarely hung around long enough to have this conversation. 'And if it was?'

'I'd kill him.'

Mia wrapped the sheet around her and gave him a kiss on the cheek. 'You're sweet.' She wished it were enough. 'Where in the States did you say you were from?'

'Fern Creek.'

'Where's that?'

'Kentucky. It's a small town, you probably haven't heard of it.'

'What's it like there?'

'It's the kinda place where everybody grows old together, everybody knows everyone's business.' He stopped and gave her a smile. 'You want to *mally* me so I take you there?'

She laughed and punched him playfully on the arm so he would not see how much the idea disgusted her. He misunderstood her. She wasn't one of those girls; she was playing an entirely different game. Flicking on the light at the wall, the room seemed smaller than it had been an hour before. She was repelled by the plain brown sheets and dark print curtains. The smell of Tide on the linen and the strong scent of his cologne on her skin were suffocating.

She picked her clothes from the floor. 'I have to go.'

'Do you want to hang out next weekend?'

'I'll call you,' she lied.

The base looked different in the blue morning light. An artificial, miniature America.

At the subway station, Mia wiped the dark eyeliner from her face and scrubbed herself with dispenser soap from the public toilets. She pulled out a fresh T-shirt, a pair of jogging pants and hiking boots from her rucksack.

The trains had not yet started running. In any case she preferred the bus. She wanted to take in the city. Watching it go by calmed her, made her feel she was moving forwards, not returning to old habits.

She turned the corner onto the street. It was strangely eerie in the early morning light. The streets were deserted. A short distance ahead, smoke was rising from the middle of the street. A fire. She heard the rattling whirr of an engine. As she walked towards the bus stop, she saw that there had been an accident. A car had driven into a street cart and had a large crack in the windshield. Whoever was involved would have been lucky to survive.

Just as the bus arrived, she caught sight of the diplomatic license plates. British. An Embassy car. She ran across the street towards it.

A man sat with his face buried in the airbag. The driver's door was jammed. The passenger's side was badly damaged. She went back to the driver's side and knocked on the window. The driver was unconscious. She took out the clothes she had worn the night before and, wrapping them around her fist, punched at the glass several times. This seemed to rouse the driver. The car was thick with the smell of whisky. She tugged on the driver's arm, nearly dropping it when she saw who it was.

Thomas's face was streaked with blood. The source of it seemed to be a gash above his eyebrow. She checked his arms, the rest of his limp body. She detected no other serious injury. She pulled him out onto the side of the road. He groaned and opened his eyes a little.

She held his face. 'Are you okay?'

He said something she couldn't make out.

'What happened?'

'How bad is it?' he asked. He seemed to be having trouble staying conscious. 'I'm finished.'

A passerby squinted at them from across the street. She became conscious of the Embassy plates. She needed to assess how much damage had been done.

The car was still running. She sat in the driver's seat and put it into reverse. There was a shriek of metal as something dislodged itself from underneath the car. Once it was free of the obstruction, it began to move. The engine sounded as though it were going to cut out at any moment. She put the car into drive and crept forward, wondering where she could possibly abandon it so that it wouldn't attract any unwanted attention.

She saw an underground car park on the other side of the road. Thankfully the parking attendant was asleep. She drove down to the lowest level, to the space furthest from the lifts. When she stepped out of the car, she saw that the front bumper had come away, hinging only on a thin strip of metal. She was able to lift off the front license plate, loosened from its screws by the impact, with ease. It was the back set, which had not been subject to damage in the crash, that presented a greater challenge. She got on her knees, the only tool at her disposal the heel of the shoes she had worn the evening before, to free the metal plate that would expose him.

When she returned to him, Thomas was still lying across the pavement, his face so slack against the pavement that he appeared dead. She tried talking to him and looked around for witnesses, conscious of the blood.

Several minutes passed before a taxi appeared. The cab driver helped her lift Thomas from the street. He did not stir and lay inside the car with his chin against his shoulder like a wounded saint. Perhaps there was some truth in what Charles had said. He had a history of trouble in his last posting. The car was Embassy property. He could have killed someone. Even if he managed to evade questions from the police, he would be in trouble with the Ambassador.

They pulled into the Emergency Room and she half carried him across her body to lift him into the lobby. They brought a stretcher for him. As they lay him down in his shroud of blood and vomit, he let out a soft groan. A nurse tugged at her arm, tearing her away.

'You'll have to fill out some forms.'

The nurse led her back behind the lobby and handed her a clipboard and a pen.

Name. Thomas Dalton, she wrote, deciding not to write out his full name. Just in case.

Address. Mia scribbled her own address and phone number.

Occupation. She hastily wrote, English teacher.

'It's not an exam, you know,' the nurse said after a while.

Mia gave her a weak smile, handing the forms through the window and onto the nurse's desk. 'It must be the shock,' she said quickly. 'All that blood.'

With that she turned the corner onto the emergency ward. She drew back the curtain around the bed they had left him in.

And she found it empty. He was gone.

It was only on the street that he became aware of the blood snaking down his arm. His first instinct had been to free himself of the bed. Unlatch himself from the IV. He found his wallet in his pocket. The memory of how he had arrived at the hospital was harder to attain. He caught sight of his reflection in the pharmacy window. A large dressing covered his eyebrow. His shirt was stained with blood. He looked like a man who had walked away from a plane wreck.

What was he going to tell Felicity?

He walked to the line of taxis waiting outside the hospital and mumbled his address to a taxi driver who asked him to repeat himself several times before he understood where Thomas wanted to go. He squeezed his eyes shut against the thunderclap of pain that reverberated inside his head. What was there to tell? How would he explain what had happened to the car?

There was no traffic to buy him more time. As the taxi drew to a halt in front of his house, he realized that he would have to explain

75

more than just the car. She would want to know where he had been.

After fumbling with his keys at the door with unsteady hands, he paused for a moment in the garden. He could feel the sweat under his dressing. The heat did nothing to quell his nausea. He stood paralysed with indecision, feeling the sharp spasm building upward momentum just below his sternum. Then he was prostrate before Felicity's roses, expelling an unceremonious offering of bile. He groaned, pushing against the bush. Moments later, when he was feeling better, it was thirst that drew him towards the house.

The front door betrayed his entrance. The creak of it elicited Felicity's footsteps across the bedroom upstairs, the landing, the stairs. He knew by the heavy footfall of her steps that she had been waiting for him. That there would be no lamb dinner waiting for him. Her steps slowed as she descended the stairs.

'My God, Tom, are you all right? What happened?'

What had happened? He had come to on the pavement, his car nowhere in sight. Only a piece of it spinning ominously on the road before he lost consciousness again.

He staggered forward, feigning more instability than he felt. She led him by the elbow onto the sofa, like a stranger guiding the blind. He closed his eyes for a moment. What would he tell the Embassy? Was it better to confess and resign? By now someone would have reported the car. The diplomatic license plates a glaring accusation. They would piece it together before he even said a word. He did not have the capacity to lie. She would know about his drinking. But to reveal that he had crashed the car? Then she would know it was serious.

'I don't know,' he began. It was the only honest answer he could give. 'I'm finished, I'm a mess,' he said, without looking at her. He felt tears sting his eyes. 'I'm sorry.'

★

She watched him from the doorway of the bathroom. He lay in the bathtub, the water now tepid, feeling the ache of alcohol as it left his body.

'I rang the office and told them you hit your head fixing the kitchen cabinet.' She paused. 'God knows, I've talked about the state of this house enough for it to be believable. I said you'd be in tomorrow.'

He opened his mouth, grateful but unable to say so. Her lie would be exposed as soon as his car was found. They would put the pieces together when they saw the state of him. He chose not to tell her so.

'Thank you.'

'What's going on? The stench of you, how did this happen?' She sank down in the doorway and looked down at her hands, now gathered in her lap. It was the same look that she had had when she had learned of the incident in the Ambassador's residence in Phnom Penh. She was ashamed of him.

'You know these Koreans . . .' he trailed off, remembering exactly how the Ambassador had put it, 'they'll drink you under the table. A Korean minister suggested we go to a bar. You know what it's like here. You can't say no.'

'What on earth happened to your head?'

'I stood up too quickly . . . hit my head at the bar,' he offered. He wasn't sure it was convincing.

Felicity looked incredulous.

'But with everything that's happened . . .' she stopped herself. 'It can't happen again. I thought we had a deal. Isn't that why you don't want me working for the paper? Will you at least try? There won't be any second chances, they made that clear.'

'I know that,' he said, suddenly feeling guilty. She still thought he had almost been sacked because of her story. She didn't know it had been his drinking.

'You didn't drive home in this state, did you?'

'Of course not, I took a taxi,' he snapped. 'I had the car taken in for servicing. I was having engine trouble.' He immediately regretted the lie. It was all about to unravel around him. He squeezed his eyes shut. 'Everything's a mess. How did we end up here?'

When he opened his eyes, she was standing over him. For a moment it looked as though she were about to touch him. Then she drew back and sat beside the bathtub instead.

He took hold of her wrist.

She shook him off. 'I was foolish to think things are getting better.'

'I want things to be better,' he admitted. He sat a little straighter in the bathtub. 'I didn't before. I'm sorry, I will try.'

He could see that she was holding back all her questions, fighting back the journalist in her. For now, his apologies seemed to soften her. In that moment he meant it. He wanted to be better. If he could get away with it this time, he would change. He would stop drinking. He would even try to make it work with Felicity.

'Aren't you going home?' one of the girls asked her.

Kyung-ha looked up from her sewing. Outside the shop, night had already descended. The tiny wall clock pointed to nine o'clock. Kyung-ha looked at the pile accumulating on her desk. The hem on the skirt she was working on would not straighten. It hadn't always been this difficult.

'Once I've finished this,' she replied.

The girl looked from the skirt back to Kyung-ha. 'I hope whoever it is comes back for it. I don't know how women just forget about their designer things like that.'

'They probably just go out and buy something new and then don't think about the old pieces again.'

'But then why drop off the items in the first place?' she said, shaking her head.

'Maybe they'll come back,' the other said.

Kyung-ha looked up in the direction of the storeroom. It was filled with bags of designer clothes that had been forgotten by their owners. On occasion the girls would borrow these clothes, but they would always return them. Just in case customers came to reclaim them. Though they never did.

'I don't know how you do it. I can't concentrate for that long anymore. I must be getting old.'

'When I started working I had to miss my lunch break if I made a mistake,' Kyung-ha said.

She thought back to the bleak days before she had found Jun-su. The diet of dusty, watery yoghurts and stale confectionery. She remembered the loneliness of those days when she couldn't even talk to the other girls over the sound of the sewing machines. Every night she brushed the fibrous dust out of her hair. Her fingers became so calloused even now she could not feel the tips of them.

'That was a long time ago. I had a nasty guy for a boss. Making passes at the young factory girls who were too tired to fight him.'

'Back then, you'd have to promise your first-born to your boss.'

'Not that married women worked then.'

Kyung-ha didn't contradict her. She had learned over the years not to talk about the past. It had never led to any good.

The women continued to chat as they gathered their things.

'Go well,' Kyung-ha said as they walked out of the door.

Kyung-ha cut the thread to sever the stitching she had done for the hem of the skirt. Her fingers were stiff and ached when she tried, as she had done all day, to fold the hem straight. She counted the pieces that were piled on the edge of her table. Years ago she would have gone through the pile in just a few hours. But with the state of her hands, she found it difficult to hold fabric straight.

Her fingers were curling into claws. The mark of a sinner. In entrusting the boy to her care, the Lord was reminding her that he had not forgotten what she had done. Kyung-ha pushed these thoughts out of her mind and turned on the iron to flatten the fold. She couldn't count how many times she had done this. It had not even come close to be passably straight. Everything took twice the time that it had in the past. The iron was heavy and unsteady in her hands. As she moved the skirt onto the sewing machine, she felt the pull of the past as she often did when she did not keep her fingers moving. As she stitched, she imagined she were re-stitching the past, creating pouches in the fabric where she preferred not to remember.

In those pouches she kept Jong-ho.

She examined the skirt in the light. Her effort had produced another failure. Her vision blurred from looking at it for so long. She was postponing going home where she would have to see Hyun-min again.

She worked for almost an hour after the girls left, her back aching. She would have to try again in the morning. As she gathered her bags, she went to the storeroom and picked out a plain black jacket and a pair of trousers to wear to church on Sunday. She switched off the lights and locked the shop door behind her.

She caught the bus home and watched the city go by, a growing knot in her stomach as she drew closer to home. Kyung-ha could hardly bring herself to speak to the boy. In the few days that he had been staying in their home, she had kept conversation to a minimum. She offered him food and asked him how he slept. Then she would have to leave the room and watch him from the edge of her bedroom door. The slope of his shoulders. The way he mindlessly chewed the Crunky chocolates she gave him. Mostly, it was in the way that he moved. The awkward, jutting movements of boys who grew too quickly for their body.

Jong-ho had been so skinny.

She feared smothering Hyun-min in her arms, and so she had to leave the rooms that contained him. He seemed determined not to make a dent in the household with his presence. He swept the living-room floor every morning. He folded his bedding so that it fitted neatly between the TV cabinet and the crumbling medicine cabinet. His favourite orange T-shirt was always creaseless. In the mornings she found all the shoes aligned and facing the gate on the porch. Kyung-ha felt she was peering at an alternate version of events,

Jong-ho at eighteen, at home with her. To speak to him would be to break the illusion.

Taking a deep breath, she pushed through the gate and into the house. She had been saving her energy for the moment when she would have to see Hyun-min again. Yet as she walked around the house, she saw that it was empty. She checked the living room, Mia's room and the kitchen. The boy was not home.

She stood over her husband, who paused in his painting as she came in. That was all the acknowledgement there was. A hesitation in his paintbrush. Did he resent her? She looked over his shoulder at the vague, blurry landscapes. The girl often sat beside her father, trying to decipher some of these patterns. Kyung-ha didn't believe, however, that Jun-su was really trying to communicate anything. Yet, as she stood over his shoulder, she saw a sheet of calligraphy paper. Shaky vertical lines. Then an outward flick of the brush, perfectly formed. The character *ryuk*. Strength. Kyung-ha traced the brushwork with her finger. The intention was unmistakable.

There was a defiance in his silence.

He had once been a master of hide-and-seek. She had smelled the other women on his clothes as she beat the garments clean in the courtyard. She had gone to great lengths to catch him in the act. He vanished on street corners as she followed him. When she had burst into inn rooms, she would find his cigarette still burning in an ashtray beside the lipstick-stained one of his mistress, but the room would be empty. She began to lose sleep, her stomach turned by the smell of Jun-su's skin as he lay beside her. The sickly scent of frying butter wafted from his clothes. It was the smell she remembered from the American soldiers she had encountered as a child, just after the war. Every night she endured the smell of another woman. A foreigner in their bedding.

The old rage was reignited. She smacked his waterpots with the back of her hand. Spilt the dregs of his colours over his old canvases so that they became grey. A splatter covered the table, spilled onto his linen trousers. Pencils rolled across the floor, their revolutions thwarted only by the doorframe. Kyung-ha did this though she knew that she was the one who would have to rub the floors with rags, on her hands and swollen knees.

His self-containment infuriated her. He no longer needed the outside world. He had not left the house in years. There were days when he only left his room to use the bathroom. When he did not protest or respond with his dry raspy breathing, she shook him by the shoulders. But when she touched him, she felt searing pain, as though his flesh were boiling hot.

'Did you ever wonder about your son? Did you care that he lay dying while you jumped between those whores' beds?'

Thomas stepped out of the lift and into the glare of the fluorescent strip lights. He already regretted the decision to come to the office. How long before the wreckage was found, the diplomatic license plates traced back to the Embassy, to him? The gaps in his memory troubled him. Without knowing what had happened to the car, it was impossible for him to cover his own tracks, defend himself. He swung around the few cubicles by his office, his face down, hoping to pass by unnoticed.

'The Ambassador is waiting for you to begin the meeting about the FTA protests,' Mrs Oh said as he rushed by. Then he heard her gasp. 'What happened to your face?'

'I hit my head,' he mumbled. He closed the door behind him as soon as he set foot in his office. The report. It had completely slipped his mind.

Grasping for a chair, he sat down to steady himself against the vertigo. How could he tell the Ambassador that he simply hadn't written it? He had been warned. There would be no more mistakes. Perhaps he could feign the injury to the head as more substantial than Felicity had let on. He had to get his act together. There had to be a way back to his former glory. In the days before he lost control he never would have let it come to this. He would have lost sleep trying to complete the report. He had to stop. He wanted to.

There was a knock on the door. The Ambassador's secretary told him they were waiting for him.

'I'll be there in a minute,' he said, feeling resigned to the public ridicule he would endure when the Ambassador saw the blank look on his face.

He was the last to arrive at the meeting and sat down apologizing loudly to conceal his embarrassment. He didn't care to interpret the look on the Ambassador's face. Dread flooded his stomach. He was doomed. Several people stared at the bandage over his eyebrow; he felt it burn with incrimination.

'Good of you to join us,' the Ambassador said, gazing at Thomas's eyebrow. 'As I was saying, I thought we should discuss the recent protests,' he said, with another glance in his direction.

That paternal treatment brought out the child in him. A child caught with his hand down his pants in front of the whole class.

'I don't really see the point, this sort of clash is a dime a dozen in this country,' Paul said.

'Not on this scale,' someone else pitched in.

'Thomas, what do you think?' the Ambassador asked.

The Ambassador was trying to humiliate him in front of everyone. What did he really know about the issue? He had hardly been paying attention. He tried to clear his head of the fog. His eyebrow throbbed.

'Well . . .'

'In your report you suggest that we might be on the cusp of a dictatorship, which I suppose would require some kind of revision in our attitude to relations between us.'

There was a bit of irritation in the way that he said this. It took him a moment to register what the Ambassador had actually said.

He was momentarily confounded. What report? He looked around the table to see whether this was some kind of extended joke. 'You'll have to forgive me,' he said, rubbing his head. 'I seem to have left my copy of the report on my desk . . .'

Paul handed him several pages across the table. He coughed to mask the laugh that rose in him. Had he written this? Impossible. He was losing his mind.

'Just because the President is trying to clear up this mess that's happening in the centre of the city, that doesn't mean he's suddenly a dictator,' Paul said.

'Yes, but I agree with Thomas,' Samantha chipped in, 'that with various ministers handing in their resignations, the President may be able to select others who might be more sympathetic to his agenda.'

'There's also the possibility that the President might resign,' Paul countered.

'I'm merely suggesting . . .' Thomas began, realizing that he had to say something. He met Mia's eyes across the table. She was staring at him keenly. 'That the situation is unstable. A number of scenarios are likely, but the President's dictatorial tactics illustrate a frightening trend.'

'Interesting,' The Ambassador said, nodding. 'We should keep a close eye on the situation and revise our current policies,' he said.

They moved on to discussing Boeing's chief executive's upcoming visit. Thomas hardly listened, wondering what on earth had just happened. Someone had written the report and turned it in to the Ambassador as if it were his work. He caught Mia's eye across the table again. She didn't seem to be listening either.

When the meeting was over, everyone stood up to leave. Thomas was about to slip away when the Ambassador called for him.

'You seem to have sustained quite an injury there,' he said.

'It looks worse that it is.'

'When you have a minute, I'd like a word.'

'Of course,' he replied.

Once the Ambassador had left the room, he grimaced. Was it possible that he already knew about the accident? He ruled out this idea. If he knew he wouldn't have sat through the charade of the meeting.

The report lay on the table in front of him. He picked it up and re-read a few paragraphs. He had to find out who had circulated it.

He floated back to his office from the boardroom. He had had his share of drunken moments, but was it possible that he had more substantial lapses in his memory than he realized?

Mia came in and closed the door behind her, leaned with her back against it, her arms behind her. 'You're here.'

'Where else would I be?'

'How is your head?'

'It seems to be the least of my problems.'

'You're worried about the report . . .'

'I'm baffled, quite frankly,' he said.

She was staring at him, her mouth slightly open. Her dark eyes were performing an excavation. He looked away to stop her from finding whatever it was she was looking for. He sat down at his desk, hoping that it would encourage her to leave. But she stood, unmoving.

What did she want from him? Her presence was full of expectation. Then the two bewildering things came together in his mind, the pieces fitting perfectly.

'You wrote the report?' he asked her.

She nodded. 'I told them you had asked me to send it yesterday while you were out.'

He laughed out of not knowing what to think. 'You needn't have bothered. I'm finished here. When Nigel finds out—'

'The Ambassador doesn't have to know.'

'No,' he shook his head. 'Not about the report. Never mind.'

There was something else. He was still several steps behind. He could see that on her face.

'You don't remember . . .' she said.

He froze. 'What do you mean?'

'The car, the hospital. When I came back from filling out the forms, you were gone.'

She crossed the room.

He became conscious of the small distance between them.

'You mean . . .' He touched his head. 'How is that possible?'

'I saw your car from across the street. I carried you out and took you to the Emergency Room.'

He stared at her, incredulous. 'You mean you just happened to be there?'

She nodded.

It took him a few moments to understand what this meant.

He found himself distracted by a strand of black hair that fell into her eyes. He began to search her for more details: the pleasant jut of her collarbone at the edge of her shirt, a sliver of olive skin from the gap between the buttons between her breasts. He looked away.

'You mean no one knows about this?'

'I got your car off the street as soon as I could. It's in a safe place. It's in bad shape, but I think I know a place that will be able to fix it.'

For hours he had walked around with the weight of failure in his stomach. He had not even dared to hope for a second chance. Yet here stood the bearer of secrets. An unexpected heroine. It was as though he were seeing her for the first time. Her dark, hot eyes. Her slim arms in the short-sleeved shirt. The hint of a scar at the edge of her collarbone. Relief flooded through him, like a gush of water against his parched throat.

'I don't know what to say,' he said, too embarrassed to thank her.

★

The Ambassador stood by the window watering the avocado plants with his back to Thomas for several moments. Thomas was unsure whether to stand or sit.

'Sit down, we should have a chat.'

The leather armchair by the coffee table was too soft. He felt himself sinking into it, unable to straighten himself out. The elation of getting away with it had subsided as he considered what it might be that the Ambassador wanted.

'This report,' The Ambassador said, his eyebrows furrowed. 'Where did it come from?'

His heart sank. Of course. The Ambassador suspected that it wasn't his work. 'Well . . .'

'You mustn't misunderstand. I see you've taken to heart what we discussed at our last meeting. You certainly seem to be pulling yourself together.'

Thomas searched for sarcasm in what the Ambassador had just said.

'I mean this report. It's so utterly different from what I've seen of your work recently. I hadn't realized that you'd invested so much in getting acquainted with the situation. Has someone been helping you with this?'

He was reluctant to respond; he had certainly not been expecting this. 'Mia Kim helped me with some translations and offered her input.'

The Ambassador nodded as if in agreement with some internal thought. There was a long pause. Thomas wondered if this was an invitation to confess.

'I was impressed with the report and it's made me think . . .' The Ambassador paused as if considering what he was about to say. 'I wondered whether I might interest you in a slightly different project.'

Thomas's head snapped up.

'The NIS are tightening up security and they've asked us to perform a few security audits. Spot checks, if you like.'

'The intelligence service?'

The Ambassador nodded. 'Rather curious: they thought we might do an audit report on Mia Kim.'

'Mia Kim?' he repeated.

'They'd like an assessment along the following lines: is she trustworthy with confidential information? Could she be the source of a leak to the Embassy's security walls? Does she have any questionable alliances? An independent background check. That sort of thing.'

Thomas felt a tightening in his chest. It seemed possible that this was an elaborate ruse designed to get him to confess that Mia had covered for him.

'Was there something in particular that's prompted the NIS to pursue this?' he asked.

'If there is they haven't disclosed it,' he said. Then as if to persuade him, offered, 'Of course you understand that a project like this holds a great deal of weight in the service.'

The Ambassador did not have to continue. He was offering an opportunity to win back what he had lost. Thomas didn't know what to say to this. Just several hours before he had thought he had lost his job and would be damned for ever.

Mia walked into the kitchen to find her uncle sitting beside her stepmother. Despite everything that had passed between them, her heart still lifted at the sight of him. At least until she saw the new contours of his misery. The slackening of his generous cheeks. The enlargement of his bulbous nose against his withering skin. His ageing was a betrayal of the man she had once loved.

'He wouldn't just leave without saying anything,' he said.

Mia had thought nothing of the rolled-up futon in the living room when she had returned after discovering the accident. But later she found that Hyun-min had not returned one afternoon after saying that he was going for a walk. It had now been two days although the backpack he had brought with him was still tucked neatly under the chair in the living room.

'You don't think . . . ?' Kyung-ha began. She didn't finish that sentence.

'The kid's always had a heavy mouth. I don't know who he talks to. Even before this thing with Myung-chul. I have this feeling that it might be something else . . .' Her uncle rubbed his fist on the table as though trying to quash a disturbing thought. 'Do you have anything to drink?'

Kyung-ha brought out a bottle from the back cabinet.

Her uncle tipped the soju into a glass.

'Mia,' he said, without turning around. 'Why don't you sit down instead of standing around like you don't see us? Drink with your uncle.'

She sat down.

'This business I'm in is drying the blood in my veins,' he said. His face had reddened from the drink. Her uncle was not a man who could tolerate his liquor. 'You're a smart girl. It's good that you got out of the school when you did.'

She let the soju sting her lips. The distance between them felt like an intrusive visitor.

'He'll be back,' she said.

'We can hope, that's all,' he said.

'Have you tried looking for him at his old apartment?' Mia asked.

'Why would he go back there?' her stepmother chipped in. Then she seemed to change her mind. 'You should check, Mia.'

Mia shot her stepmother a look. She did not respect the distance that Mia needed to keep from Hyun-min. She held her tongue. Remarks of this kind would only be met with comments about her insolence. Her stepmother gave her a scrap of paper with an address on it.

Her uncle said nothing, hardly seeming to hear the exchange. He seemed preoccupied with listening to his own internal self-accusations.

Reluctantly, Mia got to her feet. She would do it for her uncle. For old times' sake.

Her uncle had been the hero of her childhood. She had been a mute child and he had consoled her with a spam radio, coaxing her to speak. Convinced that she was stuck between languages, he had tuned into the BBC World Service and had begun translating English words as they listened to the reports. When her stepmother had found out, she had thrown him out of the house. A spam radio would have them all arrested, she had said, they could be accused of using it to listen to North Korean radio programmes.

They had begun to grow apart when Mia was hospitalized as a teenager. Her uncle had brought her some comic books and sat in his chair clenching and unclenching his hands, leaning back and then forwards again. 'Jesus.'

He rolled the papers that he held in his hands as he spoke softly so the other patients could not hear, 'You know, you could have died.'

Mia had nodded. Her jaws had been wired shut. Nonchalance had been difficult to convey with a broken shoulder.

'Your mother . . . it's not something I know much about.' She had watched his Adam's apple move up and down his throat as he swallowed. He began to lecture her about the hardships of the North Korean defectors he had at his school. 'What are we going to do with you? It's like you want to make things difficult for yourself. The kids at my school, they weren't only abandoned, but starving. Traded for food and money by their parents. You've got nothing on them, kid…'

She let her uncle's words wander in and out of her consciousness. All she had wanted was to empty her head of words. Mia felt burdened with stories of their hardships when she was not even clear of her own story.

Mia had looked away, disappointed that he didn't understand. The last thing she remembered before waking up in hospital was the sight of blood on the girls' white socks, the stained hems of their skirts. Pain had been a welcome distraction to her failed attempt to bleed herself of her Englishness. As far as she could tell, her blood remained a noxious mix of madness. She had refused the morphine they offered, waved the nurses off with her crooked fingers.

It was only when her father had come to visit her in hospital that she had eventually succumbed to the morphine. As a child Mia had spent many hours at his feet, stretching the corners of his mouth, trying to create wrinkles on the sides of his eyes, moulding his expressions with her hands. She'd had temper tantrums when Kyung-ha yanked her to her feet as she sat in front of her father trying to read his thoughts. She had hit her father and he had not even tried to defend himself. As she had grown up she had found her father's silence a thing of solace, a soothing place to escape from a cacophony of conflicting stories. But as he sat beside her in hospital, she grew suspicious of his silence, a manipulative, heavy thing of irritating loudness.

The next time her uncle came to visit, it was with a stack of letters. 'You need something to do, kid. Translate these for me, will you?'

Eventually boredom got the better of her and she did as her uncle asked. Slowly, she found a way to hold her pen so she could write, despite the thick casts on her hands. The letters always began in the same fashion:

Dear _____,

I am the director of a school for North Korean defectors and only wish for a moment of your time. As you may know, the Korean peninsula has been at war for almost fifty years. Our students are those who have risked their lives in order to cross the border. Many of them have lost their parents to famine. Some have parents who have been sentenced to hard labour or the firing squads. Our school is unique . . .

She began the translations fascinated by the no man's lands that stretched open as she carried words like wounded victims from one language to another. Lost in the world of words, she began to believe that if she found the perfect translation, even she herself would make sense.

She never went back to school. She sat her high school exams with the North Korean defectors at her uncle's school. She had kept her distance from them and continued to work there, helping him with his administrative duties.

Later, when her legs had healed and she could walk without pain, she began to take the long bus ride to the bottom of a hiking trail. At the top she would look down at the airfields of Gimpo, watching the planes take off and land. Was it possible to be nostalgic for a home you never had? She tried to fold away her preoccupations about her mother, but in the absence of any more information, her imaginations about the English loomed larger. If she could not rid herself of the Englishness that had alienated her everywhere she went, she would have to try to understand them.

It was there that she had uncovered her ambition to be a translator and interpreter. Her uncle had wanted her to stay and work for him. He lectured her on the good she would be doing with a skill that was so hard to come by, so useful. But she did not want to be in a community that hosted those who were perpetually lost. She had wanted to find a place to belong. And when she had seen the opportunity at the British Embassy she had leapt at the chance. But he had not understood it. His heart had room for the suffering of defectors, but had no eyes to see her own.

That had been almost four years before.

She got off the bus in Mapo. How had Hyun-min and his roommate had managed to get an apartment so centrally? As far as she knew, defectors were allocated apartments in Suwon, or in different cities. She wondered if Hyun-min or Myung-chul had some significant connections, or strings they had pulled. Perhaps they had traded important information to win them more privileges from the South Korean government.

The apartment block rose fifteen storeys high above a busy market where vendors sold eels and fresh crabs out of red plastic buckets.

She walked through the entrance and inspected the mailbox for apartment 214. It was unmarked by names. She walked up the stairs but hesitated before putting the key her uncle had given her in the lock.

She knocked instead. 'Hyun-min?'

There was no answer.

She opened the door. She didn't know what she had been expecting. A dead body, perhaps, remnants of suicide. She did not expect to find the collection of black-and-white portraits. Photographs had been hung with washing pins across a line from the edges of the room. Two dozen faces blinked back at her as she moved through the room. A fabric screen divided the living room. On the other side of it she found trays for developing prints and an ancient printing machine. There was a small room with nothing but a low desk, a cracked mother of pearl dresser and a neat stack of clothes. She avoided the bathroom.

She sat on the futon that had been rolled neatly into a corner. It was probably what Hyun-min had slept on. She recognised his neatness. She was surprised by how clean and homely the apartment felt. There was nothing in the apartment that pointed to great unhappiness.

There was also no sign that Hyun-min had recently been there.

How many days had it been since his last drink? It was too painful to try to remember. He kept losing count, the thread of his thoughts fraying as he neared the end of them. Mostly he was distracted by the pounding in his head, the throbbing cut under his eyebrow. And the heat. The humidity made his headache worse. He closed the door leading to the garden, turned on the air conditioning, then wandered from room to room, looking for a cooler spot where he might finally fall asleep.

His hands were trembling. And it wasn't just the alcohol. There was another source of anxiety. It was something to do with Mia. The way she stood with her back against his door. Her eyes an empty stomach. Concerned for him. But there was something else, wasn't there? He would not think about that now. It was enough to try to keep his hands steady. He had been given a second chance.

He saw Felicity sitting on the sofa as he walked past the living room, sitting in a dressing gown, her hair tied back into a messy ponytail.

'Sorry, I don't want to disturb you,' he said, about to venture upstairs when he saw their wedding photographs spread across the coffee table. 'What are you doing?'

'Just taking a moment to enjoy the peace and quiet. I haven't got to rush off anywhere this morning.' She put the mug she held in her hands on the coffee table and patted the sofa beside her. 'Why don't you join me? I was taking a gentle trip down Memory Lane.'

He considered this for a moment and then, for lack of a decent excuse, sat beside her.

'You look tired, darling. Why don't I get you a cup of tea?'

'That's all right.' He could hear the clock on the mantelpiece ticking. 'Is that a new clock? Don't think I've seen it before.'

'I bought it from Insa-dong a month ago.'

'Ah-ha.'

They sat on the sofa, their eyes surveying the pristine living room. Despite their warming relationship, the lack of things they had to say to each other seemed to grow larger in the room. The more he thought of something to say, the more ridiculous it sounded in his head.

'When do you think we'll have the car back? I'd like to do the shopping and it would be more convenient than taking a taxi.'

He hesitated, reluctant to continue the lie. 'I'm not sure. End of the week, perhaps?'

'That seems an awfully long time for a bit of servicing, especially for a new car.'

'I didn't think you would mind. You always say how much you hate driving here,' he said. 'But I'll speak to someone at the office to follow it up.'

'Yes, do,' Felicity said. Then, 'how have things been, since . . . ?'

There was no trace of hardness in her voice. Her hazel eyes had a hint of vulnerability about them.

He knew she wanted to ask him more about the night of the accident, but he could hardly think through the fog of his headache. He gave her shoulder a squeeze. It felt like a fatherly thing to do and he dropped his hand, not knowing quite where to put it. He thought about telling her about his meeting with the Ambassador. Successful completion of the project could mean a new posting, somewhere

where he could have a real impact. There had been a time when he wouldn't have hesitated in telling Felicity everything. But they had long grown accustomed to not discussing their work.

'I'm fine.' He squeezed his eyes shut and rubbed them with his fingers. When he opened his eyes she was still looking at him. 'What is it?'

She smiled a little. 'It's funny, I . . .' She stopped herself, leaning her head against the palm of her hand. He was afraid she might initiate a discussion about the state of things between them but all she said was, 'You're so tense, Tom.' Her hands were on him then. 'It's only me.'

He felt the urge to lie down. He put his head on her lap. She inspected the dressing over his eye.

'It's healing rather well, isn't it? How did you say you got it? You were terribly vague.'

'Let's not talk about it now,' he said.

'Tom,' she began. 'I want us to attempt to talk to each other, somehow.'

'I'm not trying to be difficult,' he said. 'I'm not feeling well. My head feels as though it's about to split open.'

She put her hands through his hair and began to massage him. He couldn't remember the last time she had touched him like this. The pulsating knot seemed to weaken. It felt like a seduction. He resisted the coaxing of her hands. It would be surrender, she would have the control. Despite himself, he felt himself relax. He had forgotten how soothing her hands could be. The veranda door thumped lightly against the frame, he heard the first drops of rain. Maybe he had been wrong about everything.

'I know we've both been terribly busy . . .' She began and kept talking. He listened to the softness in her voice, edging him towards sleep. Her hands seemed to dissolve his headache. Perhaps not all had been lost. Perhaps their marriage could be salvaged.

He felt a tightness in his briefs, he began to feel more alert, excited. He turned on her lap. Her skin smelled of tea and biscuits. He slid his hand in the gap of her dressing gown. She was wearing nothing underneath. How long had it been since he had touched her like this? She moaned at his touch. How much they had evolved since they had first made love as university students. She had grown into her body, become more comfortable with herself. He raised himself against the soft cushions of the sofa and buried his face against her breasts. He ran his fingers through her hair and kissed her. He tugged at her dressing gown and undid his trousers. She did not resist him. She was open and willing. She was at her most vulnerable during sex. He had forgotten. He had resisted making love to her as an act of reasserting his power. He did not want to use sex as a weapon. They had become used to making love in a perfunctory, ordered manner, though he could not remember the last time they had done so.

Afterwards, they lay on the sofa, clutching at the other's clammy skin, and fell into a light sleep. As he hovered above consciousness, he thought how marriage was like that — a tide drew them apart and then brought them together again, sometimes unexpectedly. Perhaps there was nothing wrong at all.

When he opened his eyes, Felicity had disappeared and he looked about the dark living room, feeling abandoned. His headache returned to its former glory. He needed her hands. He found her in the kitchen, showered and fully dressed; looking intently at the laptop she had set up there.

She hardly looked up at him as he went to kiss her. He wrinkled his nose at the perfume she had grown attached to. It smelled of sour grapes.

Walking out of the kitchen, he looked back at her and wondered if the tide wasn't about their marriage, but Felicity herself, who drew back further every time and returned less and less frequently.

In his study, he opened the bottom drawer and found the bottle of whisky he kept hidden under the Amnesty files he had brought back from Phnom Penh. He stood for a moment in the darkness without switching on the lamp. Half a glass of whisky couldn't hurt. The monster in his head had begun to scream. He squeezed his eyes and lit a cigarette.

The Ambassador was offering him a promotion. A cleaning of the slate. Mia had attended to him just when he needed it. He owed her his career. He knew nothing about her, had scarcely noticed her before. It was unlikely he would find anything surprising about her. A few speeding tickets, perhaps.

He shut the drawer and closed his eyes, waiting for the starving monster in his head to weaken and die.

'Say, Kyung-ha-shi, don't you have a daughter?'

Kyung-ha paused as she sliced the spring onions on the cutting board and was slow to look up. The women who usually volunteered to prepare the church lunch rarely paid her any attention.

'Yes,' she said, reluctant to explain. Discussion of the girl would only lead to trouble.

There was a pause. An invitation to elaborate. Kyung-ha ignored it. 'Did you see what Mrs Kong was wearing today?' one of the other volunteers said.

Soon-hee let out a cry. 'Did I see it? What was there to see? It was so tiny. Where were the buttons on her shirt?'

She let out a quiet breath, relieved their attention had been diverted. Mrs Kong was the favourite point of gossip among the ladies who helped with the lunches. Mrs Kong had spent many years living in California and it had been rumoured that she had returned to Seoul after the collapse of her business, a shop selling jeans. She had been married at least three times to men almost half her age. She had insisted on organizing the rice donations from the congregation for the poor but had never once dirtied her hands with the daily cleaning chores around the church.

Setting aside the spring onions, Kyung-ha wiped down the edges of the sink. 'Maybe you should have offered to sew a few back on for her,' she said, enjoying the rare opportunity to banter.

'You know she's always been a bit . . . glamorous,' Myung-ja said.

Soon-hee dropped a plate in the sink. 'Glamorous is too nice for what that woman is. Does she think she's twenty-five? A woman of our age shouldn't have long hair like that. Don't even get me started on the skirt,' Soon-hee said, shaking a soapy glove in Myung-ja's face.

'I think it's kind of . . . interesting. It's different,' Myung-ja suggested. She put all the plates away and took a watermelon out of the fridge. 'Maybe we're just getting old. Have you seen the girls and their hot pants these days? I'm so embarrassed I don't know where to look when I'm walking. One of these days I'm going to hurt myself. It's not just once or twice I've bumped into something or other.'

'I'm not talking about street fashion. This is a church, not some kind of brothel. You know,' Soon-hee lowered her voice, 'I've heard that she's had plastic surgery.'

Kyung-ha shrugged, though she agreed with them both. The country was not what it used to be. They were being infected with the West's loose morals. She remembered Jun-su joking about her glowing red cheeks in the dark on their wedding night. Those were the days when the film censor went wild because there was a scandalous scene where a couple were sitting on their bed and then slumped over just before it moved onto the next scene. Even so, she felt obliged not to outwardly judge others. It was sinful. 'So what if she has. Mary Magdalene—'

'Stop it. I don't care if she is a hooker, she's just so proud of it. Can't she cover up, at least pretend a little?'

Myung-ja seemed to lose interest in the subject. She was staring intently at Kyung-ha again. 'Anyway, what were we talking about? I remember, your daughter, Kyung-ha, how old is she?'

'She's almost thirty,' Kyung-ha said nervously.

'And she's not married?' Myung-ja seemed inspired by the possibilities. 'I have a nephew who's still single. We should set them up.'

'I don't think so . . .'

'*Aigoo*,' Myung-ja said, misunderstanding Kyung-ha's hesitation, 'You've got to let go at some point. You don't expect her to stay at home with you for ever?'

Kyung-ha bit her tongue at the irony of it. She said nothing. When she looked up, she saw that Myung-ja was offended. Perhaps she thought that Kyung-ha was saying that her nephew might not be good enough for Mia.

'She's a handful. That's all.'

Myung-ja softened at this. 'You should arrange it for her. It's only going to get harder to arrange these things after thirty.'

'I'll talk to her about it,' she lied. 'She's very strong-willed.'

That much was true.

As she walked home, Kyung-ha stopped every so often to ease the burn in her legs. Why hadn't she said that Mia was married, or in a very serious relationship? Then she could have avoided all of their questions. But she had lied enough about their circumstances as it was. What would happen if they saw the girl? All the questions she would have to answer about the girl and her father. It had happened before. She was no stranger to the way that neighbours viewed their family. A cripple, a girl of mixed blood and sin, and herself. She had been astounded by versions of her own life story. She had heard all sorts of interpretations, the most shocking of which was that Kyung-ha had prostituted herself with a GI to make ends meet for her disabled husband.

Kyung-ha slid the living room door aside to let in the light from the courtyard. As she did so, the loose glass in the door, held together with yellow masking tape, rattled. Her back felt bruised and beaten. The balls of her feet ached.

Looking out over the wilting hibiscus plant lining the courtyard walls, she postponed cooking for a few more moments. Several mosquitoes and fruit flies had met their sticky end on a piece of hanging insect tape on the porch. It was their *palja*, their ordained fate. To be drawn in to an apparent treat before suffering an exhausting death.

How could she explain what she had done? When she had learned of the girl's existence she had gone to the adoption agency and had offered to take her. She had done it with all the ease of holding her hands in boiling water. Even as good Christians they would never believe that she had taken her in out of Christian love, though she tried as much as she could to appear devout. She pushed the thought to the corners of her mind. There were some things that were better left buried, even if it meant living a lie. She had already made her deal with God. They had an understanding. She was paying every day for what she had done.

Hyun-min walked into the living room just as Kyung-ha was about to turn into the kitchen.

'Hyun-min ah . . .' Her chiding words lodged themselves in her throat. She could hardly bring herself to look at him. He looked as though he hadn't eaten in several days. His cheeks had grown slack, his skin, pale. His hands were dirty, his fingernails, black. There were dark circles under his eyes. He had become more ghostly in his appearance.

'What happened to you?'

He looked almost irritated at the question. 'Nothing. Don't worry about me,' he said.

Kyung-ha bit her tongue, fighting back the urge to slap him. She wanted to rage against his nonchalance. How oblivious he was to their worry. 'Don't worry? Is that all you can say? You said you were going for a walk. We thought you'd thrown yourself off a bridge. You couldn't call us?'

He looked as though it hadn't occurred to him before.

'I didn't know that it mattered,' he said.

'This isn't a hotel. There are people who live here who worry about you.' He looked confused.

A glaze of self-protection came over his eyes. There was a self-sufficiency in his movements that struck her as precocious. It struck Kyung-ha that the boy had never had anyone to hold him accountable.

Worse, he'd never been loved by anyone.

From her desk Mia could see Thomas reading in his office, his head propped up against his hand, the repeated stroke of the eyebrow, as if he needed soothing. His attention seemed impenetrable. Had she imagined it? That look he had given her when she had told him about the car. There had been a charge between them. Then suddenly she sensed a change.

The hours stretched into days. Still there was nothing. She was perpetually in a state of waiting for something to happen. She wasted long minutes in the kitchen stirring hot drinks she could not bear to consume in this humid weather in the hope that he might walk in.

Now, finally, there was an excuse.

Covering up the damage to the car was not the simple task she had imagined it would be. An imported car had to be sent to an authorized garage where the parts' serial numbers would be logged and repairs matched off with corresponding invoices. She spent several hours trying to find a link in the paper trail that could be broken. Eventually she had been able to persuade someone at the garage to produce two separate invoices.

Mia hesitated as she put her hand to his door, overcome with doubt. Then she knocked softly and went in without waiting to be invited in. He was seated by the window, looking out over the palace.

'I wanted to know if everything was okay,' she said.

He looked at her blankly.

She didn't think it would be so hard to speak to him.

'Did the Ambassador? I mean . . . do you think he knows that I wrote it?' she asked.

'No, I don't believe so,' he said with a tight-lipped smile. He looked down at his feet. 'But thank you.'

His formality was a sudden foreign presence in the room.

'Your cut. It looks a lot better,' she said, lamely.

She waited a moment but he said nothing in response to this.

'The garage called. Your car's ready,' she said.

He looked up with a blank expression as though he had no idea what she was talking about. A fleeting horror passed over his face.

'Of course, thank you. I'm in your debt,' he said. He grew quiet again.

She didn't know what she had expected. He had expressed his gratitude. What more was there? She had spent those hours attempting to fix an arrangement with his car, thrilled with the camaraderie of their secret. Now there was nothing between them.

'Okay, then,' she found herself saying. And there it was again. The swollen tongue.

She turned to leave when he stood up. He ran his hand through his air, his eyebrows furrowed as though he were about to say something painful.

'Why don't we get out of here for a bit?'

The blue light of the bar made his face look cold and statuesque. Around them red-faced students knocked over their drinks and raised their voices in incoherent protest. She had miscalculated her choice of place. She couldn't help noticing the cheap, peeling lacquer of the bar. Was he uncomfortable in this habitat of the locals? She wondered if she should have taken him to a place where they would find expats. Thomas fingered his cufflink, weaving the back of it in and out of his shirt. He wore melancholy like a pigment of his skin; she wanted to touch him to see if it would rub off.

'You must think I'm irresponsible,' he began.

'No. Just unhappy,' she said. 'Why?'

'Everyone goes through phases of being unhappy, don't they? It's not always all that specific—'

'You don't like it here.'

He threw her a glance. 'It's not that I don't like it, exactly—'

'I don't like it here. If I lived in England I would never leave.'

'Everyone feels like that about their hometown,' he said.

She ignored the remark, slighted by how quickly she had been dismissed. He assumed that this place was home, when she had never felt it to be. This place where her presence was always questioned.

'And anyway, you seem perfectly happy –' he stole a glance in her direction – 'with your job.'

'There's more to it than the work,' she said.

'Is that right?' He was studying her. He wanted something from her and she had no idea what it was. This, she realized, was what unsettled her. She could not read him.

'Why do you do it? Forgive me for saying this, but you'd make twice what you earn as a corporate interpreter,' he said.

'I like working at the Embassy,' she said. 'With freelance work you're all over the place. You're dipping in and out of meetings with new people all the time. You don't really belong anywhere.'

He looked at her for a moment after she had stopped talking. His eyes lingered on her lips as though he was expecting more, then he looked out of the window.

'Some people would say that they enjoy the freedom of that,' he said, looking into the bottom of his glass as though disappointed by the emptiness of it. 'Isn't it funny. To work day in, day out with a roomful of people who are perfect strangers. There's something of an artifice about that. You say that about freelance work, but there's something similar to be said about working in an embassy. After every posting you pack up and leave and you begin again.'

He retreated into some private thought.

She wanted to ask him about his notebook.

'What did your wife say, about your accident?'

He let out a little laugh, 'Well, she quite possibly would have a lot to say on that. If she knew what really happened.'

'Do you have many secrets from your wife?' The question was more flirtatious than she had intended.

'More than I should,' he said, simply, without taking his eyes off her. She was the first to look away.

He ran his finger around the rim of his glass. 'Can I rest assured that this debacle with the car. It's just between us?'

'Of course.'

'You helped me to cover up my indiscretions without even thinking about it. Why?'

'If you were fired, I'd have to work for Charles and he's a pain,' she said. It was partially true. She didn't say that she didn't want to see him leave. He was a mystery she hadn't unravelled yet.

Thomas hung back for several moments before following her as she walked to the subway. He could still feel her lips on his cheek. She had kissed him unexpectedly as they parted. His anxiety about why she had helped him as much as she had began to fade. There was no need for conspiracy. It was simple.

He studied her as she walked with all the grace of a sullen teenager, hands in her pockets, her stick-like calves, a slight drag of the heel. By looking only at her shoulders he might have guessed that she was walking through a windstorm. She turned the corner towards the subway station, and he hurried past the Anglican Church, the soft hum of organ practice.

An audit required that he get to know her but she was strangely closed to him. She had a way of deflecting his questions and turning them around on him. The report would be a portrait, an assessment of security, but in order to do it, he needed to separate what was habitual, what was not.

Her attentiveness did not escape him. It was as though she had studied him. As though she had been reading his thoughts. That alone was not a reason to be suspicious. Perhaps she was particularly talented with people.

What had she meant when she said that there was more to it than the work?

When he thought back to how he had seen her before, he realized that he thought of her as he had thought of all the Asian women in the office. Efficient. She was prepared for meetings, but very quiet. And she had been so considerate, taking him to a bar where they could freely discuss his situation. She hardly touched her drink. A delicate creature. There was nothing about her to arouse suspicion. Yet as they stood in the bar he became fascinated by what secrets she might conceal. She seemed to care so dearly about covering up his misdemeanours.

She disappeared into the crowd of people coming out of the subway station at City Hall. The traffic on the main road was heavy; cars inched forward impatiently every thirty seconds, making little progress. Red brake lights pulsed as far as he could see in every direction. He ran a little. Once he was down in the subway it would be easy to lose her. Through the sea of heads rising out of the station, he caught sight of her bumping into a stranger and carrying on. Seoul was a city where strangers did not apologize to one another. It was liberating. London was full of empty, pre-emptive apologies.

When he had applied for a job at the Foreign Office he had no idea that it would lead him down foreign streets following a local girl. But there were a lot of things he had not expected. The feelings of helplessness. The social boredom. He could have done what his brother had done and gone to work in the City instead, equally restless there. No, anything was better than that.

It was noticeably cooler underground. He hung back at the top of the stairs, waiting until she had reached the platform and disappeared from view. Then he ventured slowly towards the tracks, making sure he was a good distance from her. He was a good head taller than everyone else. If she looked in his direction, she was sure to see him. He kept close to the stairs until the train arrived.

He kept an eye on her from the next carriage. She was absorbed in a book, the title of which he could not quite make out. She had the manner of someone not entirely absorbed in her own thoughts, but was guarded, a person used to being observed, but rarely admired. Her eyes challenged those who stared at her. Seeing her absorbed in her reading, he realized how often she regarded him with the look of a prisoner awaiting a verdict. In profile, her face was slender, though the tip of her nose was a little plump, a button mushroom. Her downcast stare gave her eyes a feline appearance, almost playful. It crept up on him slowly, the realization that she was beautiful. Everything about her suggested that she was harmless.

She had seemed more at ease when she'd turned the questions on him. Perhaps it was a habit of Asian reticence. The Cambodians had been secretive. If in doubt about anything, they retreated into silence. It had been so difficult to get them to talk. Older people in particular had learned that it was best not to speak about the past. To hide their identity was safer in a past that implicated them in so much. He felt his stomach knot with regret. He had failed in Phnom Penh. If he successfully completed the tasks the Ambassador had set him, he could rebuild his career. The better the posting the more influence he could assert.

A flood of people swept into the carriage at Yongsan Station.

Passengers pushed as they fought for space and he lost sight of her. He leaped to his feet and jumped onto the platform. He stood for a moment, feeling ridiculous; why had he done this? He had acted impulsively in following her. The platform was beginning to empty and he had lost her.

Kyung-ha took to the wooden floors with a wet rag. Tried to wipe away the guilt in circular motions. She moved the boy's futon aside and cleaned the floor under it, setting aside the backpack in doing so. She was conscious of living with a stranger. She knew nothing about him. She watched him often as he moved about the house. He had the manner of an old man and spent a lot of time lost in thought, as though he were a philosopher or a mathematician, contemplating a complex puzzle. It was easy to forget that he was only eighteen. He was unusually tidy, folding his clothes neatly under the chair in the living room and then putting the futon on top. Every night he unpacked and in the morning repacked, as though he wanted to be prepared to leave at any moment. His bag bulged; she couldn't imagine what he kept in it as he had hardly changed his clothes since he arrived. He seemed destined for invisibility and it was hard to know whether it was a manner he had adopted or whether invisibility had chosen him. In his orderliness he announced himself as a perpetual guest. He slipped outside at odd hours. Occasionally she thought she heard him talking on the phone, but she didn't even know if he had one.

Fearing the meditative act would be over before she felt better, she rinsed the rag and was about to start again when she heard a sound outside.

There was a shadow that moved across the gaps of the rusting gate. Kyung-ha crossed the courtyard. A young girl stood on the other side of the gate. She looked no older than sixteen, with short hair and a sharp fringe.

'Who are you?' Kyung-ha asked.

The girl withdrew immediately. Kyung-ha pressed the lock on the gate and opened it, half expecting the girl to run, the whole visit a practical joke. But the girl did not seem to see her, seemed to be looking around her. She got on her tiptoes and seemed to be intent on looking for something inside the courtyard.

'What are you looking for?' she asked.

Finally, the girl stared at Kyung-ha, as though unsure that they were speaking the same language. 'I was looking for someone,' she said at last.

Kyung-ha caught the accent immediately. She didn't carry herself as the other defectors did, but her words gave her away. 'Are you a friend of Hyun-min?'

The girl smiled a little shyly, evidently relieved. 'He's here?'

Kyung-ha opened the gate a little wider and called out, 'Hyun-min?'

There was no answer.

'Come inside, I'll get him.'

The girl looked hesitant to step into the courtyard. 'I just need to give him this letter.'

'A letter?'

She looked reluctant to say any more.

'Wait here. I'll call him for you,' Kyung-ha said.

Hyun-min was nowhere to be seen. She tapped on the bathroom door. She heard the halting of running water.

'There's a girl here.'

There was no response. She wasn't sure that he'd heard her and was about to repeat what she had said when he replied, 'I'll come out.'

She went to the kitchen and boiled some water. She took out some leftover watermelon she had brought home from church. Could it be that he had spent those nights at this young woman's house? She felt relieved. She had ascribed such darkness to his disappearance when the truth was simple and obvious. Why hadn't she considered that Hyun-min might have a girlfriend? She cut the watermelon into cubes and put them on a plate. She was about to enter the living room when she caught the tension in Hyun-min's voice.

'Answer the question. How did you find me?'

The girl's voice was quiet. She sounded afraid. 'I thought . . .'

'Who told you I was here?'

'That's what people have been saying. At the school. That you handle the letters now. That you know where—'

'Shut up. Don't say any more.'

Kyung-ha almost dropped the plate in her hands. She had never heard Hyun-min speak like that before.

'Isn't it true? Everyone says you and Myung-chul were in it together . . .'

'Get out.'

'Stop. That hurts,' she said.

Kyung-ha followed the sound of their voices as they moved further away until she was standing in the living room, overlooking the courtyard.

'Get out. Tell whoever it is spreading the rumour that I don't know anything about the letters.'

'But . . .' the girl stammered. She was still holding the letter in her hand.

'Swear it.'

'My letter . . .'

'Tell anyone where I am and your family's dead. Do you understand what I'm saying?' Hyun-min pushed the girl out of the gate.

He turned back towards the house but froze when he saw

Kyung-ha watching him. She crossed the courtyard to him, incredulous. 'What was that?'

'Don't concern yourself with it,' Hyun-min said.

'What did she mean . . . about you and Myung-chul?'

'I said don't worry about it.'

'Was he in some kind of trouble?'

'No. I don't know what she was talking about. Just leave it,' he said and walked out of the gate.

Kyung-ha put down the plate and followed him out onto the street. She saw the blur of his figure at the bottom of the hill and decided not to pursue him in the heat. As she turned back to the house, she became aware of someone beside her.

It was the girl. Visibly shaken. A crumpled letter in her hand.

'Is he always like this?' Kyung-ha asked her.

The girl shook her head. 'Always? No. I don't know. I've never met him before.'

This surprised Kyung-ha. 'Then, why . . .'

The girl wiped her cheeks and seemed to recompose herself. '*Ahjumma*, will you do something for me? I just want him to deliver a letter.'

'What kind of letter?'

'A letter to my family,' she said, thrusting the envelope into Kyung-ha's hands.

It was addressed simply to Mother and Father. Kyung-ha read the address. *Pyongyang*, it said.

'Will you give it to him? He'll change his mind. I know he will.' Her eyes were wide and dark. Full of anxiety.

'*Haksaeng*, what makes you think he would be able to deliver something like this?'

The girl looked frightened, as though she had realized she had made a mistake. Her mouth fell open. She trembled a little. 'Please, it's my last hope. It has to be . . .' her voice trailed off, her mind suddenly elsewhere.

Kyung-ha felt her impatience stretched and ready to snap. 'Why would you give Hyun-min something like this?'

This seemed to break the girl out of her trance and fear returned to her eyes. 'If you don't know, then I can't tell you.'

Kyung-ha knew implicitly that it would be easier to push the girl than to get answers from Hyun-min. She decided to try a different approach. 'I can make sure that Hyun-min gets this letter, if you tell me what you think he'll do with it.'

'They say Myung-chul was a messenger . . . before he . . . died. He would deliver letters to Pyongyang, Chongjin. Anywhere.'

Kyung-ha's heart stopped, her thoughts immediately drawn to Hyun-min's unexplained absence.

'What are you saying about Hyun-min? That he—'

The girl's eyes returned to the dream-like state and then met Kyung-ha's. 'They say he can cross the border from the South to the North and get back in a day.'

Monsoon

The deafening rains arrived in the middle of the summer.

There wasn't a step they could take out of the Embassy building, towards the old palace walls, that left them unscathed by water. Yet Thomas continued to insist on taking Mia to lunch. Weeks had passed since his car had been restored, yet he led her to quiet restaurants with private rooms, taking her further and further from the office. As if he still owed her something.

They walked in the rain, down the narrow alleys between the parts of the city centre that hadn't been restored, his hand on the small of her back, the other holding an umbrella over them.

Wherever they ate, it was always in a private room or in the corners least visible from the entrance. Mia sat in her wet clothes as he asked endless questions about her and her life, as though she were some rare species he had never encountered before. Any time she had tried to divert the conversation, or ask him questions about himself, he managed to turn it around back at her. A leisurely game played by the bored. She felt hunted. He wanted to see how far she would run. She wondered how long she could stretch her lies. Was she ever truly comfortable in his company? She still had trouble speaking around him, careful of her slips of language, afraid that he might question her foreignness.

'Is it your mother or your father who's English?'

'My mother,' she said.

'Your mother was English?' Thomas leaned forward. 'That's unusual, isn't it? You didn't mention how your parents met . . . ?' he said.

She dropped her cutlery to earn herself more time. Of all the stories that Mia had twisted out of Kyung-ha, this was one that had been impossible to piece together. There were many versions that had been implied, but nothing that even resembled the beginnings of a story she could believe. What could she say about her mother? How could she explain that she hardly knew who her father was, a silent invalid with eerie paintings?

Thomas leaned forward, expecting an answer. The cut above his eye had receded and was fading into a pink scar.

'My father is practically English. He grew up in England, which is where he met my mother, you know, at Cambridge. After my mother passed away, he had a nervous breakdown and that's when we moved back,' she said.

In the absence of a real story, any story would do.

'Really? Cambridge? Which college?'

She tried to remember the name of the college that she had read on Thomas's file. It took her a few moments to recall it. She took a bite of her spaghetti and dabbed at the corners of her mouth, trying to buy more time. 'John's.'

'You mean St John's? What an extraordinary coincidence. I went to the same college. Where did your father go to secondary school?'

Mia squeezed her knife, resisting the temptation to throw it on her plate. 'If I had known he was of so much interest I would have invited him to lunch,' she said.

The silence was ugly. She was cornered. They would never again be alone like this. 'I'm sorry. I didn't mean to pry.' He looked at his plate. He seemed to be considering whether or not to say something. 'I just find you rather fascinating.'

Her face grew hot. She took a few mouthfuls of water to weigh the word. She felt she was auditioning for a part without knowing what role it was.

He laughed a little and then quickly grew serious again. 'I feel we're on an unequal footing here. You know a few secrets of mine and I know almost nothing about you.'

Mia picked up the spoon on the table and twirled it, not sure what he expected her to say. She checked her watch, thinking it might be time to leave. She cultivated stories, liked culling the details of other people's lives. She was the one who asked questions. She thought of her father hunched over his strange painting in the lamplight, her stepmother's heating pads stuck to her back. How could she tell him about this?

When she looked up, he was still staring at her intently. He was testing her. The intimacy of the private dining area was suggestive. He was different. Married. It changed the rules. He was more cautious. She hated that it was on his terms. She would have to find a way to change that. Outside, a foot of mist rose against the hiss of rain. It would not be so hard to get to the heart of his intentions. All she needed was a place.

'I'm an open book,' she said with a smile.

The apartment was as she had last seen it.

She turned on the light and blinked at the black-and-white portraits hanging in the room. All the faces unsmiling and sombre, yet the eyes alive, watching her next move. She was drawn to a photo of a young man with an unshaven face. A name had been written in neat handwriting on the back of it. Myung-chul Lee. Hyun-min's roommate. Goosepumps broke the surface of her skin. Squeezing the wooden clothespins, she released the photographs. All of them had names written on the back of them. She put them in a pile by the sink and made herself a cup of coffee.

She examined the bookshelves. There were several engineering textbooks. She found an English dictionary and opened it. Under F she looked for the word 'fascinating'. His curiosity had been provoked, that was what he had meant. But did people become curious of those of their own kind? In suggesting fascination, had he not already put some distance between them? She feared she was an island on the horizon of a passing ship, a pencil smudge of a word that one couldn't quite make out. Was fascination not a hungry animal that wanted to satiate itself and then move on, forgetting the plight of its meal?

She closed the dictionary, suddenly impatient.

She peered into the bedroom. At the hanging clothes. Still there was no sign that Hyun-min had been there. Her uncle had petitioned for the extension of the lease in case Hyun-min wanted to move back in. She stepped into the room and folded the clothes. Put them in a drawer. She looked around her. What was missing? What would convince Thomas that she lived here?

By late afternoon thunderstorms took siege over the city. An artillery of rain fell against the pavements, beating down the maple leaves in the Embassy compound. Mia watched the lightning illuminate the palace rooftops, moving floodlights flickering on and off in the darkness.

'You'd better not take the subway this evening. There've been reports of flooding,' Charles said.

'I know.'

'We could run across the street and find some supper until the storm passes.'

'I can't. I've got plans.'

'I suppose they involve catching a cold?'

'I think I'll be all right, thanks, Dad.'

She waited for him to disappear. Over the partition, she saw

Thomas raise the strap of his satchel over his shoulder. She leaped at the opportunity to go to him.

'Will you drive in this?'

'I don't see why not.'

'I was wondering if I could ask you for a ride,' she said.

'Of course.'

As they got in his car, Thomas put the key in the ignition and said, 'Where to?'

'My place.'

'Certainly, madam,' he said, jovially, but the mood quickly changed. They drove in silence, the only sound the windscreen wipers and the crackling of rain against glass. Thomas seemed engrossed in thought, he hardly looked at her. He was undecided. He seemed to be wrestling with the morality of it. Perhaps he was thinking of his wife, of the permanence of vows.

'So this is where they keep you?' he said, as they pulled in front of the apartment block. He stared at the building for several moments. There was no hint of anxiety, no desperation to leave. He turned off the engine and tapped the steering wheel.

That was all the sign that she needed.

'Would you like to see it?'

'Why not?' he said, almost cheerfully. By the time they stepped into the lift he was no longer smiling. He could still change his mind. The men she usually seduced were not so conflicted.

On the other side of the door, there was no pretence of drinks or the view.

She leaned closer to him; her cheek tingled at the nearness of his cheek. It was still possible to withdraw. To brush it off as a whisper. She was gritting her teeth, rolling her lips into her mouth, biting her lips instead. Then she pressed them against the stubble on his jaw.

He didn't flinch.

He stroked the length of her chin, held her face, directed her mouth to his. She kept her eyes open. His were closed. He was frowning slightly. The look of a musician who searched for the right chord. She closed her eyes. She couldn't breathe. Her heart was swollen. It squashed her lungs. Crushed her stomach.

'Hold on,' she said. It had never been like this before. This was foreign territory.

He kept his hand on her neck. A thumb on her jaw. Her memory, sheet-white, a blank page, she was a girl without a past. She couldn't recall how she had done this before.

He grasped her by her elbows. She sucked in another breath. He was pushing her deeper into the room. There was something in his tenderness that made her feel breakable. A sudden glimpse of life as it could have been. The revelation of an absence.

'This —' she gasped to catch her breath — 'is a bad idea.'

She stepped away from him.

'What is it?' he said, then almost immediately, 'I'm sorry.'

She couldn't look at him. She knew he misunderstood. 'Don't say anything.'

He turned to face the door and then turned back. Tried to meet her eye. 'I thought . . .'

'So did I,' she said.

What was this? The shaking hand. The unsteadiness in the knees. She pushed him out of the door and turned the lock.

She had wanted to slip into his skin for a moment, just to know what it was like. She never thought, for a moment, that this would be anything other than a game.

Kyung-ha stood outside Mia's door. She could hear Mia tapping what sounded like a pen against the surface of her desk. The smell of cigarette smoke wafted from the cracks. She had never before confided in the girl, but she had to tell somebody. If she could say it out loud, she would be able to hear how absurd it sounded. The young girl's visit had unnerved her, but she had chosen to believe Hyun-min when he said that he knew nothing about it. After all, getting to Pyongyang and back in one day? It was impossible.

Then a second letter had arrived on her doorstep. Then another. Then a stack of envelopes bound together with a rubber band. It was clear that more than one person believed that such a thing was possible. Although Kyung-ha tried to quash these thoughts, they expanded in her mind. She could not get involved. She would not. She had done enough damage once before.

'What do you want? I know you're there,' the girl said from the other side of the door.

Kyung-ha opened it to find Mia sitting on her chair, a leg up on the seat, her elbow on her knee, a cigarette in her hand.

'Take it outside, will you? You'll bring the house down with fire one day.'

Mia stubbed out the cigarette and straightened herself out. 'You're up late.'

'I can't sleep with your restless tapping.'

There was a moment of awkward silence. Mia looked at her suspiciously. She rarely came to the girl's room. The walls were yellowed with cigarette smoke. Her desk was cluttered with papers. There was something else as well. A growing impatience. The girl wanted something and her desire filled the house like a balloon about to burst. She marvelled at how little she understood the girl, what her preoccupations were and how she viewed her future. Earlier that day Myung-ja had pestered her again about arranging a date with Mia and her nephew. She couldn't imagine how she would present the girl and her salacious ways. She had no energy to pursue the girl's temptations. Not when there were so many other pressing things at hand: heavy, worrying concerns about Hyun-min.

'The boy . . .' she began. She had no idea how to broach the subject. 'Where do you think he disappears to?'

Mia shrugged. 'Who knows? Why don't you ask him?'

'Maybe he'll talk to you . . .' It was the wrong thing to say. The lazy look on the girl's face disappeared.

'And why is that? You think we have something in common? We're both rejects? Is that it?'

Kyung-ha said nothing, surprised by the outburst.

'Just leave him alone. He came back, didn't he? What's the big deal?'

It was pointless trying to talk to the girl. If it didn't concern her, she wasn't interested. Just when she thought Mia had settled a little into her heart, she would do something, put up an act of defiance and resistance, and then evidence of her whiteness would spring from her and she would be cast out of her heart.

'Never mind,' she said with a scowl and left the room. Kyung-ha closed the door and stood in the darkness at the top of the stairs. A momentary silence and then the tapping began again. Something was growing inside the girl, a bird preparing to take flight. She grew paler by the day, her changing body a ripening fruit.

Kyung-ha descended the narrow staircase, gripping the banister on each side with her hands. The pile of letters that she had left out on top of the TV set remained untouched. She refused to be drawn into the mystery of it. She would not get involved. Not this time.

'You scared me.' Mia felt the wall for the light switch. 'What are you doing sitting there in the dark?'

'Habit,' he said.

'Creep,' she said as she walked towards the stairs.

'I feel safer in the dark,' he said. She could just make out his outline as he sat against the cabinet. 'Back in the North, during the day you had to be watching out all the time. A frown at the wrong moment. A look of distaste at something and someone could report you. They would say that you were disloyal to the state. That you were showing signs of dissatisfaction. Then sometimes at night we'd have these power cuts and it was like I could finally breathe.'

There was a long silence.

Mia stood on the stairs for a few minutes, not knowing what to say.

Hyun-min shifted wearily. 'It's not a mystery. What Myung-chul did. He was disappointed.'

She hated the way he spoke to her as though it were natural for her to understand. 'What makes you think I get it?'

'Because I see the way everyone looks at you too.'

She did not want to hear any more. They were not the same. Some stories needed thicker, unbroken skin. Her bare feet slapped the stairs as she flew from him. She stood with the door against her damp back. The muffled roar of the unforgiving city rushed in through the open window. She unzipped her skirt and let it fall to the floor. She shred her shirt the way *they* had once done. With bare, biro-marked fingers. Their vulture-like nails. They had marked their hate on her body. In their eyes she was acceptable only as a presence. If she had remained quiet, they would have not touched her. They alleviated every fear of their own standing, of their broken homes and their uncertain futures, with every kick against her bones. They assured themselves of their own place by demarcating lines on her body. A permanent reminder that lines existed. And should not be crossed.

Mia was sixteen when her stepmother had dragged her out of the local police station by her hair. They had been caught – her skirt high around her thighs, his buttons reflecting the glare of the police car's headlights. The sergeant had been arrested and later, discharged from the army.

'Filthy, disgraceful, sinful child,' Kyung-ha had said as she pulled Mia onto the street. 'Lord knows how I'll show my face at church. It's in your blood. You're a poisoned child.'

Kyung-ha had walked ahead of Mia in the blue morning light and Mia had stopped to steady herself against a wall. She had been drunk and felt the vomit rising in her throat. The stench of the waste placed outside by the residents of the street had fanned the flames of her nausea and she shut her eyes in concentration, trying to resist a second wave.

'Are you pregnant?'

Mia had wiped her mouth with the back of her hand. 'Don't think so.'

Her stepmother had come towards her. For a moment Mia had thought she was about to offer her sympathy. Then she had caught the slap across her cheek.

The sting left her hungry for more. 'That's it?'

'Filthy child,' she muttered, shaking her head. 'If you're pregnant you're out of my house. Do you understand?' She sounded more tired than angry. 'You'll end up like your mother.'

It seemed to be the last resort, the final profanity left in her stepmother's book of unmentionables. Mia glared at her. 'You don't know anything about her.'

'And you do?' Kyung-ha shook her head. 'She didn't disappear. She left you. Do you understand what I'm saying? Threw you away like you were trash.'

'I'm getting pretty tired of your stories,' she said. Then she had felt as though she had needed a tug of the hair, another slap across the face. But Kyung-ha's face had become subdued. The anger had receded.

Mia pulled out her packet of cigarettes from her bag and smoked one; sure her stepmother would fly at her in a rage at any moment. 'What?'

'What kind of mother does that?' Kyung-ha's eyes swept Mia's ruffled hair, her eyes and her face. 'You're a mixed-up child, it's not your fault you've got troubled blood. When you start mixing the races, it creates craziness. That's why you struggle to find your place. This is what happens when the Lord's word is disobeyed. You were born in sin, so how can you help it?'

'Stop it.' Mia tossed her cigarette aside. 'I'm not listening to this.' She slung her bag over her shoulder, blowing the smoke out hard as she passed her stepmother.

As she walked home, Mia had felt the rage gathering in her veins. There had been times when she had been angrier with Kyung-ha. It was easier to rail against her slippery lies and twisted stories than to confront the truth. She did not know her mother. All she had been left with was her mother's legacy – green eyes and light-brown hair which she had dyed black since middle school. She had been given her mother's pinkish, pale skin. In that moment, what she wanted most was to wring herself of that poison, that tainted blood.

When she got home, she had locked herself in the bathroom and sat on the toilet seat, sucking wildly on cigarettes, tugging at her hair. She sat there cross-legged, the ash dropping from her quivering hand onto the tiles. She inspected her face in the mirror, searching for traces of her mother in her own reflection. She looked nothing like her father. What was it about her that had been so repulsive? She scratched at her skin. Her light-brown hair had begun to show at the roots. All of it was incriminating. She wanted to exorcise her mother from her body. Spotting a razor in the cabinet, she took the blade and ran it across her long hair, watching the great lengths of it collapse onto the tiled floor.

At school, matters had been made worse by her uncle's work. When the girls had become bored of teasing her for being white, they had begun calling her a communist. It was the first thing that every Korean child learned, that to be different was wrong. Mia had every reason in the book to be hated. That morning she decided that if they wanted to crucify her, she would let them. She walked to school with a plan, ignoring the stares of those who passed her on the street.

Mia walked down the wooden school corridors, dragging her school bag behind her. If she survived it would be a rite of passage. There was only one girl in the class for the job. Jiwon was known as the queen. She ruled over the other girls with blades she kept hidden in her uniform. The fates of all the outcast schoolgirls rested in her hands. If younger students did not stop and bow to her in the corridor, they would be taught a lesson about respecting one's elders in the storeroom between classes.

There had been a rumour at school about Jiwon's mother. No one dared to talk about it on campus.

Mia walked to the back where Jiwon sat and rapped on her desk. 'Hey. I've got a question.'

All the girls in the classroom froze.

Jiwon's eyes narrowed. Her chair scraped across the wooden floor.

'Did you get your hair chewed off by a rat or something? What the hell is wrong with you, white girl?'

Mia hid her shaking hand behind her back and leaned in close. 'Is it true that your mother is a hooker? Is that why you're so pissed off all the time?'

The flaming look in Jiwon's eyes had given Mia hope.

'We're going to talk after school,' Jiwon said, running her finger across her neck.

Their teacher cleared her throat and the other girls scattered and found their seats.

Mia had slumped into her chair and waited. For the fists against her ribs. The razorblades they kept in their wallets. Their fingernails across her face.

As part of their high school education, they learned that there were certain corners of the school that one went to only to be broken. The toilets on the fifth floor, where the mirrors were held together with brown duct tape. The rooftop that was sealed off after Kim Mijin broke her neck. Few girls came back to warn others about the bunker in the basement. Those girls with buck teeth who talked too much. Those who gossiped with a lisp or a stutter. Had skin too pale. Wore poverty too much like pride.

That day Mia had dragged her heels across the gravel of the schoolyard after class. Rubbing her feet in the ground, she dusted her greying tennis shoes as she marked out her steps, looking over her shoulder towards the school building.

'Don't take too long, ladies,' she murmured.

She hunted her predators in the deserted schoolyard. The smell of fishcakes and spicy soupy *dukbokki* sold from the back of a van had lured all her classmates to safety outside the school walls. She ran her hand over the uneven lengths of her short hair and waited until she could be sure that they would follow her.

She had entered a maze of quiet alleyways, running with light, expectant feet. They were not far behind.

'Hey, freak!' Jiwon called out.

One of the girls forced her to kneel with a baseball bat to the back of the knees. There was a crack, the sound of a home run echoing in a stadium, her knees shattered on concrete. She felt the swell and split of them as Jiwon held her prostrate.

'I don't need a reason to shave that white skin off your body. But to provoke me? I almost love the guts.'

She punctuated this with a fist to the stomach that had Mia dizzy and transcendent.

'Freak,' she said.

Mia had been afraid she would leave it at that. She gave her best smile. Her mouth was moist and salty; she felt the sting of acidic, poisoned blood rising in her throat and coating her gums.

Jiwon frowned. The thin lines of her charcoal-pencilled eyebrows became rigid. She looked at Mia as though she were the dogshit on the soles of her shoes. 'You lost your mind? Will you look at that?' she said to the other girls.

'We were having a conversation, remember? Before class . . .' Mia said, cleaning the bloody front row of her teeth with her tongue. 'About your mother.'

'What did you say?'

'I was explaining,' she said. Her knees pulsed as though they had hearts of their own. 'About how we're not that different. Your mother works on Hooker Hill, right? How many GIs do you think she sleeps with a night? Fifty? You could have come out just as white as me, don't you think?'

She saw the glint of metal. A razor landed by Jiwon's foot. Mia saw the rubber of her tennis shoes had split and gaped like an open mouth. Jiwon picked up the razor with her long manicured fingernails.

'You're not thinking straight. A mutt like you must get confused a lot. That mixing gets in your brain. Do you know what you're saying? Or who you're talking to?'

Mia paused. Jiwon bent over her and popped a few of the buttons of her uniform with her nails. Red pepper breathed. The smell of *kimchi* embedded in their skin. The other three girls, long-haired, their skirts rolled up to reveal the middle of their thighs, drew closer.

'Admit it. You're scared of me because you can see that we're alike. I could be your sister,' Mia said.

She felt a pinprick. She remembered the sound of ripping satin. An unzipping of skin. Cleaving with small razorblades that punctured the spaces between the ribs that later they would break. She had been ready to feel it all – the pop and snap, the dissolution of her body as it was broken open. But she had only been able to hear it in the end, the thuds and groans of those girls so hard at work.

Kyung-ha nearly tripped over the stack of packages on the doorstep, bound neatly together with string and wrapped in plastic to shield them against the rain. The letters had been one thing to ignore, this was another. Kyung-ha took them into the kitchen and threw them on the counter. The packages felt soft. Whatever was in them seemed perishable. She raised the stack to her nose. Ginseng. Spirit mushrooms. Dried curled snakes. Over the years she had fed Jun-su plenty of Chinese herbal concoctions and knew their price. No one would abandon such expensive medicines without believing that they were going somewhere.

Kyung-ha picked up the telephone, dialled her brother-in-law's number. She let it ring once before hanging up. She could not become involved.

Hyun-min was asleep in the living room with his arm over his eyes. There were several bruises along the length of his arm. Small cuts on his legs.

She shook him awake.

'Hyun-min, ah, that girl with the letter who came by the other day . . .' Kyung-ha began.

Tension rose in his shoulders.

'I told you, I don't know who she is.'

She was careful not to push, sensing the need to tread carefully. 'She mentioned something about a letter . . . something about it being delivered to Pyongyang.'

'A lot of defectors come here and lose their minds.'

She studied the green bruising on his forearms, the film of sweat that had appeared on his upper lip. The courtyard was filled with the cacophony of the hard rain on concrete. She sensed an opportunity to ask him the question that she had wanted to ask him since he had come to the house. 'Were you and Myung-chul close?'

'He was a friend,' he said, his eyebrows furrowed as though he were trying to see something small. He swallowed and then grew self-conscious. Shrugging, he said, 'I didn't know him that well.'

'You're not alone. You can talk . . .' she began, before seeing that Hyun-min was not listening.

Kyung-ha waited for the other volunteers to leave so she might speak to the Reverend alone. He had a habit of asking favours, even personal ones, of the volunteers who stayed after the services, but she was willing to risk this for his advice.

'You dropped something, Reverend.'

'Ah – you're still here.' He checked the floors around him and picked up the photograph. 'For the wedding invitations. My daughter wouldn't be too happy if I lost those.'

'Yes, Reverend.'

'I was wondering whether I could ask a favour.'

'A favour?' she asked, as if she hadn't been expecting it.

'I was hoping to have a few people over for a dinner at the church. I could use a little help with the cooking.'

'I can do that.'

'Good.'

Kyung-ha said nothing. Unsure of how to manoeuvre the

conversation to where she needed it to go. Would she be endangering Hyun-min or anyone else in talking about it?

'Reverend, I have to ask you something.'

He seemed a little weary. 'What is it?'

'I have a defector living at my house. He came to me because of some trouble. I don't know how to reach out to him.'

He gave this a moment's thought. 'It's an issue close to my heart. Our relationship with our people in the North. It's something I worry about. I have family in Pyongyang. A younger brother, actually. We were separated at the beginning of the war. I was just a child then. I often wonder what happened to him. We should do more events to support our brothers and sons from the North. Do some fundraising for them. Tell them about the word of God. Nurture them.'

The Reverend's enthusiasm made her a bit bolder.

'I'm worried about him. I have a feeling something else is going on,' she began carefully. 'I had a visit from another defector who seemed to think that he could deliver messages across the border.'

The Reverend leaned in with keen interest.

'How do you mean?'

'This girl said something impossible. It doesn't make sense. She said it was rumoured that he could make it across the border and back in a day.'

'That would mean that the border is being crossed directly, without passage through China.' The Reverend frowned slightly. 'Who is she?'

She had expected him to dismiss the suggestion immediately. But the look on his face chilled her. What had Hyun-min brought into her home?

'I don't know the girl—'

The Reverend raised his hand, as if to say that he didn't need to hear any more. 'I'd like to meet him. This defector. What is his name?'

'Hyun-min.'

'Bring him to church; show him that he has friends here. We'll make him feel welcome.'

Why had she not thought of it before? Involving him with the church would give them something to do together. That evening, Kyung-ha lured Hyun-min into the kitchen with the smell of *kalbi-jim* to try a different approach. His eyes lit up at the sight of the short beef ribs and she watched him eat, slowly.

'You're too thin, Hyun-min,' she began. 'A boy like you needs to eat. You're still growing.'

He shrugged, noncommittal. He ate the meat in the bowl with an earnest look.

'Hyun-min ah. You should come with me to church sometime.'

'Why?'

'It's a good way to meet people. Aren't you lonely? Do you have any friends here?'

He said nothing in reply to this and scraped his spoon against the bottom of his bowl.

She was afraid that was the end of it, but he said, 'I know about the Bible.'

'You do?'

'I used to cross the river into China. When things got bad and we got hungry. I used to go there once a week. Then one time I met these missionaries, they bought me something to eat, told me about the Bible, they asked me if I wanted to defect, that I wouldn't go hungry again if I did.'

'I didn't know that,' Kyung-ha said. Now that he had finished eating, she was afraid that he would leave. She didn't want to push him. She put some dried squid over an open flame until the edges of it curled and became crisp, before cutting it up for him to snack on.

'Something I could never work out. About this God. I mean, he wrote the Bible himself?' Hyun-min chewed on a stick of the squid without closing his mouth.

'Not exactly,' she said, pouring herself a glass of cold barley tea.

He peered at the squid in his hand. Half of it was wet and brown with his spit. He seemed to be trying to work out whether there was a better way of eating it. There was something child-like about the gesture.

'So you know about Jesus?'

Hyun-min nodded. He now attempted to attack the squid with his back teeth and bared his front in an exaggerated grimace. She couldn't help laughing at him. A white crust covered his chin. She reached across the table between them. She licked her thumb and wiped at his chin. He allowed the gesture. Another sign, she thought, that he was settling down. Warming to her.

'He didn't write it.' Hyun-min said with conviction.

'No, his disciples did.'

Hyun-min nodded, as if this seemed to make sense. 'What if they were phonies?'

'Who were?'

'The disciples.' Hyun-min reached for a chopstick-thin piece of squid. 'How do you know that they didn't just try to change stuff around to make a better story?'

'Hyun-min. This is holy scripture we're talking about.' She couldn't help the sting in her voice. Instantly she tried to retract it. It was no way to encourage the boy. 'The Bible is a holy text. It's blasphemy to say that ordinary men changed the word of God.'

Hyun-min swayed his head as though he could go either way in response to that. 'Comrade Park used to adjust the numbers of boys at the orphanage so that we could get more rice rations. Every year he would add extra numbers so that we'd get more rice. But the newspapers reported that the number of orphans had gone down. What if it was like that?'

It was the first time that Hyun-min had directly mentioned the orphanage. They had had fundraising events at the church for orphanages in North Korea. During presentations missionaries had painted a grim picture of the children's lives. Of younger children who died of dysentery. Of time spent by the older children searching for edible weeds. She wanted to ask him who Comrade Park was but didn't want to push him.

'That's why we have faith, Hyun-min. That's what religion is about.'

He stared at her without blinking and for a moment she thought she saw Jong-ho, not Hyun-min, before her. She had to look away.

'I make you uncomfortable. You don't want to hear stories like this.'

'No, I—'

'It's okay. I'm used to it,' he said.

The fan on the floor between them began to squeak with every rotation. Hyun-min slapped away a mosquito just above his knee.

'So this God. Can he be in two places at once?' he asked.

'He's everywhere.'

Her reply silenced him. He seemed to be contemplating this with great seriousness.

Kyung-ha braved the moment. She did not know how long it would be before it came again. 'This Comrade Park. Who is he?'

'Sorry.' He had a strange look on his face, as though he sure whether to smile or not.

'Why are you sorry?'

Hyun-min shrugged.

'You know, you can tell me anything.' Kyung-ha thought she might push a little. 'What was he like?'

Hyun-min played with the squid, wrapping it around his fingers. He stole a glance at Kyung-ha and then put the squid on the table. 'He was strict. He didn't like talking much. If one of us got caught stealing from the black market, he beat us with branches. I know he cried when the younger kids died. When the famine started, he called me into his office. He said he needed to know whether he could trust me. He was like a father to me. I said he could. He had found a safe path where he could cross the river to China. The river shrank in the summer. Comrade Park began giving me pots and pans, irons and bricks to take across the border to exchange for medicine and food. That's how we survived.'

'Where is Comrade Park now?' she asked gently.

She saw on his face that that was a question too far.

'I'm going to take a walk,' he said, getting to his feet.

'Hyun-min ah . . .'

She was about to follow him when she saw them – two brown paper packages, one neatly stacked on top of the other, tucked under the gate and out of the rain.

'Do sit down and all that,' the Ambassador said, waving his hand, his eyes fixated on the screen.

Thomas sat down. He had a good idea why he was there but he needed more time. Had he misinterpreted those lingering looks, the slight quiver of her hand as she held an umbrella for him when he stepped out of his car and into the rain?

'And it's all right, is it?'

'Of course. Excellent.' Thomas was unsure what he was appraising but guessed that enthusiasm would be winning.

'So.' The Ambassador stroked his chin absent-mindedly. 'How are things going with this . . .' He seemed lost in his own thoughts again, momentarily. 'How was your visit to the National Assembly?'

'It was nothing out of the ordinary.'

'Of course.'

Silence fell between them.

'I thought Mrs Moon circulated the notes on the visit?'

'Yes, so she did.' The Ambassador leaned forward in his chair.

They both knew that this had nothing to do with why he had been called in.

'Are you making any progress with the audit?'

Thomas crossed his arms and shifted uncomfortably in his seat. The air conditioning seemed to have been turned down or off completely. Hadn't she invited him to the apartment? She had kissed him and not the other way around. He had been ready to take it further but had no idea what to make of her elaborate performance as she asked him to leave. They had been circling each other for days.

He cleared his throat.

'Nothing of significance, no.'

The Ambassador nodded. 'Keep at it.'

Thomas wiped his hands on his trousers.

'Forgive me for saying this,' he said. He tugged on his collar. 'But I thought this was a routine security audit. Have you had some intelligence suggesting that Mia . . .' Thomas paused. Calling her by her first name sounded overfamiliar. 'Miss Kim has been compromised?'

The Ambassador shook his head and gathered his hands over his chest and looked towards the ceiling. 'It's delicate. If it were anyone else and any other role it would be a different matter. The thing about interpreters is –' he clenched his fist – 'you want to own them.'

This disturbed him. He sensed there was something that wasn't being disclosed. 'You would tell me, wouldn't you? If you knew something. I mean, do you think Miss Kim is working for someone else? Or has she breached security in some way already?'

The Ambassador shook his head at this, as if the very suggestion was something that could not be said out loud. 'The NIS are pooling their resources. After this beef protest, they need to be sure that they have all their dissidents under control. They've asked for our help and it's a bit heavy-handed but I feel we have to comply, security audits are standard practice after all.'

'But, and forgive the question, why Miss Kim?'

The Ambassador laid his hands on the table and Thomas sensed that he was testing his patience.

'It's best if this assessment is done from the point of view of an impartial investigator.'

'So you can't tell me what you know.' Thomas wiped his forehead and closed his eyes. 'I'm not sure I'm the best person for this.'

The Ambassador raised his eyebrows and tipped his head towards him. 'Why do you say that?'

His throat was dry. It had been a mistake to say this. It had been curious how she had avoided his questions. How neatly she had seemed to fix problems. He had crossed the line of impartiality.

The Ambassador sat back in his chair and looked at him disapprovingly. 'I would have said the contrary. With your enthusiasm in dealing with locals, I would have thought you were the perfect candidate. I'm singing your praises in your latest appraisal about your recovery.'

The Ambassador had got him and they both knew it. Thomas would not admit to incompetence. 'You're right. Of course. Just a momentary crisis of confidence. Don't think anything of it. I'll get you everything you need to know,' Thomas said. He hated how feeble that sounded.

Thomas weaved through the narrow market lined with rows of stalls selling fresh fish and pulses or red rice cakes from an open pan. Some sellers sat on the ground, splitting pea pods into large metal buckets. And just like that the heavy skies burst. As the rain came down he stood in the uncovered alleyway while old ladies pushed past him. He waited, the rain gathering in a neat stream under his chin, torn. He had rung her impulsively, asking her if they could talk. She had suggested they meet in the apartment.

It had been the first direct exchange since she had asked him to leave. Since then they had retreated from their elaborate routines of lingering looks and suggestive words. They had fallen back on formalities. What was he doing? He could neither move forward nor turn back. She had covered for him. Didn't he owe it to her to warn her? The street vendors began packing up their goods, staring at him. A woman, who had been observing him from her stall, thrust an umbrella into his hands, and waved him off, muttering at him in Korean. He nodded gratefully and tried to offer her some money but she refused him.

The apartment building was in sight. He could still turn back. To investigate her as the Ambassador wished was to betray her. It had to be a misunderstanding. He would tell her. Better yet, she could help him. It would become a joke. He would interview her. Is there any reason why the Korean government might suspect you of being suspicious in any way? he would ask. Perhaps they would even laugh about it.

When he entered the apartment, she was standing in the kitchen with a mug in her hands. Her T-shirt was slipping off her shoulder, revealing a small valley hidden behind her collarbone. He had crossed the city, preparing what he was going to say. Now in her presence those words dissipated.

Three strides and he had her face in his hands. He could hardly breathe. He was too sober. He felt everything. He ripped the T-shirt off her shoulder. Her small hands on his waist. Her mouth was cool, her tongue grainy and sweet, a ripe English pear.

He pulled away, suddenly.

'I shouldn't be here,' he said. 'But I felt I should warn you . . .'

'Don't. It's better if you don't say it. It's all a game of pretend anyway, isn't it?'

He hesitated. What did she mean by that? 'Is it?'

She turned her face from him, her breath on his shoulder. Outside, he heard shouting over the unrelenting rain.

'You don't have to give me the speech about being a married man. It doesn't change anything. I don't know what I'm doing with you either.'

For a moment he thought she had changed her mind about him

again, but her hand was on his cheek, guiding his face to hers. He had come resolved to tell her about the audit, but he could not bring himself to interrupt the moment. Was this not the real reason he had come there?

To touch the length of her, unwrap her.

'How did you get this number?' Kyung-ha asked, gripping the phone.

'The Reverend had it. He asked me to help him with dinner. Something about some generous donors to the church. You know how he is,' Myung-ja said.

'He asked me too,' she said.

'I know. He wanted me to let you know that it's been postponed until next week. One of the donors has gone to America, his daughter has had an accident.'

'Next week?'

'Anyway, I've talked to my nephew. He says he has time to meet your daughter on Saturday.'

Kyung-ha had hoped that Myung-ja had forgotten about this.

'Mia, she . . .' Kyung-ha hated to lie. 'She's going on a business trip next week.'

'When will she be back?'

'I'm not sure.'

'We'll find another date,' Myung-ja said. There was a pause. 'You're going to have to let her grow up one day, you know.'

Kyung-ha did not try to correct her. The misunderstanding served its purpose. She put down the phone. How many times did she have to turn Myung-ja down before she would leave her alone? There was a reason she had kept her distance from these women. She could not be subject to their judgement. That was not the only thing that was bothering her. Hyun-min hadn't been home in almost a week. Every night, Kyung-ha stayed up waiting for him, reading passages from Isaiah or cooking his favourite snacks. Several nights in a row she had fallen asleep in the living room and had woken in the early hours of the morning to see that his bedding was untouched.

When she slept she dreamed she walked through a field of broken bones towards the red-brick facade of Seodaemun Prison again. Waiting for him to be brought out, before they released him and he folded onto his knees, before she saw what the hours inside the prison had done to his body. When she woke, she immediately discarded the memories that seeped into her dreams.

Her anxieties were rooted in her uncertainty of Hyun-min's whereabouts. Could there be any truth to the defectors' belief in a route that allowed the delivery of letters across the border? She couldn't think how such a thing was possible. She tried not to think about what it might mean for them if he were caught.

Kyung-ha eyed the backpack that Hyun-min had left tucked under the chair in the living room. It was lighter than she expected. She unzipped it, afraid of what she would find.

She pulled out a change of underwear, a tightly rolled T-shirt. Underneath these items were dozens of letters bound together with red rubber bands.

She picked one thin envelope, marked with an address in Seoul. Kyung-ha ripped it open.

Dearest Brother,

It's been almost sixty years and still I remember you as though it were yesterday. I wonder how you have grown old. They say a habit formed at three years old lasts a lifetime. Do you still scratch your nose when you tell a lie? I saw you that day when you followed our father, after he had expressly told us to stay at home and wait for his return. You didn't know I was watching you, but I saw you walking through the gate and following him as he went to do business in Seoul. Did he catch you following him? Was it too late to turn you away? By the time he saw that you were behind him, it must have been too late. The border closed and that was it.

Over the years I have thought about contacting you many times but I've hesitated. Not just because of the obstacles impeding our communication. There are ways, risky, but effective ways nonetheless. I asked myself, aren't the differences between us too great, how will we talk? What will we talk about? How can I explain what has happened to me and our family over this lifetime? How do I explain to you what life is like here?

I've hesitated for so long that now I am an old man. I wonder if you remember me and our mother and how it was before we were separated. I wonder if those memories are real enough, dear enough to your heart that you might grant my dying wish. It is all right for me to suffer. But I wish for more for my son and his family. Will you help them if they come to you in the South? It would give me some final peace of mind to know that they are being well looked after, better than I was able to look after them—

Kyung-ha heard the gate. She rose to her feet as Hyun-min came in. He stared at the letters in her hand.

'The girl says you can deliver these, is that true?'

He stared at the ground.

'Is that why you keep disappearing?'

'Don't worry about it.'

He had begun to adopt the same tone that Mia used when speaking to her.

'Don't worry about it? You selfish, insolent boy. Do you have any idea how many people have been losing their minds worrying about you? How do I know that you're not dead somewhere or that you're not in hospital? You don't think to call, not even to say that you're still alive?'

Hyun-min blinked several times. He seemed surprised by her outburst. 'I'm sorry.'

His ignorance of why she should be angry enraged her even more. Jun-su had looked at her the same way when he came home after spending the night at another woman's house.

'Explain all of this,' she said, throwing his backpack onto the floor. Letters spilled out of it.

Hyun-min picked up an envelope from the top of the pile. Ran his finger over the address.

'What have you brought into this house?' Kyung-ha said.

He shook his head a little. 'These letters aren't mine. They're nothing to do with me. It's Myung-chul . . .' he began. 'He was obsessed by this story—'

'Are you in some kind of trouble?'

He said nothing for a moment.

She went to him and put her hands on his shoulders. He flinched. 'Was Myung-chul in trouble?'

Hyun-min was quiet for a long time before he began to speak.

'Myung-chul was obsessed by this story he'd heard about an underground tunnel. The rumour is that it was built by a special division of the North Korean army in charge of constructing tunnels under the Demilitarized Zone. One winter, they became separated from the main division by a snowstorm. While they were trapped together, one by one they became convinced that they wanted to defect to the South. All they could think about was a better life. In the South, they said to each other, the winters wouldn't be as harsh. They began sharing stories of things that they had heard about South Korea. Some said that men could have many women and with riches could have many wives. Others said that they had heard that everyone was rich in the South. They made a pact that they would dig a tunnel to the South that only they would know about. It was narrower than the kind they were used to digging – just large enough so that only one man could go through at a time. When the first man died of starvation, they ate his body to stay alive and finish the tunnel. They said it took them months to finish it. And when they finally broke through to the other side, only three of the men had survived. When one of them started talking about going back for his family, one of the other men killed him. Then the remaining two men began to fight about the tunnel. One said that it was just a means of getting to the South and that the tunnel should be destroyed, the other said that it should be kept and used, but only for very special use. They fought and the man who wanted to keep the tunnel killed the other.'

Hyun-min turned the letter over in his hands and broke the seal. She noticed the dirt under his fingernails.

'Myung-chul was obsessed by it. He found it hard to live here. He missed home. He'd worked hard to get where he was, but people still treated him like a foreigner, stiffened when they caught onto his accent, that kind of thing. He used to pack his bag on a Friday and wouldn't come back for days. Sometimes I thought he had left for good. Then he would come back saying he had been on a long walk across the city. It looked suspicious, you know? Then he got this idea that he would build a tunnel himself. He had all these structural sketches in our apartment. It used to drive me crazy. I didn't want to get involved with that. The rumour started circulating among other defectors too. They started coming to him with letters and pills and vitamins and heirlooms and photographs. People showing up at all the time because they thought that he could get this stuff across the border. He wasn't sleeping at all after a while. He was stressed out. All those hopeful faces. Some even came to him saying that they wanted to go back. He couldn't say it, that he hadn't found the tunnel. So he had that hanging over his head too. All those unanswered letters. People started to think that their family members, the ones who they were writing to, were dead. Brokers – guys who smuggle people across the border – all wanted to know where the tunnel was. I think that's why he did it. It drove him crazy.'

Kyung-ha nodded, sadly. She looked into the courtyard and then back at Hyun-min. There were dark shadows under his eyes. For a moment the story settled her worries, though it did nothing to explain where he had been. There was something he wasn't saying and she grasped for it in the growing darkness.

They sat on the porch, feeling the cooling heat as the night drew in. Hyun-min stole a glance at her, as though he were unsure of whether she believed him. Kyung-ha stood up, wanting to wash off the feeling of uncleanliness. She caught sight of the envelope she had opened.

Addressed to a district in Seoul.

If the tunnel was a myth, how was she holding a letter from Pyongyang in her hands? Her eyes met Hyun-min's.

'It's just a stupid story,' he said, without looking away. 'You're not going to report me to the authorities, are you?'

'No,' Kyung-ha said.

The question was like a shot through the heart.

He had called Mia suddenly, to say that he wanted to see her. She raced against him to cross the city to the apartment that she had led him to a week before. When he came in, his hair soaking wet from the rain, she saw that his mood had changed since they had spoken. He said very little. He seemed on the verge of saying something, but hung back, neither sitting down or taking off his raincoat. She didn't have time for his excuses, or whatever it was that he wanted to say to justify what he was doing. She saw that he hadn't really come to talk.

After a week of avoiding each other, he didn't give her a chance to be uncertain. When he put his hands on her face this time she wasn't shaking. She had given it too much thought before. He ripped her T-shirt and she felt the press of his warm skin against her bare stomach. When he backed off, not once taking his eyes off her, it was to resurrect old excuses. But she knew he hadn't come all that way to resist her. She slipped her fingers inside the waistband of his trousers. There was no hesitation. Whatever he had done to justify this to himself had been done. The top button of his trousers fell to the floor as she tugged at it. His face was burrowed in her neck as he pushed her back towards the futon in the living room. She pretended to resist a little, she wanted to know how much he wanted it. She wanted him to fight for it. He did.

He ripped off the remainder of her shirt and as it fell away, her scars were exposed in the light. He pulled back. She didn't want him to stop. She took his hand and put it firmly on her buttock. With her other hand at the back of his neck, she pulled him towards her. Pushed him backwards until he was on his back. This was her old self. Why had she been afraid of this?

She crouched over him. Placed his hands on her breasts. Placed hers on his chest and slid them down to his erection. He tensed at her touch. She took his hand so he was holding her underwear aside and then pulled him inside her. He closed his eyes, gripped her waist. She stopped him. Touched his cheek, waited for him to look at her. And only then did they begin to move together.

Later she caught him studying her scars, tracing the length of them with his fingers.

'What happened?' he asked.

'It's an old story. From a lifetime ago.' She rolled over onto her stomach so he couldn't look at them anymore. 'Are they ugly?' She had never asked anyone that before. 'Don't answer.'

Magpies bickered in the courtyard below. Thomas stood in his office watching them shredding their feed among themselves. His head was filled with screaming cross-currents which he could not quiet. The glisten of her olive skin. Moist. The smell of mould beneath the scent of the rain. Her mouth had tasted of cheap cigarettes. Her skin was paper-thin over her collarbones. She was harmless. Frail, almost. He had unwrapped her from her clothes and saw scars running across the length of her ribs, under her breasts, criss-crossed against the jutting bones of her pelvis. It was almost as though separate sections of skin had been stitched together. He thought of the Aboriginal tribes who scarred themselves as a rite of passage.

He had been as horrified as he was fascinated. Frailty didn't survive such violence. Her body celebrated pain. There was so much about her that he didn't know. He had asked her about the scars and she had murmured something about a former life. Perhaps the Ambassador did have reason to suspect her of something.

He had had a choice. He had resisted her at first. Then he had felt her breath on his cheek and he was only thinking of how much he wanted her. He had spent all day trying not to think about it, throwing himself into work, looking over the itinerary for a policy minister's visit, getting back to Paul about the minister's visit. Lurking at the end of every conversation he had was that feeling of suspension over the same conclusion. That no matter how he assessed it, sleeping with her had been a mistake. An unnecessary confusion. But he was insatiably curious about her.

Thomas stepped away from the window. Mia was not at her desk. There was no turning back now.

Autumn

The rains continued to fall for a month, washing the pavements clean of the yellow desert dust that blew in from the west. Floods rose in the valleys, bringing traffic to a halt in several corners of the city.

'Darling,' Thomas said on the phone to Felicity, 'the water's up to my knees here. I don't know if I dare venture out in this. I think I'd better stay here. As it is, I've got a lot of work to do.'

In those nights that he could get away they lay in the apartment, speaking little, listening only to the rush of rain on the streets beneath their urgent whispering breaths.

By the time the monsoon was over and the August heat made it too hot to touch each other, they met by the river, the only place where the breeze carried over the water.

'I can hardly touch you in this heat. It's insufferable. I can't imagine a different hell.'

'I know,' she said. 'But I'd have the weather this way all year long if I could.'

He tried not to take offence. She struck him as distant and cold when she spoke like this.

'You think I'm strange,' she said.

'Strange isn't the word.'

'Is that it? You won't say how you feel?'

'Isn't that the agreement between us? We tell each other as little as we can. Isn't that right?' he said, turning away from her and leaning against the railing overlooking the river, feeling the warm wind in his hair. She said nothing. She was disappointed in him. 'I'm sorry. I don't want to quarrel.'

There was a long pause.

'I have to be very careful about what I say around you,' she said.

'Why is that?'

'I think you know why.'

When he was not with her, he had taken to reading a thick volume of Korean history. He avoided reading the employee documents and other files that the Ambassador had given him. Without any context or background, the bare facts meant nothing.

He was hungry to learn, consuming the history of the rapid development of the country with fervour, feeling it to be a small step towards regaining something he had lost before he had come to Seoul.

He thought of Mia's report and her suggestion that the country was headed towards a dictatorship. The protests had been shut down with authoritarian efficiency.

'Makes for rather exciting reading, doesn't it? Quite a tumultuous fifty years the country's had, really,' Felicity commented, picking up his reading glasses from the floor and placing them on his lap.

'I didn't know you knew so much about the country's history.'

Felicity closed her book. 'I did my homework, darling.'

At the start of the posting, he had skimmed a condensed history of the country. It had been a half-hearted attempt. He had gathered scraps of basic information as he went along, but had generally veered away from committing to knowing too much.

Felicity was studying him, her head cocked to one side. 'What's sparked this fresh interest?'

He ignored the question.

'Tom,' Felicity began.

He looked up and thought that he saw trepidation on her face. 'What is it?'

'There's something I must discuss with you.' She looked cautious. He felt his lips grow taut.

'I know how you feel about the paper. But Giles wants to give me a column. It would cross over into politics, occasionally. We've discussed our confidentiality conundrum at length. Supposing we discuss my work before it goes to print?'

Immediately he felt weary. 'If I object? Will you abandon the story?' he said.

'I'm hoping it wouldn't come to that, of course.' Her face fell.

'Does it have to be politics?' He felt cruel, he was still punishing her. 'Listen. I'm sorry,' he said. 'Perhaps the three of us could have lunch and discuss how it would work.'

'I'll put you first, of course. I won't touch anything contentious.' Her face brightened. She kissed him suddenly on the cheek and then she disappeared to make a phone call.

The Ambassador was unhappy with him again.

'You've gone quiet on the delicate matter of our audit.'

Thomas could see the accusation. The Ambassador suspected his incompetence. 'I need some more time.'

'It's been two months.' The Ambassador put his hands in his pockets. 'The NIS are starting to get a little impatient. Have you nothing to write?'

He thought of the photographs he had taken from the kitchen counter in her apartment. All of them named portraits. They lay abandoned in the bottom of a drawer in his study. He thought of the slide of her chin in the valley of his shoulder. The lightness of her fingers on his back, the narrowness of her hips. The lingering smoky sweetness of her mouth.

'Just give me a little more time. Just a little more.'

Though they were becoming accustomed to Hyun-min's frequent absences, Mia couldn't help noticing the effect his desertions were having on her stepmother. Every night, Mia caught Kyung-ha waiting for him on the porch, gazing at the gate. Or setting out an extra spoon and a set of chopsticks at the dinner table. The fridge was bursting with Tupperware boxes containing red-chilli-fried squid, Hyun-min's favourite. She caught Kyung-ha attempting to sew on a missing button of his washed-out denim shirt with her crooked fingers.

Mia found herself whispering or tiptoeing around the house as though loud noises would be disrespectful of his absence. Her stepmother's sadness became a kind of politeness. There were no lectures on respect, no admonitions on smoking. Mia had provoked her by spilling her seaweed soup onto her lap during dinner and her stepmother had merely turned her face and pretended that she hadn't noticed.

She often found her stepmother sitting on the porch, as though waiting alone would somehow bring him back.

'I wish he wouldn't be out so late,' she said.

What was it about Hyun-min that she loved so much? He never talked back. Used words that no one used anymore. Perhaps they reminded Kyung-ha of another time, before the war. It was also because he was a boy. Mia knew that that alone meant he was worth more in Kyung-ha's eyes.

'He can take care of himself, you know. He doesn't need you to protect him.' She had intended to console her but once the words were out they sounded bitter.

In the moonlight, her stepmother looked haggard and small. 'I know that,' she said, softly. 'But that's not the heart of a parent.'

They looked at each other for a moment, conscious of the admission that had been made. Kyung-ha's eyes were worn. They had sunk in their sockets. Her stepmother said nothing, would not look at her still. Instead she looked into her palms, as if in contemplation of the lines drawn there.

'What would I know about that?' Mia said. She elbowed a clay pot where Kyung-ha had planted an orchid she had brought home from the church, convinced that it would bloom again. It shattered on the gravel. For a moment Mia thought she saw the old flames in her stepmother's eyes. Then she seemed to let it go.

She sighed. Her ankles clicked as she rose to her feet. 'I'll clear it up.'

Her stepmother's preoccupation with Hyun-min's disappearance was so great that it was a surprise when Kyung-ha sought Mia out one evening.

'Is he back?' she asked, looking at all the food on the table. 'I guess not. Since you're suddenly wondering where I've been.'

'I need you to do something on Saturday.'

'He'll come back if he wants to. I'm not going to look for Hyun-min again,' she said. She expected a slap across the face or a smack of some kind for that, but her stepmother was looking at her feet.

'It's nothing to do with him.'

Mia tensed; her stepmother's tone was unfamiliar.

'I need you to meet someone.'

She let the strangeness of the statement sink in. Her stepmother had never introduced her to anyone. They had rarely been out together. She had assumed that her stepmother was ashamed of her.

'What for?'

'Just have a cup of coffee with the guy and then go.'

'What are you talking about?'

Kyung-ha turned her attention back to the frying pan as though it had all been agreed. 'There's a woman at the church whose nephew would like to meet you. It's just a coffee . . .'

Then she realized what her stepmother was saying. 'You set up a *suhn* for me?' She didn't understand. 'Why?'

'I don't know why her nephew wants to waste his time, but she's insisting.'

'That doesn't make any sense.'

'How long are you going to remain a child? When will you start caring about other people? At your age you need to be a bit more serious about life. How much longer will you free-float your way through things?'

'You're not doing this for me,' she said, expecting Kyung-ha to deny it.

Kyung-ha said softly, 'Just be there. That's all you have to do.'

'So how about this ball on Saturday?' Charles asked, resting his arm on the partition.

'What ball?'

'The fundraiser. For the Anglo-Korean Foundation.'

'What about it?' Mia asked, hardly looking up from her work.

'As luck would have it, a spare ticket seems to have found its way into my hands. Would you like to be my date?'

She looked at him doubtfully. 'Not really.'

She didn't know how she would explain the arrangement that Kyung-ha had made for her on Saturday evening when she hardly understood it herself. When she looked up at Charles she saw that she had offended him. 'I'm sorry, I don't really do dress-up.'

'That's a shame. I'd have thought you'd clean up really well,' he said with a smile and she knew she was forgiven. 'I suppose I'll have to ask Mrs Moon instead.'

They both laughed a little at this.

'I don't think her husband would approve.'

'How about a drink this evening then?'

She caught sight of Thomas waiting for her by the lift.

'I can't.'

'Miss Lee,' he said, flashing Mia a teasing look as he turned to their colleague, 'I don't suppose you're free this Saturday?'

'What was that about?' Thomas asked her as their paths joined along the palace walls.

'Charles asked me to go with him to the ball on Saturday.'

'What did you say?'

'I think I'll go,' she said, testing him.

'I suppose anyone will do? Even if it is Charles?'

Mia reached out to touch him. She had never seen him angry. He had never given himself away.

He caught her hand. 'Don't let me get in the way if you'd like to spend the evening with him.'

Then she began to smile.

He was jealous.

★

Kyung-ha fastened the last button of the blouse she had put on Mia. It was long-sleeved, made of silk, with frills hanging over her chest. She had borrowed it from the storeroom that night. She had resisted the *suhn* for months and then decided that it was better to let the date, the failure of it, unfold. If she knew the girl at all, she knew it would not lead to anything. All she needed was for the girl not to embarrass her.

'Be careful with this. Don't eat anything. Use a straw if you have to drink. If this comes back stained—'

'Okay. I get it,' the girl said quietly.

The rosy glow that crept on the girl's cheeks brought out the whiteness of her skin. It would be impossible to hide. How would she be able to explain the whiteness of the child, the fact that she was not hers at all, to the women at the church? She had been distracted, and had let them talk her into it. She could feel their judgement and scorn already. Kyung-ha felt hardness in her stomach as though she had swallowed a large seed.

The girl was strangely quiet. Compliant.

The girl's eyes had become greener as the years went by. She had thrown her outside as a child, but she had only returned home at the end of the day with whiter skin than before. Yet Kyung-ha could not eschew her duties. After all, she had spent years trying to prove to herself that she could and did love the girl. There were times when she felt sorry for her. She was a lonely child without an anchor. A child lost in reverie. Suddenly, the dread that she was feeling fell away. Perhaps the *suhn* was a good idea after all. If the girl would not do it for herself, it was her duty to yank her into adulthood. She owed her that much. It was her duty to find the girl a family of her own.

Mia picked up the dress she had left with the concierge in the hotel.

It had been pointless to try to tell her stepmother that she had other plans. No use explaining that she had to go to the Embassy's annual fundraiser ball. She had suggested her date should meet her for coffee at the hotel lobby. Now, as she passed the coffee shop, she considered going straight to the ball instead. But she needed to make her point.

She found the toilet and pulled out the black silk dress from the paper bag. Inside the cubicle, she stripped off the clothes Kyung-ha had given her and threw on her other dress. Creases had appeared on Kyung-ha's face as she had examined Mia. With every look there had been a new reason for dissatisfaction. They had both known that the clothes did not suit her. She sucked in her breath as she pulled the zip up along her side. Loosening the tight bun that Kyung-ha had insisted on, she brushed out the hair spray and stood for a moment appreciating the cool air descending from the vent on her bare back. She turned around to ensure, again, that the lower edges of her dress covered the jutting points of her scars.

Kyung-ha had drawn Mia's eyebrows with a charcoal pencil which was at odds with the colour of her hair. The effect was severe. She looked a little unhinged, which was no bad thing, given her plan.

She reversed the effect, though, with a dab of lotion and some tissue paper. She applied eyeliner and mascara and took a step back. With the finishing touch of black eyeshadow, she had taken herself out of the running as a potential candidate for marriage. To a Korean man, she knew, her appearance would be inappropriate for a date. It didn't send the right message. Korean men seemed to place women in two categories – those they married and those they slept with. She turned to assess her dress from the other side.

The armour was perfect. She could not fault the intent inherent in her appearance. Had she not done this a thousand times before? Yet tonight, there it was. A feeling like she couldn't breathe.

All of the tables in the coffee shop were taken. Several people took turns eyeing her dress. He was sitting alone, tapping the edge of his mobile against the table. She was sure it was him, though he was older than she had been expecting. A man who had spent his youth on trading desks and late nights at the office, who wanted a family as an afterthought. His hair looked sharp, propped up by too much gel. His eyes widened as she approached him. He cracked his knuckles before he stood up and offered his hand.

She ignored this and sat down. There was no time to waste with civilities. She reached for the pack of cigarettes in her handbag.

He cleared his throat and sat down.

'Are you Mia?' he said in English. He had an American accent. Kyung-ha had said that he had gone to Harvard or Princeton or some Ivy League school. 'I'm Young-suk.'

Mia nodded and sat back in her chair. 'Do you mind if I smoke?'

His mouth tightened.

'I get nervous, you know.' She realized he might misinterpret this; she didn't want to encourage him.

He smiled a little and, as if to demonstrate his generosity, said, 'Sure, sure.'

'Do you want one?'

He raised both his hands in a show of palms. 'I don't drink or smoke.'
She made a face.

'I exercise a lot.' He paused and seemed to reconsider. 'Your mother mentioned you're an avid hiker.'

'She's not my mother,' she said, sharply. 'What else did she tell you about me?' She gave him a chance to think about it. As she had expected he took the opportunity to steal a glance at the edge of her dress across her thigh. 'I'm not such a great hiker these days. I've found I've . . . outgrown that interest.'

'So what are you interested in?'

She paused and took a drag of her cigarette, holding his gaze. 'Diplomacy.'

He nodded. 'That's right. You're an interpreter. Impressive. I didn't know you were so crazy about your job, though.'

'I'm passionate, if that's what you mean.' Mia leaned forward in her chair and stubbed out her cigarette. She shrugged a little.

'That's . . .' His voice trailed off. He looked lost for a moment. He began to talk about himself. His job at a securities firm where he was an analyst. His love of Miles Davis and live jazz music. His voice got smaller and smaller as he continued on, as though he were losing faith in his own words. Her hands were twice the size of his. She imagined what might have happened if she had sat across from him in the clothes Kyung-ha had prepared for her. Covered her mouth when she smiled. They would see each other once a week, perhaps. Hold hands after several months. Declare their intention to marry after six months. Perhaps then he would try to kiss her and she would bashfully let him. Their wedding would take place in a wedding hall, a concrete conveyer belt of weddings, where guests would eat in the canteen downstairs without bothering to watch the ceremony. Would she last a year before the facade crumbled, before she burst at the seams, needing to breathe, wanting more, wanting to speak English, wanting to be in England?

He over emphasized his 'r's and spoke in an exaggerated American way. Mia lit another cigarette without asking. She could tell by the way that he looked at her that he was one of those men who believed that the only women who smoked openly in public were prostitutes. It wore her down. This culture of questions and placement. It was social courtesy to immediately reveal one's intellect, where one had gone to university, one's class; to answer questions about her family and her relationship status and age. An artillery of questions. Men like him suffocated her. The English let her be. They were generous in their politeness.

She realized he had stopped speaking.

'You haven't touched your drink,' he said.

He had ordered lemonade for her while he was waiting. She drank the whole glass without stopping and wiped the remains from her chin, exaggerating a grimace. 'That's so sour.'

She felt sorry when she saw the look on his face. It was wrong to mock ordinary dreams. He could have been genuine. Lonely. But not lonely enough to go for a woman like her. It was time to drive the final stake. She uncrossed her legs, lit another cigarette and crossed her legs again, inhaled sharply and asked him. 'So, do you like to fuck?'

He gave her a lopsided smile which made her like him a little less. He seemed to understand, finally, that she wasn't taking the meeting seriously. 'I'm a good catch, you know. Do you know how many girls would love to be in your position? You're not exactly what I was expecting. You're lucky I'm still here. I'm an open-minded kind of guy. So I thought, why not?'

'I'm leaving now.'

He grabbed her wrist as she stood up. 'I'm your break, kid. You should think twice about what you're doing. A girl like you doesn't get too many chances.'

'Pervert.' She tugged against his grip and raised her voice, 'No I will not go upstairs to sleep with you.'

Several guests looked over to them, alarmed. A waiter made his way towards them. He leaned back in his chair and buttoned his jacket, staring down at his drink, redness creeping up his cheeks.

'Is everything okay here?' The waiter asked.

'He wants the bill,' she said, walking away.

The ballroom was warm though the patio doors hung open to the chilly autumn air. Waiters hurriedly weaved between the red-faced guests, as if attending to an urgent problem. Mia hung back at the entrance, looking for Thomas.

'I thought you weren't coming,' Charles said as she came in. He kissed her hand, theatrically. He whispered in her ear. 'You're on some sort of man-eating prowl, I presume?'

'Not that it's any of your business,' she said.

'Join me for a drink?'

She nodded, unable to find an excuse not to. His hand lingered on her back as he led her past the tables and towards the bar. She stepped aside, hoping to get a better view of the ballroom from the other side of the crowd. David Hewer, one of the senior diplomats, chatted to Charles for a few minutes before noticing her. 'You look very well. Are you enjoying the party?'

Her cheeks warmed. 'It's great.'

'I always feel that if you've been to one, you've been to them all,' David said.

She felt a little ashamed at having been in awe of the party, at that.

'Nonsense. These canapés are wonderful,' Charles said.

'Mrs Hewer and I thought we might throw you a dinner party in December to commiserate your leaving us for England. What do you say?'

'That's very generous. I'd like that very much, though I don't much like the idea of my leaving.'

David seemed to notice her again and said as an afterthought, 'You must come as well. Rumour has it that Charles has formed quite an attachment to you?'

She avoided meeting his eyes.

'He's a good friend,' she said.

She made an escape by claiming to need the toilet and slipped out onto the patio. The swimming pool, several floors below, looked inviting. Further away, a parade of orange lights lit up the bridge over the black river. Thomas stood with his back to the party, talking to Paul, one of the diplomats in his department. Mia hung back a moment and watched him. His hair was slicked back and had lost its curl. He had shaved. He seemed younger. It was in seeing him in his element that meant she could finally place the noose-like thought around her neck. She was no longer the hunter. He was nothing like the GIs that she consumed and discarded. She could not wash herself of this desire for him.

Paul caught her eye and smiled, beckoning her over.

There was no option of hiding, or sliding back into the ballroom. Her cheeks warmed. 'Hello.'

'That's quite a dress,' Thomas said.

Was it her imagination or had a hiss escaped his lips as he said this? She tensed, aware of some misalignment that she could not place.

Mia stole a look at Paul and then muttered, 'Thanks.'

'I always feel women dress far too conservatively at these events, so well done for shaking a bit of life into the party,' Paul said. He took a swig of his drink and then, turning back to Thomas, said, 'Where is that gorgeous wife of yours?'

'I believe she's cornered the Ambassador,' Thomas replied. 'Perhaps you should go and rescue him.'

It was only then she realized he was drunk. There was an awkward silence.

She looked into her glass, now empty, and handed it to Paul. 'Would you mind?'

He looked surprised, but muttered that he would be happy to and disappeared into the ballroom.

Thomas turned back towards the river. A speck of ash landed on his shoulder. She reached out to wipe it away, then, hesitating, dropped her hand back to her side.

'How much have you had? I thought you'd stopped this,' she said.

'It's a party, Mia, it's what people do.'

'Not like this. You can't let anyone see you like this,' she said.

'I suppose you'd like to get rid of me.'

'I don't know what you're talking about.'

'Would you care to dance?' He saw the look on her face and laughed. 'It's not such an appalling suggestion is it?'

'No, but what if someone were to see—'

'You worry too much.'

His hands were on her waist, his breath on her cheek. She looked anxiously over his shoulder to see if anyone was watching them. He was unpredictable when he had had a drink.

'Why have you started this again?'

He ignored the question. 'Where were you earlier this evening?'

'Stuck in traffic. I was late, I took a taxi,' she found herself saying, not knowing why she lied.

'That's funny, I could have sworn I saw you in the lobby earlier.'

'You must be seeing me everywhere you go,' she said, trying to make a joke of it. She couldn't imagine trying to explain the blind date to him. He didn't laugh. 'It must have been someone else.'

The music came to an end and she stepped away from him, conscious of their closeness. Thomas reached into his jacket pocket and pulled out his pack of cigarettes, never taking his eyes off her.

'Mia . . .' he began. 'What are you hiding?'

She laughed a little. Was that what this was about? Was he still jealous of Charles?

'Tom,' Felicity's voice broke the spell. Mia took a step back from him quickly.

'Mia.' Felicity turned to her with a smile. 'Hello, again. Lovely dress,' she said, turning her attention to Thomas immediately, making Mia think that she hated it.

'How are you?' Mia said, barely able to muster a smile.

'I'm afraid I'm not feeling so well.' Felicity put her hand on Thomas's shoulder. 'Tom, do you mind if we go home?'

'You've met?' Thomas asked, bemused.

'Months ago. You remember that awful mess we had with the plumbing. Mia was kind enough to sort it out for us. Did I not mention it?'

Thomas shook his head. Felicity put her hands on his waist. They said goodnight and Mia watched them leave. Thomas gave her a backward glance as he walked into the ballroom. Mia turned back, her shoulders hunched over the balcony railing. She stared at the glass in her hand and then tipped the remainder of the wine over the edge.

The ballroom had cleared out a little.

She felt a hand on her arm.

'There you are,' Charles said with a smile. 'I hope you're not thinking of leaving.'

'I'm tired,' she said, realizing how deflated she felt.

'The night's still young,' he said. 'How about a dance?'

'No, thanks.' She pointed to her feet.

He looked a little disappointed. 'Well, if that's the case you'd better have a drink to numb the pain. Here, have a sip of this and we'll put your feet up.'

He took her hand and pulled her back into the ballroom. She sank into the nearest seat. Her feet were aching. He took off her shoes. He kneaded her right foot with his hands. 'You really do look beautiful this evening.'

He was looking at her intently. There was something tender in his eyes. She was trapped, her foot in his hand.

'Where's your date?'

'Don't have one,' he said, taking her other foot.

'Miss Lee turned you down as well?'

He gave her a tired half smile. 'Who will you tease when I'm gone?'

'I'll be okay.'

He put her foot down and sat back in his chair. His mood seemed to change, suddenly. 'He's married, you know. Not to mention that he's a mess.'

She was so surprised that she didn't know how to respond.

'You deserve better, can you not see that? Or do you only love what's bad for you?'

A few guests looked over in their direction. She didn't like his tone. 'Don't patronise me. You don't know anything about how I feel.'

'What about how I feel, then?'

She turned away from him, grasping her bag and shoes. She didn't want to hear it.

He grabbed her hand as she stood up. 'Why won't you take me seriously?'

'I thought we were friends.'

He let go of her hand. He looked angry. 'Are you in love with him?'

'Don't be stupid.'

He said nothing for a moment. Then he seemed to change his mind. When he spoke he was light-hearted again.

'How about that dance then?'

'If I must,' she said.

'You say this now, but you'll miss me when I'm gone.'

'I doubt it,' she said.

He was shorter than Thomas, softer. When they danced, they were almost eye to eye. She drew in closer to him to look over his shoulder. He spun her around and then pulled her towards him again. She laughed a little. That was the thing about Charles, he never stayed serious for too long.

'I wouldn't leave for England, you know,' he said, as the song ended. 'If you asked me not to.'

'Thank goodness for proper air conditioning,' Felicity said, switching on their bedroom light as she removed her heels. 'I don't know how we survived that first year in Phnom Penh, do you?'

Thomas paused at the mention of Phnom Penhh before slowly placing his dinner jacket on a hanger. He wouldn't be drawn in now. There was a murkiness that filled his head with the recollection of another detail.

He had gone to the ball resolute. Ready to tell her everything. He had written an innocuous report and was ready to hand it over to the Ambassador. But, strangely, he had felt that he owed it to Mia to tell her. He had waited anxiously for her to arrive at the party. Had wandered into the lobby to avoid the lure of drink. He had been nervously fingering his cufflink when it had dropped on the floor. That's when he saw it: Mia's easy manner with the stranger. He was frozen, bent over on the floor as he saw her touching this man's knee. She nodded as he spoke, as though she agreed with everything that he said. It had pained him to see it. Was she this way with other men? It was presumptive of him to think that she looked at only him in that way. He had deluded himself in thinking himself privileged. And what right did he have to possess her? He had watched them from behind one of the pillars in the lobby before turning back upstairs to the party. He had reached for the first drink he could. The burn in his throat had calmed him. He had had another. Another after that.

'You've been very quiet all evening. You're not still cross with me?' Felicity sat down at her dressing table. 'You're just going to have to trust me about the paper, Tom.'

He didn't feel like indulging her. 'All right, let's not talk about it now.'

He went into the bathroom and turned on the taps, undid the buttons of his shirt. He splashed water on his face and willed himself to quiet his mind. He had never seen her dressed as she was before. She was wearing a short, tight-fitting black dress, her black hair loose and wild. The way other men had seen her was not lost on him.

There was something else that bothered him. How had Felicity not mentioned that Mia had been in their home? He shut off the taps and went back into the bedroom. 'You said you'd met Mia?'

'Yes, it was the evening we had the plumbers round. It was kind of her to come. She didn't have to do that.'

'You didn't tell me.'

'What's the matter?'

He stepped into the bedroom and started getting changed. 'Nothing, just work.'

A shadow crossed her face. She looked hurt but seemed determined not to show it. She set down her brush and took off her earrings.

'Such curious people, the Koreans, aren't they? I spoke to Mrs Song for the first time tonight, I can never remember her Christian name, though I suppose it's not Christian if it's Korean, is it? Anyway, it was fascinating. I mean, they're so overfamiliar. It was almost like an interrogation. She asked how old I was, I think that's quite important here, you know, like in Japan, though they aren't so direct in Japan, are they? I might ask John the next time I see him.' Felicity unclasped her necklace and paused, fingering the links between the jewels. 'She asked why we didn't have any children. Can you imagine? To ask something like that, within hours of an introduction. Even my mother daren't ask.'

It was his cue to retreat. He put down the toothbrush.

Felicity appeared at the door and watched him. 'Tom, have you been listening to a word I've said?'

'Of course.' Thomas paused, burying his face in a towel so that he would not have to look at her. 'Listen, I've just remembered I promised Nigel something. I'm sorry, I know I'm distracted.'

He kissed her chastely on her forehead and then moved into the bedroom and lit a cigarette.

'Will you unzip me before you go down, please?'

Thomas unzipped her dress, a cigarette between his lips, his face turned away from her hair.

She sat back down at her dresser, unmoving. She was on the verge of snapping at him. He could feel it building and her suppressing it.

'I wish you wouldn't smoke in here,' she said, reaching for the bedroom window.

He turned to leave.

'Tom?'

He hesitated in the doorway. He didn't want to be drawn into a fight. 'Yes?'

'I think you might've had a glass too many tonight.'

He kept his eyes on a tiny stain on the carpet, marvelling how it had missed Felicity's hawkish eye. 'I've got it under control. Don't worry.'

'Tom . . .' she began, then seemed to change her mind. 'Goodnight.'

She turned out the light and he went down to his study, where he poured himself a glass of brandy. He recalled Mia's easy smile at something the man had said. It had seemed oddly subservient. She was a woman of many faces. A chameleon.

She had been in their home. He knocked back the glass. He needed to know who that man was. What he was to her. He poured himself another glass. She was resourceful. What else was she capable of? She had never reassured him of her affections. It suddenly seemed reasonable to him to investigate her. There was no harm in it. If he uncovered nothing, then so be it.

He turned on his computer and began to type an email to the Ambassador.

Nigel, he wrote. *I'd like some help from the NIS in identifying someone.*

Hyun-min sat in the pew alone. He had recovered the colour in his cheeks, though his face remained hollow and dark. Kyung-ha blew out the final three candles at the altar and gathered the rag in her hands.

She put a hand on his shoulder. 'Where have you been? I've been so worried.'

'I came for the service,' Hyun-min said meekly. There was a pause. 'I'm trying to understand your God.'

Kyung-ha nudged him along the pew and sat down beside him. 'What is it you don't understand?'

'There are no photographs of him in your home.'

Kyung-ha hesitated. It took her a few moments to understand what he meant. She had seen Jong-ho in his face so often that the reminders of the border he had crossed surprised her. She didn't pretend to know what the world he had left behind was like, though she had seen the framed photos of Kim Il-sung and Kim Jong-il in photographs of North Koreans' homes. When he did not speak, it was so easy to forget that he had come from a different world, where leaders were worshipped. People were idolized. Where Nationalism was a religion.

Before she could respond, he said, with two ridges appearing between his eyebrows, 'to pray. Is it kind of like wishing?'

Kyung-ha opened her mouth in reply and then shut it again, unsure of exactly how to put it. Praying was like exercising a muscle. The more she prayed, the more effectively her voice would be heard by God. She imagined God to be overwhelmed by a sea of voices and thought that it could only be a good thing if her voice was strong and persistent, so that he might hear what she had to say over all the other competing voices.

'Imagine, Hyun-min, that there is a being out there. Who is benevolent. Who has loved you from the beginning. Who is listening to your desires and has the power to grant them.'

Hyun-min nodded, as though he were taking this in. 'Do you have to close your eyes?'

'Not necessarily, but it helps you to concentrate.'

Hyun-min closed his eyes and gathered his hands. 'Now what?'

'Well, you could start by saying, dear Lord, thank you for the blessings you've given us.'

Hyun-min opened his eyes and stared in front of him.

'What is it that you want to pray for?'

Hyun-min opened his mouth to say something and then seemed to change his mind. She saw that he wanted to speak. He bit his lip. He seemed so much younger than eighteen. It was only when he searched her eyes that she saw how he avoided her. He was not her Jong-ho, who had not been old enough to become so guarded.

'Not to feel so guilty all the time,' he said, finally. 'What can your God do about that?'

'Why would you feel guilty?'

'I look around me and I think about how unfair it all is. To have so much food that it goes to waste, when I know that not so far away from here I knew boys who died because their stomachs were so hungry they ate themselves. Now I'm here. I can't enjoy it. I never told Comrade Park that I was leaving. I just didn't go back one day, after crossing the border to trade for some medicines.'

'The man is like a father to you. I'm sure he's forgiving.' She resisted the temptation to take his hand. She didn't know what else to say. 'The best thing is to pray. Until God shows you the way to let go of the guilt.'

'Is that what you pray about?'

'Mostly.' She thought of Jong-ho. 'I pray for my son.'

'Mia had a brother?'

'No,' she said quickly. She had never thought of it that way. Jong-ho had been all hers. Nothing to do with the girl. 'She's Jun-su's child.'

Hyun-min glanced down the aisle, as though he could see Jong-ho, and then back at her.

'He died. Pneumonia,' she added quickly. 'He was very young.'

Except this wasn't strictly true. He had been murdered by her pride. She had protected him with superstition but in none of the ways that mattered. When he was still a bundle she would touch the rolls of fat on his arms and check for the telltale wrinkle just short of the bend of his elbows. That prophecy of poverty. It was absent. He would not grow up to be poor. She didn't have the words to express her love. All she felt was an irresistible urge to bite him, like a mother cat taking a kitten in her mouth to move him. She was afraid of how precious he was. Afraid of showing that she loved him too much. So with every affectionate nudge, she called him 'the idiot', a baby 'the size of a rat's eye'. She denied that he was precious, so the evil spirits would pass on by.

Hyun-min looked at her, as though he sensed that there was more to it than she had said.

'He was sick because of me. I took him to the factory . . .' How did she explain to him that she had used her own son to punish her husband for philandering? She had left their home in a hurry. They had slept among that fibrous dust. 'It took me so long to see how sick he was. I left him alone to look for a doctor.'

She looked around, half expecting to see Jong-ho sitting in the pews. She did not want to say the last part. That her son had died alone.

Instead, she looked at Hyun-min and said, 'You remind me of him.'

Before Hyun-min could say anything, the doors swung open and the Reverend came in, with several volunteers.

'Is this our friend?' said the Reverend.

Kyung-ha nodded reluctantly, not wanting Hyun-min to think that she had been talking about him.

'Welcome. I'm Reverend Hwang. Sit down, get comfortable, we could get something cold to drink . . .' he said, looking hopefully at the volunteers who had accompanied him into the church.

'I'll get you something,' Kyung-ha murmured hastily, trying not to make eye contact with the women who stood at the end of the pew. The evening before, Mia's blind date's mother had called her angrily, berating her for Mia's lack of manners. It was bad enough that they had learned the truth of Kyung-ha's circumstances. She did not want them to interrogate her relationship with Hyun-min as well.

She walked ahead of them, hoping not to have to talk to them, but she heard them talking behind her as she went to the kitchen.

'These fundraising lunches aren't worth the effort. Compared to how much effort we put in, I don't think we raise that much money,' one woman said.

'Whenever the lunches are over and I'm throwing out all the food that's leftover, I think about how ironic it is that we're cooking to raise money for starving North Korean children,' another woman said.

'This is the second fundraising lunch for the North Koreans this month, what about the elderly in our city? Don't they need looking after? It breaks my heart,' a third woman said.

Kyung-ha pushed past the door through to the kitchen. Once they were all in the kitchen together, the women stopped talking. She could hear them begin to chop the vegetables in silence. She knew what was coming. The women busied themselves with their work – coating the vegetables in oil before frying them with the glass noodles, boiling the soups.

One of the women came close to Kyung-ha and said, 'You didn't say where you were from. How you met your husband.'

'That was a long time ago.'

'I hear your daughter is foreign.'

'She's my husband's daughter,' Kyung-ha said in shame. This had happened many times before. Every time they moved it was the same. She would build camaraderie with the women around her. Then they would see the girl and rumours would begin to circulate. Kyung-ha had learned over the years when to try to explain and when to leave. She wiped her hands on her apron and left the kitchen with the two glasses of cold barley tea almost spilling over in her hands.

Once it had been a point of pride. She was the wife of a professor. A revolutionary. She had enjoyed the prestige of it after all of the lonely years she had spent working in a factory. It was the kind of rags-to-riches tale that people only saw in the movies. During the early days, she had replayed the story in her mind, over and over. How she had been drawn to him, recognized his face as he stood among a crowd of students at the university. He had been like an older brother when they were younger, growing up in the countryside. Now she wondered often what might have happened if she had walked straight past him. What if she hadn't recognized him among the crowd of students?

In the bleak days before she had married Jun-su, she had sustained herself with a job sewing buttonholes in women's shirts at a factory.

She had never imagined that she would ever go back to the factory after marriage. A professor's wife – her new responsibilities had entailed serving tea and meals to his colleagues. She had spent the time in the kitchen listening to snippets of their conversations.

'This country is whoring itself to the Americans. Our economy may be growing but it's only the rich who are getting richer. We're not being liberated.'

'You see what's happening in the factories? It's the workers who are the revolutionaries. They're resisting these capitalist pigs. They are the ones who are at the forefront of the socialist revolution. Like Kyung-ha-shi – you are our hero, do you know that?' Jun-su's colleague Il Hyung had said to her. Kyung-ha didn't know how sewing buttonholes had anything to do with the government or revolution. The men had begun to scheme about infiltrating the factories, disguised as workers, so that they could add to the resistance. Then Jun-su had been fired from the university for lecturing against the economic measures proposed by the President.

Every day he spoke of getting a job in a factory and had persuaded Kyung-ha to go back to the job she had had before she was married. His job never materialized. She had supported them.

The President had implemented another ambitious growth plan which her supervisor quoted as he leaned over all the girls' sewing stations. She would come home, her fingers raw and bleeding, her lower back aching from crouching in the same position so long and find Jun-su sprawled out asleep on the sofa with a book over his face. Some nights his colleagues from the university would be there and Kyung-ha had served plates of food to them, too tired to argue, thinking of her supervisor, a man who took pride in wearing a waistcoat and smoking imported cigarettes, and who would read out newspaper headlines announcing the arrests of dissidents, as though he were warning them. Those intellectuals knew nothing of what it meant to sit in front of a sewing machine, stitching sleeves onto shirts. Jun-su's colleagues praised her calloused, ruptured fingers, while they winced over their paper cuts from turning over the pages of their textbooks. The factory manager was a man who read the newspaper between circling the girls and overseeing their work, shouting abuse if they fumbled. He was the only one in the factory with true power. Then Kyung-ha would have to lie down for three sacred hours of sleep, while her raw fingers throbbed and back ached.

She had done this for almost six months, when the foreign smells appeared. The scents of other women and their fancy soaps. She had begun to follow him. But he was clever and slippery. She never knew how he concealed the evidence. She had followed him to a basement room, sure to catch him with her, whoever she was. She had waited outside, unable, now that she had him, to open the door. Then the curfew siren had sounded. Pedestrians cleared the streets. She had no option but to go inside if she wanted to avoid arrest. She had kept her eyes on the floor. The room smelled of ink and the paraffin stove in the centre of it. She looked up to find Jun-su standing over a mimeograph machine. His colleagues stared at her, with looks of relief and irritation.

'What is this?' She picked up a leaflet. It was the kind that was thrown from the city's high-rise buildings. 'Our movements of transformation aim to obtain a national liberation and people's democracy.'

Marxist texts were strewn across the tables.

Jun-su had grabbed her by the arm and pulled her into a storeroom. 'Are you crazy? What are you doing here?'

'I thought you were going somewhere else.'

'The less you know the better. It's for your protection. You know that we could both be arrested if they found out about this? If we're both locked up, what would happen to Jong-ho?'

She had felt ashamed at first. Her domestic preoccupations seemed small when laid beside his larger ideals of democracy for the country.

But then she had shaken her head. 'I'm sure it's convenient for you. For when you go and see her.'

It was the first time she had spoken of the other woman. 'Are you thinking of Jong-ho when you go to her?'

Jun-su hadn't even blinked. 'I'm your husband and Jong-ho's father. Nothing is going to change that. Why do you have to be so narrow-minded? It's exactly this kind of narrow-minded thinking that's got us here. Can't you see that? We have to live by example—'

'Who is she? Watered-down ink, like you? Does she talk just like you? I hope you talk each other to death.'

When she had come home the next morning, her mother-in-law had shaken her head, taking long drags of a filtered cigarette, as if to ask what Kyung-ha had expected. 'A factory girl like you, with so much pride. I don't know how you work there at all.'

Later, when her mother-in-law had taken her nap, Kyung-ha had packed a bag and had taken Jong-ho to the factory. She had confused anger with courage. She had shut the gate to Jun-su's house and led Jong-ho by the hand without a plan. Without thinking it through. Without any consideration for the boy.

The women believed her to be a sinner. They were right. But they didn't know what she had done.

Mia lay awake in the darkness, watching the crawl of moonlight across the ceiling, listening to the rise and fall of Thomas's breaths beside her. Nothing ruptured the tranquillity of his sleep. The window above them was open and brought in the saccharine smell of autumn, the dying season. It made her wonder how their story would end. She got up to close it. When she lay beside him again he rolled away from her. It was her vulnerability that she resented more than his need for independence.

Footsteps sounded in the corridor and came to a halt outside of the apartment door. There was a knock. Mia rose from the futon and threw on her skirt and T-shirt.

The man on the other side of the door had white hair. A brown weathered face that narrated a life of labour in the countryside. His breath was stale and heavy.

'What's this?' he said immediately. 'Where's the kid?'

His eyes took a while to focus and then he spent several moments looking at her.

'Who are you?' she asked.

'You a Yankee?' His North Korean accent was noticeable immediately.

'What do you want?' she said, narrowing the gap between the door and the frame.

'Russian?'

She almost slammed the door on his fingers.

'Where's the kid?'

'I don't know who you're looking for.' It was almost two in the morning. She wondered if he had lost his mind.

He eyed her suspiciously. 'Have they taken him in?'

'Who?'

'I'm not going to name him. I don't even know who you are.'

She began to close the door. 'You've got the wrong address.'

He squeezed his knee in the gap in the door. 'Will you give him this?' He thrust an envelope into her hands. 'I know I'm not supposed to come here like this. He told me not to. But it's important. I've made the final arrangements. My family need to know.'

She looked over her shoulder, afraid that the sound of their voices had woken Thomas. She crept outside and closed the door behind her.

'Are you talking about Myung-chul?'

The man cringed at the sound of his name. 'Someone will hear you.'

'He's dead.'

He looked afraid and looked over his shoulder as though he were sure they were being watched.

'Those sons of a bitches killed him,' he muttered under his breath.

'What did you say?'

He looked at her in horror. 'What about the other one?'

'What do you mean, they killed him?'

'Have they found it?'

'Found what?'

'The tunnel,' he said almost immediately.

'What tunnel?' she said, sharply.

★

Thomas stirred.

She was not beside him. He lay with his eyes closed, waiting for her to return to him, slow to surface from the depth of his sleep. Slowly he became aware of her voice. The unfamiliarity of it speaking another language. There was something in it that brought him quicker to the surface, breaking his slumber permanently. An urgency, the deliberate whisper. He saw her outline against the sliver of light entering from the street. Another voice. He reached for his watch. It was just after two. After she closed the door, she stood breathing heavily before crossing the room to lie beside him.

He turned to her, feigning having just woken. 'What was that?'

'What was what?'

'I thought you were talking to someone.'

She paused. Kissed him on the forehead.

'You must have been dreaming,' she said.

Mia stepped off the bus and into the cold. She had to speak to her uncle. She turned the corner into the narrow alley leading to the school. He would reassure her. The School for Defectors, one half of the second floor, was really only a couple of classrooms. Behind them there was the narrow office her uncle worked in. The lights had long since gone out in the stairwell and the bulbs had not been replaced. In the days that Mia had worked with her uncle, the letters she wrote to government bodies asking for funding had talked about the school as a foundation from which the defectors could begin rebuilding their lives, a place of rehabilitation where they could be fostered and cared for as they learned to adapt to capitalism and Korean culture in the South. She had been careful not to use the word 're-education'. She imagined that those who read the letters, if they read them at all, would picture the school as a cosy building, lovingly decorated with brightly painted walls.

Mia peered through the glass windows into one of the classrooms where some students watched their teacher as she spoke, while others wore looks of distraction and stared out of the window. The class was split between a few who seemed to have made some awful fashion decisions, to others who were over-dressed. No one seemed to know what to do with the overwhelming reality of suddenly having choices. Her uncle had once shown her a North Korean hair-salon menu where women chose one of the 'designated' haircuts outlined by the government. There were eighteen options. Mostly bobs. A few longer permed styles. Mia had observed that the girls who defected, having become accustomed to these limited choices, often adopted fashions of the most popular South Korean actresses and mimicked the slow, careful pauses of the characters they played in drama series.

The short hallway was brightly lit. The door to his office was open. Mia stood in the doorway and watched her uncle as he patted his desk, searching for something with his fingers, not taking his eyes off the paper he held in his other hand. She hesitated as she held her knuckles against the door.

Her uncle looked up for a fraction of a second and then went back to looking for something among the piles of papers.

Mia leaned her head against the door. He wasn't going to make it easy. But she had known this. 'Can we talk?'

He was engrossed in reading the paper, his glasses propped up at the end of his pink nose. 'I've got all these receipts and accounts to get through.'

'Audit time again? You'd think this were a listed company or something, the number of times you get audited.'

He tapped a button on the small calculator. 'This government,' he said, shaking his head. 'Anything to keep me from doing any decent work with these kids.'

'Do you want some help?' she offered, shyly.

He dropped his hand and looked directly over his glasses at her for the first time. 'Why would you want to do something like that? Aren't you a little too big and important to be dirtying your hands with my accounting work? The Embassy not giving you enough work these days?'

She stared at the mess of wires under his desk. 'It's about Myung-chul.'

Her uncle looked away.

'Was there ever any . . .' She didn't know quite how to put it. 'I mean, do you know why he . . . ?'

He put down his papers and shook his head.

'There was no note?'

Her uncle looked at her with curiosity. 'Why are you taking an interest in this suddenly? You don't care about any of them. I thought you wanted nothing to do with any of it. You've acted like they're lepers intent on giving you their disease. Why would you come here to dig up what I'm painfully trying to bury?'

'I'm sorry,' she said, simply.

'He was so bright. Not like so many of the kids here. You think any of these kids have got the kind of drive to catch up and study harder than the ones born here? So many of them don't understand what competition means, you know that? But Myung-chul did. Yonsei University suited him.'

'What if . . .'

Their eyes met.

'What if he didn't kill himself?'

Her uncle's shoulder became rigid. 'Why would you say something like that?'

She explained about her late-night visitor, explaining that she had gone to the apartment looking for Hyun-min.

'There was nothing to suggest his death was suspicious. Just let it go.'

'What about what he said about the tunnel? We should go to the NIS,' she said. 'We should report this.'

'No,' he said, shaking his head. 'I can't do that to my students here. They have it hard enough as it is. To have the NIS here asking

194

questions, treating them like suspects or potential spies. No,' he repeated.

'What about—'

'Defectors want to leave the past behind them. They want to be people on their own terms, not defined by the fact they crossed a border. They don't want their lives turned upside down and interrogated every time something like this happens.'

'It wouldn't necessarily involve the school . . .'

He shook his head again. 'We're talking about a small population of defectors living in this city. Myung-chul and Hyun-min both attended this school. There would be questions.'

'What about Hyun-min?'

The scaffolding outside obstructed the window. The air in the office was dense and unmoving. Her uncle seemed to forget that she was there for several moments.

'Forget about it, Mia. I know you don't want to get involved in this. You've made that clear.'

'I see you're still not used to the Korean way,' Mr Paik said as Thomas fiddled with his chopsticks. 'Do you want a fork?'

He shook his head, not wanting to admit defeat. He had never got the hang of metal chopsticks, not even in Phnom Penh.

Mr Paik turned the barbecued beef on the grill. He had suggested the meeting after Thomas had sent him the photograph of the dilapidated building he had followed Mia to the night after the unexpected nighttime visitor. Thomas crossed and uncrossed his legs, trying his best to hide his discomfort on the floor. Mr Paik poured soju into each of their shot glasses.

Thomas picked up his drink. It was easiest to give in.

There was nothing about Mr Paik that suggested he was a spook. He had a friendly face and a rounded stomach that bulged from his white shirt. It was impossible to tell what age he was – he seemed to be in his late twenties, but it was unlikely that he would have risen to the ranks of the NIS so young. Mr Paik laid a few cuts of beef on Thomas's plate. The gesture felt paternal, both caring and suffocating.

'It happens. Every time there's a new government, everyone scrambles to prove themselves in the government reorganization. The agency is the busiest it's been in years.' He had a decidedly American accent, which also made Thomas uneasy. Mr Paik wrapped a lettuce leaf around a slice of beef and put some soybean paste on it before putting it in his mouth. He chewed carefully and then said, 'You understand why we've had to push back many of our investigations to other bodies. We're truncated.'

'So what do you think of all this?' Thomas said. He didn't know how to ask him what he really wanted. He pushed the beef on his plate around with the chopsticks.

Mr Paik emptied the shot glass into his mouth and wiped at the edges of his lips. 'I'm surprised she was able to clear all your security checks in the first place. Her uncle runs a school for North Korean defectors. Teenagers. None of them politically motivated. Her father was arrested for being a communist sympathizer during the dictatorship.'

Mr Paik took a small sip from his shot glass and put a few more pieces of beef on Thomas's plate. 'Her father was a professor of politics. Really young for what he did. A country boy. He won a scholarship to Seoul National University. I don't need to tell you that this is a society that favours age over talent. He taught at Yonsei when I was a student there. He was fired from the university just before Park Chung-hee's assassination. Something about his brother's involvement with communist texts. They thought it was unsuitable for a professor of politics to have family who had such obvious sympathies for the North Koreans. After Chun Doo-hwan came to power all the activism went underground, but he had a reputation for being something of a revolutionary.' He paused and cleared his throat.

Thomas emptied the shot glass into his mouth. He poured himself another shot and then, seeing that Mr Paik's shot glass was also empty, poured him one.

'So his time in Cambridge was a period of exile?'

Mr Paik gave him a funny look and took a moment to pick a piece of lettuce from between his teeth, not once taking his eyes off Thomas. 'He was never at Cambridge.'

Another outright lie. 'Where is he now?'

'Still around. No longer active, as far as we know. He didn't come out of prison the same man.'

'He was imprisoned?'

'For some time.'

'What about her mother?'

'I'll see what we have on file. You should talk to the Holt Agency, they might be able to tell you something.'

'Holt?'

'It's an international adoption agency. She was left there as a child.'

The soju gave him an acidic taste at the back of his mouth. He blinked to bring the blurred edges of Mr Paik's face back into focus. It was the right thing to do – to consult other sources. He had spent too much time following her. His eyelids felt heavy, his mouth slow to move. She was misleading him. Mr Paik handed him several more shots. His face had reddened but otherwise he seemed untouched by the drink. Strangely he felt as if Mr Paik was intentionally trying to get him drunk, as though *he* were the subject of interrogation and needed to be loosened up. He drank some water, tried to dilute his anxieties, and concentrate.

'About that photograph I sent you,' Thomas said. 'I wondered whether you had any information . . . ?'

'Yes,' Mr Paik replied. His eyes were drooping slightly, but his words remained crisp. 'You followed her to the school her uncle runs for North Korean defectors.'

He pulled out the photographs from his satchel. 'Could you help me with these photographs? I found them in her apartment. I thought they might be relevant.'

Mr. Paik inspected each photograph for several moments. Slowly, meticulously.

Thomas couldn't read what he was thinking.

'Let me have a look into it,' Mr Paik said.

He decided to ask what it was that he had been wanting to ask all along. 'This man that I saw in the hotel lobby. I was hoping you might have been able to identify him.'

'I got your memo. What makes you think that he's relevant to the investigation?'

'I thought he might be someone close to her.'

'There's nothing in our records that ties them together. He's a trader. Pretty uninspiring file. Bit of a porn habit.'

'You don't think they're intimately acquainted?'

Mr Paik shook his head. 'Doesn't look like it.'

He felt strangely relieved.

When they parted, Mr Paik said, 'Listen, if you ever need anything. A translator, a sounding board, whatever, let me know.'

'That's generous, thank you,' Thomas said. Hadn't Mr Paik said that the agency was overwhelmed? Had there been something in their conversation that had led him to believe that more resources could be dedicated in this direction?

The door to the apartment was open. She sat by the window, looking out at the stretch of the afternoon sun, a cigarette between her fingers. Orange light spilled onto her hair, bringing out the strains of brown in it. He could hear the distant sound of the vendors calling out in the street below, their language perfectly foreign. Her cigarette burned to the filter and ash fell to the floor by her bare foot. She didn't seem to notice. It was as though she had been waiting for him for a long time.

She leaned her head back against the windowsill as he approached and smiled. He didn't know what to think. Her mouth tasted sweet and bitter; it had become harder to separate the tastes. She pulled up her skirt and wrapped her legs around him. He broke away from the kiss, unbuttoned her shirt. The revelation of old scars. Under her breasts and across her ribs. Every time he asked her about them she found a way to distract him. He buried his head in her chest and then licked the scars, as though he would discover their histories this way.

Her head was heavy on his shoulder. He lay blinking, fully awake, looking up at the snaking crack in the ceiling. In the corner of the room a cobweb hung like a piece of thread. Her breathing was light.

He wondered whether she was awake and pretending to sleep. His fingers had gone numb under the weight of her but he made no effort to move. He brushed a strand of hair away from her face and watched its stillness. She was both familiar and strange to him.

He was thinking of the school her uncle ran. Her scars. Her lies and evasions. It had been months since the audit had begun. He tried not to think about his meeting with Mr Paik. He was treading water, neither progressing forwards or backwards. He ignored these thoughts out of greed. He consumed her like a starving man who gulped a feast without tasting the food. It was a mistake, but also a compulsion. The more he pulled away her clothes, the more he saw that she concealed and the more he desired her.

He watched her sleep. Her skin was taut over her ribs and her breaths were rapid like those of a small wounded animal. He wondered whether she ever slept deeply at all. There was something about the way that she slept that made him think of vagabonds, ready to react in a moment, nervous. As though she were a person who had long been on the run.

When he woke her, she made love to him with the fury of an insomniac who had been woken from deep slumber.

'I should go.'

'I'm not going to beg you to stay,' she said.

He shifted so that they were facing each other. Suddenly he felt the loneliness of his secrets. 'I find myself confused about what I'm doing here.'

'So stay until you figure it out.'

'What is all this? To you?'

She smoothed the hairs on his forearm, but wouldn't meet his eye. 'Self-preservation. You're the first person I've met who makes me feel like I'm not myself.'

What did she mean by it?

'Yet you tell me so little about you. You keep me at arm's length. You won't tell me about your family, your friends.'

'Aren't you interested because I tell you so little? When you see through me, you'll leave. Anyway,' she said, rolling onto her front. 'You're the same. You're with me now, but you're just killing time.'

She said this softly, as though she were telling a young child a story, but there was a slicing quality to what she had said.

'It's not a game.'

'Then tell me what I should think. Do you feel guilty? What would your wife think?'

'Felicity and I . . .' He realized that he didn't feel guilty enough. Because they had already been eroding for many years. 'You separate the work from relationships. What we didn't know was that our work placed us as adversaries from the beginning. We couldn't both be ambitious.'

'She's a journalist, isn't she?'

'Yes. Her job is to disseminate information to the public. Mine is often to conceal it, in the interest of other projects.'

'What happened?'

'In Phnom Penh, it became clear that one of us would have to sacrifice our jobs. She ran a story that she knew would put my job in jeopardy. I was cautioned for being indiscreet. They thought I had passed on information to Felicity that I should have kept from her. We haven't really been the same since.'

'I'm revenge.'

'No,' he sat up and rubbed his eyes. He couldn't keep his head straight. Again she had turned the questions on him. His questions led nowhere. He had to put an end to this. It was clear that being with her would only lead to more confusion. 'We should stop this. This should not be about being confused.'

Her eyes narrowed. 'It shouldn't be many things, but it is.'

'I'm sorry, but we have to end this,' he said and he meant it. He picked his clothes off the floor and got dressed.

She lit a cigarette and sat up with her elbow propped against her knee, watching him. Impassive. If she cared that he was leaving, she did nothing to show it.

It made it easier to leave.

He stepped into the stretch of dawn over the city, fighting the impulse to turn back, feeling hardened.

It was light by the time he parked his car in the side street by the house. He pulled his key out of the ignition. He closed his eyes for a moment. There was nothing concrete implicating her but he no longer believed that she was innocent. She was hiding something.

He shuddered at the thought of her scars. What if they had been a form of training in the management of pain? Or worse.

Torture.

As he opened the front door, he was greeted by the smell of coffee in the hallway and followed the scent to the kitchen. Felicity sat with her head in her hands over the kitchen table. The cafetiere by her elbow was almost empty.

'You're up.'

She looked up at him. Her hair had fallen out of its ponytail and covered the edges of her face. He could tell by the grey in the whites of her eyes that she had not slept.

'I rather thought it was a good idea,' she said. There was a pause. 'Well?'

He ran his hand through his hair. 'Would you believe me if I said it was Embassy work?'

'It depends on how much of a fool you think I am.'

Being apologetic would get him nowhere. It would imply guilt. 'I can't discuss the details with you. You know that.'

'How much longer are you going to do this? How can I apologize any more than I have, Tom?'

He leaned his head back against the cupboards and closed his eyes. 'I know.'

'Then tell me where you were last night.'

He imagined telling her about the audit. He was exhausted by the distance between them. They had once been the best of friends. 'I can't.'

'Fine.' She closed the book between her hands. 'Then I have no choice but to speak to Nigel about it.'

'As a means of achieving what, exactly?' he asked, suddenly confused.

'You know the stance the Embassy has on your drinking.'

'What?' He wished he could retract the surprise from his voice.

'Do you drive, Tom, when you drink? It's like you have some sort of death wish.'

He moved closer towards the wooden table between them. Her eyes stayed on his. Her bathrobe was slipping off her shoulders. Under the ring of light over the table, she had the look of a patient awaiting test results. Not a trace of anger. She was not trying to punish him. He realized with a shock that she still loved him. There was something between them yet that could be salvaged, if only he could bear the distance that came between them now and again. He wondered whether it was a matter of simply going through the motions and play-acting through those moments when they grew apart. He brought the edge of the bathrobe back onto her shoulder and then kept his hands on her. Even as he drew her towards him, he could not stop thinking of the silk of Mia's skin. At last he felt it, the weight of his guilt that had been suspended from him for so long.

'I'm sorry,' he said.

'You're your own worst enemy,' she said, stiff in his arms. 'You do this and then you'll accuse me of sabotaging your career.'

'I know.' She leaned her head against his chest and he knew that the danger had passed, her threats were empty.

'Things have to change.'

'I know that,' he said, softly. He ran his hands over her hair. 'I'm a mess.'

They stood in the kitchen, leaning against each other as the sunlight began to stretch across the counter; the rumble of the morning grew louder, until they eventually crept upstairs. As he fell asleep, he felt Felicity's hand on his arm, as though she were holding him back from bad dreams.

Mia watched Thomas leave from the window.

They'd been lying on the futon and she had curled herself into him. He had been on his back, careless. He could take it or leave it. She had mentioned his wife. Wanted to provoke him into confessing that he cared for her. It had been a gamble. She had wanted to push him, find out what she meant to him. Then when he suggested that it was over, she wanted him to finish it.

Wanted to prove that she would remain intact without him.

And how did he leave? Without looking back.

She stared out into the rain that had just begun falling. Abandoned again. Easily discarded.

She retreated into the room. She had watched him leave, stone-cold, unmoving. She betrayed nothing, she was sure of that. There was nothing to betray.

She went to the bathroom and stood in front of the mirror. She was intact. She turned on the tap and leaned over the rising water, gripping the edges of the sink.

It was an experiment. A failed one. But no damage had been done.

She turned to leave, but changed her mind. Reaching for the glass at the edge of the sink, she flung it hard at the mirror.

Stepping on the scattered glass on the floor, she wanted to see herself unbroken in the broken mirror.

She glared at the many visions of her face, fractured in the glass, before noticing a slip of paper which had fallen into the gap between the mirror and the wall. She tugged at it and pulled out an envelope.

Hyun-min.

As she unfolded the paper, she saw that it was no ordinary letter.

She read several lines before hastily turning it over.

It took her several moments to fully comprehend the illustration that she held in her hands.

Instructions for Hyun-min on how to find the tunnel.

In the weeks following their separation, there was a shift, a gentle nudging of the seasons, the first deep chill in the wind against her face. She was cold all the time, but ran a fever in her sleep, waking in a pool of her own sweat. The world she woke to was one she no longer understood: Thomas's sudden abandonment of her; the map that she had discovered in the apartment; the many stacks of letters that lined the living room; Hyun-min's inexplicable disappearances. How much did Hyun-min know of what Myung-chul had been up to?

She opened her eyes to the whine of the gate as it opened and closed. It was not yet dawn. She tiptoed onto the landing. From the top of the stairs, she saw Hyun-min rolling out his futon in the dark.

'Where have you been?'

She flipped the switch on the wall. He frowned against the light.

'Out,' he said.

'Where?'

He said nothing.

'Where do you go all the time? Can't you see what you're doing to everyone in this house?'

Still he said nothing.

She drew closer to him and lowered her voice. 'Are you crossing the border?'

'Why should I talk to you? You're just like the rest of them.'

She had been expecting fervent denial. But he wouldn't even look at her. She tried to breathe. The secret had been suffocating her.

'Are you?' She looked at the piles of letters. If he was crossing the border then why had this stack of letters been untouched?

'Leave him alone,' Kyung-ha said, appearing at the edge of the living room. It was the first time she had said anything to Mia since she had humiliated her with the *suhn*.

'Come with me,' Mia said, tugging on his arm. 'You're going to talk to me.'

He shook her off.

'No,' he said.

'No, what?'

'I'm not going with you.'

'I know what Myung-chul did. A guy came looking for him. It's not just a story, is it? The tunnel really exists.' She stopped short, unsure whether to tell him about Myung-chul's note right away. 'He said they killed him. And he was looking for you too.'

Hyun-min paled. 'What did you tell him?'

'I said I didn't know where you were.' She paused. 'What do they want from you?'

'I'm not telling you anything. I won't go to the Embassy.'

She hesitated, confused. 'I'm not asking you to go anywhere.'

'It's a trap. I know it. I've seen you with him. That diplomat who's always following you around.'

'What do you mean following—'

'You were at the apartment together. I saw you. What are you looking for in there?'

She didn't want to talk to him in front of Kyung-ha. 'Not everyone is out to get you.' She lowered her voice, not wanting to have to explain this to both of them. 'We had nowhere to go. He's married. That's all.'

Kyung-ha stepped down from the living room and came towards them. Mia caught the punch on the side of her cheek. The sting of it brought tears to her eye. It would bruise.

'I can smell his white sickness on you. Is he the reason you felt the need to humiliate me? You selfish, inconsiderate child.'

Her skin burned, but she refused to touch it. She wouldn't give her stepmother the satisfaction. She didn't have time for this. Her father made a sound from the next room, as though he wanted to say something, but she refused to go to him.

Kyung-ha's blindness to Hyun-min enraged her. 'Do you even know what he's involved in? How can you turn a blind eye to all this?' She felt a pulse in her cheek.

Her stepmother stood unmoved.

'He's not your son. He's dead. You think I don't hear you talking to him in the night? What are you trying to do? Keep him here? Imprisoned, like you do Appa?'

This time she knew it was coming, but she didn't move away in time. She hardly felt it the second time, her face numb. There would be bruising but she didn't care.

'Get out of this house.'

She looked from Kyung-ha to Hyun-min, who had turned away from them. He hadn't denied anything. How much longer could they ignore it? The easiest thing was to desert them. She snatched her jacket and turned out onto the street.

Light snowfall had started to fall, coating the pavement. Her face was a furnace against the cold. She would lose her job, but it was not a domestic matter. She had to tell someone. She had to report it.

'What was she talking about?' Kyung-ha said. Her breath came up her chest in gasps.

'Nothing,' he said, and then quickly added, 'I owe a little money.'

'How much?'

'Nothing I can't handle.'

'Is that why you keep disappearing?' She couldn't hold back any longer. She had to know. What had the girl meant? She had threatened him, almost driving him away. He didn't say anything.

He nodded.

'Are you doing something illegal?' She remembered the dirt under his fingernails. Was he doing some kind of manual labour?

'Don't worry.'

'How did you end up owing money?'

'The money I got from the government when I came here only lasted a while. I thought I'd be able to find a job, but it wasn't so easy. I thought I would be rich –' he let out a sad laugh – 'so I borrowed some.'

'You look like you've had a rough night,' Charles said. He had a grin on his face, as though he were satisfied with his assessment.

'Not now,' she said.

She looked over the partition again, hoping to see Thomas sitting in his office. Their avoidance of each other had become a carefully orchestrated dance.

'What was it? Late-night karaoke? Invite me next time, will . . .' His voice trailed off. She felt his eyes on the bruise on her face. She stared at the computer screen in front of her.

'What happened?'

She had never heard him sound so serious.

'Nothing,' she said quickly.

'Mia—'

'Just leave it,' she said, a little louder than she intended. Several people around them looked over their shoulders towards them.

'You know you can talk to me, don't you?' he said with a lowered voice.

'Yes, if I ever feel the need . . .' she said, pretending to type. The person she needed to speak to was Thomas.

'You haven't forgotten about tonight?'

'Tonight?'

'The Hewers' send off.'

She had.

'Promise me you'll come,' he said.

She looked over the partition again. 'Do you know where Thomas is today?'

A look of annoyance passed over his face. 'Such privileged information might belong to his secretary.'

She stood up.

'All right. Since you're so bloody eager. But if I tell you, you'll have to promise to come to dinner.'

She nodded.

'He's at a security summit at the Hyatt.'

She forced a smile. 'I'll see you tonight.'

As soon as Charles disappeared down the corridor, Mia took her phone and walked to the stairwell. She dialled Thomas's number. Waited impatiently for him to answer.

'I need to talk to you,' she said. 'When can I see you?'

There was a silence on the line.

'It's not a good idea for us to speak,' he said finally.

'It's important,' she said. 'I think I'm about to lose my mind.'

'I have a prior engagement this evening. Dinner at the Hewers'.'

'I'll see you there,' she said, hanging up.

David Hewer's knee bumped hers under the table. He whispered sorry with both palms up, giving her a tight-lipped smile before turning back to everyone to shout, 'Marmite.' Mrs Hewer squeezed his shoulder and took the dinner plates from the guests. A few people at the dinner table grimaced.

Mia grew increasingly impatient. She needed to get Thomas alone. She heard Felicity saying to Thomas, 'I've never liked Marmite, have I, darling?'

Mrs Hewer had commented on how difficult it was to get ordinary baking ingredients like caster sugar in the supermarkets and it had evolved into a game of things the Koreans wouldn't understand about the English.

'David Attenborough,' Felicity said with a smile, leaning back in her chair.

'Well, I don't know about that, I think the Koreans would appreciate the educational value of it. I think I saw a dubbed Meerkats United on one of the cable channels,' David replied.

'Well, it's not really a David Attenborough show if it's dubbed, is it? I can't imagine how one would translate his wonderful sense of humour,' someone else chipped in.

She tried to catch Thomas's eye. He would not look at her in Felicity's presence. She waited for a moment, a space, where she might squeeze in a contribution of her own. She was lost in their world of nouns. She thought of her drawer full of Thomas's reports. It wasn't enough to know his turns of phrase. She also had to fill in the spaces between them. The gaps left by their connotations. As it was their over-politeness was unbearable. Now Mia had begun to piece together the meaning of the look on David's face when she had turned up at his door. He had evidently forgotten that he had invited her to the dinner. She had been an afterthought and she should never have come. She wouldn't have, had she not needed to speak to Thomas.

Seeing that it would be impossible to get his attention, Mia touched Charles's arm and whispered in his ear, 'are you glad I kept my promise?'

He put his hand on hers. 'If I had known you'd be this agreeable to my invitations, I would have threatened to leave more often.'

She had been flirting with him like this all evening, hoping it would catch Thomas's attention. She looked across the table and saw that he had not seen this. Everyone at the table laughed except Mia.

She smiled a few moments too late, having missed the joke. Anyone looking would have seen she was elsewhere. Except that no one was. She was thinking of Hyun-min and Myung-chul. Who else knew about the tunnel? Were there any others who travelled there? She had to talk to someone about it. She would take Thomas there. He would know what to do about it.

The long dining table had been set up in the Hewers' library. Turning as if to inspect a book that was of interest, she stole a glimpse at Thomas. He had withdrawn into his corner of silence. In the candlelight his face was full of shadows. Felicity hardly seemed to notice, though when he tried to pour himself another drink she covered the top of his glass. The intimacy of it made her flinch.

Mrs Hewer returned with sorbets in delicate, oversized egg cups and opened another bottle of wine.

'A bit cruel, isn't it? Serving this to our guests? Not even proper ice cream,' Mr Hewer joked to Mia. 'She's had me on this diet, something or other about dairy, I'm sorry she's inflicting this on all of you as well.'

'I love sorbet,' Mia said. The enthusiasm seemed childish and she winced inwardly.

'Don't be silly, David, sorbet is divine,' Felicity said. Mia envied the familiarity between them. Mia put a spoonful of sorbet in her mouth and let it melt on her tongue. Let it hurt her teeth.

Mia finally caught Thomas's eye across the table. She excused herself from the table to no one in particular. In the bathroom, she washed her face with cold water. When she came out, Thomas was there, waiting.

'Meet me by the stairs,' he whispered as he passed her.

Thomas stood in the shadows beside the staircase, fiddling with a lighter. He put a hand on her face. He swept a strand of hair from her shoulder and leaned closer to her. 'I'm sorry. This isn't easy for me.'

'That's not . . .' She began to try to explain that that wasn't what she wanted to talk to him about, but then she realized she wanted to hear him say it. That he missed her.

'Charles – are you with . . .' he began to say and then seemed to change his mind. 'I hate the idea of him touching you. I can't bear it.'

She turned her cheek away from him. 'I could go home with him you know.'

'Don't.' He hooked his thumb under the strap of her dress, ran it down the inside of her bra and then back up again, squeezing her shoulder.

She put her hand on his and stopped him. 'Not here. Dinner's almost over.'

'I find myself thinking about you all the time.' He inhaled her hair and kissed her neck. 'Meet me after this. I'll come to yours. I must see you.'

'How are you going to do that?'

'Let me worry about that.'

She slipped her fingers between the buttons of his shirt and put her other hand under his jacket. He pulled back and kissed her fingers before walking away. In the apartment they would be able to talk. At the stairs, she put her hand on the cold stone of the railing when she caught movement out of the corner of her eye.

It was Charles. The look on his face told her that he had seen it all.

Back at the table, everyone was rallying for Charles to give a speech. He was wearing a salmon-pink shirt and held a carnation that he had stolen from the table. He seemed not to notice the other guests and focused only on the flower in his fingers, as if it were to be the subject of his speech.

'I'd like to raise a toast to Mr and Mrs Hewer for their hospitality this evening. What a bittersweet evening this has turned out to be. As many of you know, I've come to the end of my time in Seoul. It's a funny kind of place, isn't it?' A few people laughed. Charles paused for a long moment as he surveyed the guests. 'I'd like to raise a toast, in praise of colleagues and to old friends . . .' He looked uncertain for a moment, as though considering whether he had any friends at the table. Several people raised their glasses. His eyes wandered first to Mia, and then Thomas, '. . . to the pleasures, and the ruins, of alcohol.'

'Hear, hear,' someone said.

'It's so easy to get personal in this line of work, isn't it? We leave our comfortable homes, those villages where we grew up, the comforts of Britishness, and we thrust ourselves into the field.' He looked at Thomas. 'I suppose some of us get quite romantic about it all, secretly fancying ourselves to be anthropologists. Goodness knows, plenty of people do go native in the end.' Several guests laughed a bit at this. 'And for those who don't go that far, who don't care to get so involved in truly understanding their new environments . . . I wonder what it means to be a professional in this business? How much do you get involved with others, when you're just going to get up and leave again? How much do you love your local colleagues, invest in getting to know them and the context of their lives, when you know the next posting is around the corner?' He was almost exclusively looking at Thomas as he said this.

Mia looked away. Stared intently at the candlelight at the centre of the table. She felt Charles's gaze shift towards her.

'I myself have become very attached to this place and the people here. You know you've been in a posting too long when you feel protective of it. I'm not entirely sure how I will extricate myself.'

Mia dared to look up, to find he was still looking at her.

'Before I get any more sentimental. Let me end with a toast. To professionalism.'

Several guests exchanged bemused glances. Charles sat down again and the table erupted with the noise of several different conversations.

Mia caught Thomas saying to Charles, '. . . You are probably a bit undervalued, though everyone knows that you hardly do any work . . .'

Charles abruptly stood up, his chair falling back behind him. 'That's enough,' he shouted, then, catching himself, muttered, hardly audibly, 'I'd like a word.'

'I was only joking, there's no need for this,' Thomas said, obviously surprised.

'I'd rather not make a scene in front of these people, so if I could have a word, in private,' Charles said through gritted teeth.

Thomas got up in a leisurely manner, as though the whole thing was just a bit of horseplay. As he walked towards the end of the table, he said, 'Obviously hit a nerve . . .'

Charles turned as soon as they were in the kitchen.

'What do you think you're doing?' he said.

'It's only a joke. You've been here so long you've lost your sense of humour. I'm sorry, I didn't realize it was such a sensitive—'

'Do you love her?'

Thomas stepped back to steal a look across the hallway to the dinner party. It was evident that the guests had lost interest in their conversation. He straightened a little, understanding suddenly. 'I don't see how that's any of your business.'

'You're just fucking around, is that it?'

Thomas laughed. 'Have I offended the romantic in you? Is that the problem? Was that what your speech was about then? How pathetic.'

Charles lunged at him and gripped him by the collar. 'You're shameless. Your wife is right in front of you and you don't even look the slightest bit guilty.'

He tried break free of his grip, incredulous. 'I don't think you should concern yourself with my guilt.'

'What are you doing with her?'

'You really have spent too much time here. I never had you down as so melodramatic. Look here, it's not what you think. So I would drop it, if I were you. Don't make a spectacle of yourself, the Hewers have done a nice thing here. Let's not ruin—'

'It's the audit, isn't it?' Charles said, quietly. 'Nigel asked you.'

'I beg your pardon?'

'That's it.'

'I don't know what you're talking about.'

'Come off it, Dalton-Ellis. You don't imagine that you were top of the list for the security audit, do you? Everyone knows about the state of you. I doubt Nigel would be impressed with your research methods.'

'I doubt he would be impressed with you discussing this at all.'

'Do you have the faintest idea what you're doing? You could ruin her career, her life.'

'What would you know of it? I'm the one doing the audit. She's not suffering, I assure you. I'd even venture to say she's enjoying herself,' he said, unable to resist. 'If you want her so badly, you shouldn't have turned down the audit.'

The punch landed solidly on his cheek. He fell back against the wall. At first he felt nothing. Then the release of pain along his jaw. Thomas bent over. Several guests gasped.

'I'll have you sacked,' Charles whispered.

'Piss off,' he said, catching his breath, more annoyed by a flooding of images of the back of the cricket hut from his days at Tonbridge than by the throbbing in his face. Charles didn't have much weight behind him, but there was sting to his punch.

'You've got nothing on me.' He was sure of this, but he felt his stomach burning nonetheless.

★

Mia watched Charles and Thomas step out of the room. She looked around to see that the guests were exchanging glances, not entirely sure what had happened.

Mrs Hewer broke the silence that had fallen over the table, 'Would anyone like coffee?'

The guests dispersed, some accompanying Mrs Hewer to the kitchen, others taking the opportunity to mutter excuses to leave. Mia remained where she was, feeling the sweat on her back.

'I don't know what that was about, do you?' Mia heard Felicity say to one of the guests. Her hair was loose and fell around her shoulders. She was wearing a long green dress with thick straps which crisscrossed across her bare back. She seemed oblivious to the cold. Her freckled arms were muscular; Felicity was the kind of woman who had been skinny as a child.

The other woman shook her head. Mia tried to see Felicity through Thomas's eyes. She tried to imagine how love for a woman as seamless as she was could recede. Mia imagined that there might be some women in her situation who might lift their chins in the presence of their lovers' wives, a mixture of pride and pity. They would hunt for details of neglect, hair in disarray; fingernails unmanicured, or for obliviousness to their husbands and that would validate them. Instead, Mia felt herself shrinking back to the girl in the empty playground with dirt on her face and mud under her fingernails. Mia wondered if Felicity had ever second-guessed herself.

'That's men when they're drunk. It's just what they do, isn't it?' someone offered.

Felicity frowned a little. 'Funny. I didn't think they knew each other, really.' She tapped a polished fingernail against the eggcup in front of her. She let the thought hang.

Felicity caught sight of Mia across the table and their eyes met. She stared at Mia directly for the first time that evening, visibly studying her face and throat. Mia turned away and stared at the table.

The candle in front of them flickered as the wick sank further in the wax. She put the glass of water against her cheeks to cool them.

'What would I know anyway,' Felicity said, after a few moments, blowing out the candle between them. 'He never tells me anything.'

Felicity picked up her eggcup and stood up, apparently in search of the kitchen.

Mia saw movement in the darkness. Several guests at the end of the table gasped and got to their feet, suddenly. Thomas was bent over, holding his cheek. Charles turned away from him, shaking out his hand, stopping only when he saw that Mia was watching.

In the taxi home, Felicity was unusually animated. 'What is it between you and Charles? I didn't think he drank so much. To strike out at you like that. What you said wasn't particularly charming, granted, but to take you aside at a party, I mean really . . .'

Thomas realized he was gripping his hand into a tight fist.

'What an embarrassment. What a send-off. To think he's still got to face everyone at the office for weeks. How ironic, with his speech—'

He frowned. 'Can we not do this? I've got a splitting headache.'

Felicity closed her mouth, her lips withdrawing into a fine line.

'You wouldn't have a headache if you didn't drink so much.'

He said nothing to this. It was better to let her assume that it was his drinking. Charles's mention of the audit had unsettled him. Could it really be true that others had been approached about the audit? He found it hard to believe but how else would he know about it otherwise? He would have to wrap up the report, be done with it.

They paid the taxi driver and Felicity went straight upstairs to the bedroom without another word. In the kitchen, he unscrewed a bottle of whisky and poured himself a glass. He took a sip and then put down the glass on the counter. The accusation rung in his head. He would have to finish the audit before Charles did something foolish. What did he have to hold against her? She had lied to him. That she had some questionable relationships. That was all. Was he working hard enough? Wasn't he also afraid of what else he might find?

What a fool. He had gone native. Was he in love with her?

She closed the front door to muffle the sounds of the waning party and stepped onto the street.

'Mia.'

Charles opened the door. His shirt was wrinkled, untucked. He came towards her. She was afraid he was about to kiss her, but realized that he was examining her face.

'Did he do that to you?'

She let out a laugh when she realized what he was referring to.

He grabbed her arm. 'This isn't a joke. Has he hurt you?'

She shook him off. 'What do you think you're doing?'

'Come with me. We can't talk here.'

Charles was drunk. He had been acting erratically all evening. She didn't have time for him. She needed to speak to Thomas. Tell him about Myung-chul's note.

'Later, I need to go.'

'Just for once, will you listen to me?'

His tone of voice caught her off guard.

'You're drunk. Say what you want in the morning, not now,' she said walking away.

'It's about Dalton-Ellis.'

She turned to face him.

'There's something you should know.'

He put his hand on her shoulder and led her towards his car.

'You're not driving like this.'

'Get in the car. I just want to talk to you.'

He opened the car door for her. She sat down. After walking around the car, he sat in the driver's seat as though puzzling over where they should go.

'Break it off with him,' Charles said, suddenly.

'Is that what this is about?'

'Has he said that he loves you?' He was staring at her intently now. 'What has he promised you?'

She didn't need him to look out for her. 'Just leave it alone.'

'I'm struggling . . .' He looked a little desperate, looking from side to side, as though expecting a knock on the window behind her at any moment. 'I'm torn between what I know to be true and what I'm obliged to keep from you.'

The clock on the dashboard showed it was past midnight. She wasn't in the mood for guessing games. 'What are you talking about?'

'Just steer clear of him. For your own sake.'

'What is your problem with him?' she asked.

'If he's led you to believe that your affair is a matter of passion, then you should know that it's a lie . . .' He gripped the steering wheel.

'What are you talking about? What would you know about it?'

'To hell with this.' He sighed and then composed himself. 'He's working with the NIS. On a security audit for the new government. It seems they have reason to believe that you need to be investigated.'

She made a sound that could have been a laugh. She felt her throat constrict.

'How would you know that?' she asked.

'Someone has to liaise with the NIS. I've been doing it for years. If

I had known they would ask Dalton-Ellis, I wouldn't have refused to do the audit.'

She said nothing. Would not betray any more than had been betrayed. Aware that she had misread everything, even Charles. How easily she had dismissed him. A liaison with the NIS was no small responsibility. He had fooled everyone with his nonchalance.

She was wary, though she saw that Charles had no reason to lie to her.

'Why would they be investigating me?' she asked, though she had a good idea already. How much did Thomas know?

He squeezed her shoulder.

'I'm sure there's nothing you have to worry about with respect to the audit. What's the worst Dalton-Ellis could say about you?' he said.

Her smile was a grimace.

Myung-chul's note burned in her pocket.

Winter

Every winter the cold entered the ancient cracks in the old man's bones like a spirit possessing a body. He whimpered as she massaged his legs and tended to his aches, just as she had since the night so many years ago, when he had been released from Seodaemun Prison. He was her patient, it was punishment bestowed upon her by the Lord that she should nurse this broken man who would never speak again. Every night, she forced herself to wash him, memorizing every dip and gap in his bones. The softness in his head, the indent of his skull above the temple.

On these cold nights, she attended to him with both hands while he groaned as if he were being broken all over again. He lay on the heated floor, the skin of his cheeks slack, his face pale. Seeing that he was little comforted by the warm washcloth, Kyung-ha drew the door to his room aside and stepped into the living room.

'Hyun-min ah, run out and get some heated pads,' she said, handing him a wad of bills. They had settled into a routine domesticity, avoiding any discussions that might lead them to the hinterlands.

The boy got to his feet and put a jacket on his back, squeezed his naked feet into his shoes.

'Put on some socks – you'll catch a cold.'

'I'll be okay,' he said with a lopsided smile.

She returned to the old man. Dimmed the lights for his aching eyes. Picked up the Bible and read to him the story of their redemption.

Kyung-ha held the thin pages between her fingers, distracted by the noise. She put on her slippers and went to see whether Hyun-min had come home. Opening the gate, she half expected to see another parcel on her doorstep. As the months passed, the arrival of the letters and packages had slowed. Not knowing what to do with it all, she had resorted to throwing them in sacks which she stuffed into the large earthenware pots she kept in the courtyard for storing *kimchi*.

The cold found the parts of her that were exposed, her wrists and ankles. The doorstep was empty, there were no hopeful letters; perhaps people had grown weary of those arrows they had been shooting into the dark. She was about to retreat into the house when she noticed a figure standing on the street. A man in a long black trench coat stood on the stoop. He smelled strongly of cigarettes. His black eyes had blue rings around them.

'It's late, I know, but he won't be surprised.'

She was unsure of who he was talking to at first.

'What is this?'

The man stepped closer towards her, as if he needed no further invitation. He used the informal address, though he couldn't have been older than forty-five. 'Is he in?'

'Who are you talking about?'

He shot her a smile that revealed a set of narrow, yellow teeth. 'Is he hiding? Did he ask you to tell me that he wasn't around?'

'I don't know what this is about, why are you here? What are you doing coming to a stranger's house in the middle of the night—'

'Hyun-min,' he said. He had stopped smiling and wore the expression of a man who had worn weary of the conversation. 'Get him for me.'

She was dumbstruck by his tone.

'Get me something warm to drink. I'm thirsty.' He sat on the front step of the porch and began to untie the laces of his leather shoes.

'Who are you?'

'The kid doesn't talk about me? Get him. He can introduce us.'

'He's not here.'

His expression grew dark. He took off his gloves. He had labourer's hands. Several of his fingernails were missing. Kyung-ha had seen plenty like them when she was a child growing up in the countryside.

'My drink?'

Kyung-ha went to the kitchen. Tried to steady her trembling hands, before reaching for the copper kettle on the stove and pouring a glass of warm barley tea. When she returned to the living room, she saw that the man had made himself comfortable on the porch, smoking a cigarette plugged into a long white filter.

'When is our friend going to be back?'

'I don't know. What do you want?'

He took a drag of his cigarette. He gave her a look that made her want several more layers to wrap herself in.

'It's debt-collection time.'

Then she understood. 'How much does he owe you?'

He laughed at this and wiped the edges of his eyes with his ruined hands. 'You should ask him about it when he gets back.'

He sucked hard on the cigarette in his hand and then flicked the stub onto the ice in the courtyard.

He stood up abruptly as if to stretch out his legs after a pleasant rest. 'All right. I'll give him a bit of time. Now that I know where he lives, I can be generous. Tell him I'll be waiting for him to drop off what he owes me until the day after tomorrow, or . . .well . . . he's a smart kid, he knows what I'm capable of.'

Every touch, a sting. The warmth of his hand burned through her skin. How long could they continue like this? She felt the press of him, the slip of lies in his hot breath in her ear. How many more times could she let him inside her like this, knowing what she knew?

For weeks she wrestled with the secret. She spent their evenings together studying him, looking for falsehoods, a moment in which he might give himself away. She was looking for evidence of Charles's jealousy, that it was his lie.

'How many women did you have in Phnom Penh?'

She lay on her stomach, her elbows tucked tightly underneath her.

He pulled away. 'What makes you think there were any?'

'What is it about me, then?'

He tapped the end of his cigarette absent-mindedly while looking at her. There had been a time when she had thought any restlessness she had seen in him was a muted anguish, an indecision about how to arrange his feelings. Now she saw he was ticking off the time, like a director watching a horrible audition out of politeness. What was he assessing her for? All this time, she had been concerned about the odd Americanism which spilled from her mouth as she lay beside him. Small slips of the tongue. Awkward syllables which would not have gone unnoticed. There was something about the English that she couldn't quite ease herself into. She kept slipping up the lines, slipping up in character.

'What is it that you'd like me to tell you?'

'Tell me why you started this.'

'You've grown fond of this line of questioning. What is it that's bothering you?'

'Tell me how this is going to end.'

'If you're looking to fight, I think it may well be time for me to go,' he said, sitting up, the cigarette still in his mouth. He buttoned his shirt, reached for his trousers.

'You've never said it. You can never bring yourself to say what it is about me. I could be anybody, isn't that right?'

He was no longer looking at her. 'Perhaps you're right. You're equally evasive. You give me nothing of yourself.'

Suddenly she realized. All this time he had been searching her for details. Those relentless questions. She had taken them as the interest of a lover. Now she saw that when the audit was finished, he intended to discard her like dirty clothes.

At the door he seemed to relent. 'Mia, I care for you.'

'Liar.'

She would humiliate him as he had humiliated her. No matter how she thought about it, it was clear that she would not emerge from this unscathed.

So she would make sure that Thomas didn't either.

She had spent enough time wavering in indecision, considering talking to her uncle, or telling Charles. Yet even he was not as he seemed. How could she have misread him? She trusted no one. She could hardly trust her own judgement. It was likely that Thomas had been investigating her the whole time. What did he know of

Hyun-min? And what did Hyun-min know about Myung-chul's work? She had to assume that he had never discovered the map. She packed a bag. A torch, gloves, a canister of water, and Myung-chul's letter. If Hyun-min couldn't tell her the truth, she had to see for herself what she was potentially implicated in.

Out on the street, a taxi pulled up in front of her and she told him where to go.

'At this hour of the night, lady?'

'I'm meeting someone there.'

'That doesn't seem creepy to you?'

The cab driver drove silently as they left the city, taking a glance at her every so often in the rear-view mirror. Many miles ahead, beyond the stretch of rice paddies, lay no man's land. Mia did not know exactly how far they were from the border, was conscious only of the city rapidly receding behind them, the distant floodlights in the mountains illuminating the army barracks on the darkened horizon.

When they finally reached the bottom of the hiking trail, the driver hesitated as he counted her change.

'Listen, I don't feel right about this. This place, at this time in the night. I mean, there's nothing around. I don't want to scare you, but they used to say all sorts of this about this mountain. It's supposed to be full of spirits. I mean, before the dictatorship, this place was some kind of holy ground for shamans. Hardly anyone goes up there. You're not thinking of hiking, are you? It's going to be cold up there.'

'I've got a jacket,' she said, exasperated.

'What about your friend? Why don't I just sit here for a while? I'm not going to get much business this time of night. I could wait for your friend to get here. It just gives me the creeps you know, a pretty girl like you, out here in the middle of nowhere.'

'Really, you don't have to worry,' she said. He was getting on her nerves. She thought about just getting out and making a run for it, but decided against it. If he called the police, things would be complicated. It was better to wait it out.

'You're right,' she said. 'Maybe I should wait until it gets a bit lighter. Is that okay with you?'

'Sure, sure,' he said. 'Come to think of it, this mountain has seen a lot of action. You know, the Chinese had control of this whole area during the Battle of Imjin. Then the British beat them back. I always liked the British. They have manners. Not like the Yanks.'

She had nothing to say to this. Not wanting to encourage him, she looked out of the window and said very little, waiting for the thin line of light to appear on the horizon.

She hiked for half an hour with the winter sun in her eyes. The soles of her tennis shoes had worn thin and she almost fell several times on the frozen gravel path. The wet pine trees smelled fresh in the cold. She climbed, not stopping to catch her breath.

She swiped at a branch as she walked away from the stone trail. A miniature world lay below. In the distance, she could see snow on the mountain peaks on the horizon.

The temple described by the map was small, badly in need of repair. The wooden panels on the roof had lost their colour. The once rich reds and greens had chipped into a more uniform brown. Dust covered the floors.

She took out Myung-chul's note. She walked around the temple pavilion as it instructed. A twelve-foot Buddha, whose eyes and mouth had partially eroded, had been carved out of a rock face. She looked over her shoulder. How could people just forget about a place like this? There was no one around for miles. Climbing around the edge of the rock, she found a small cave. A pile of wishing stones had collapsed and lay scattered on the ground.

There was a hole, about a metre-and-a-half wide, at the edge of the slab of rock. She felt the edge of it with her foot and was surprised to find a ledge, which turned out to be a step. Removing the torch from her backpack, she lowered herself, feet first. Then she threw a stone ahead, testing the depth of the descent before continuing on. At the bottom of the gravel steps, she stood for a moment and felt the wall. It was solid. She shone her flash light ahead and saw a narrow tunnel ahead. She fought back the squeeze of claustrophobia and walked down the slope.

It was colder underground, though she was sheltered from the winds outside. She shivered in the darkness, the T-shirt under her jacket damp and cold against her back. Could this really be it? It didn't seem possible that a tunnel of such significance could have been kept a secret for so long. She walked forward a few steps, hesitant to continue, conscious of how alone she was. What if Myung-chul had been wrong? It was possible that there were others who knew about the tunnel.

The gravel underfoot was soft. Some parts of the tunnel were narrower than others. She guessed she couldn't be far from the demilitarized zone. How could it be that no one knew about this place? There were army barracks nearby. She walked a little, unsure of whether to keep going or turn back, when she heard a low hum in the darkness. She stopped and held her breath. On the ground were several footprints.

The whirring sound grew louder as she walked. Several paces further, she became aware of the faint smell of gasoline.

She stopped and listened for several moments. Switched off the torch. There was a tiny speck of light ahead.

Someone was down there.

Squinting against the light, she tried to keep her breaths even. Her heart was a frantic animal trapped in her chest. It was further away than it appeared at first. The air in the cave was humid and cold. She felt something soft under her foot. It took her a moment to gather the courage to look down. A dirty sleeping bag had been abandoned on the uneven ground. A figure disturbed the light. She should have come better prepared. The smell of gasoline was making her a little dizzy.

The figure stood up.

It was Hyun-min.

'By the end of the week? But—'

'I should think you've had long enough. The NIS would like to wrap this up by the end of the year.'

'I'm not sure that I have everything that they might want to know,' he said helplessly.

The Ambassador gave him a stern look. 'I appreciate your vigilance in reporting on a colleague, but this is getting embarrassing. This report should have been turned over to them months ago. Is it that you haven't had the time or is it that there some ambiguity here?'

Thomas sensed that there was more riding on his answer than just the audit report. 'I feel I have to be thorough.'

'The longer we postpone this, the more they're expecting something substantial. How else will we explain the delay?'

The Ambassador was right. He had to give them something.

'Let's get this wrapped up by the end of the week, before everyone leaves for the Christmas holidays.'

He nodded.

Back in his office, he reached for his phone. He had to confront her.

Hyun-min dropped the shovel in his hand and wiped at his forehead. 'I thought I was careful. How did you find me?'

'I found this,' she said, handing him Myung-chul's note.

He crouched over the naked light bulb on the ground, held the note over it. He squeezed his eyes shut as though he had a headache, then screwed up the note in his hand and tossed it aside.

'Who else have you told?' he said, finally.

'No one.'

'You're alone?'

She nodded.

He stared at her for several moments, as if trying to decide whether he believed her. When he looked away, he seemed to have relaxed. 'It doesn't matter. I'm almost finished.'

She looked around at the sandbags, mounds of gravel and drilling tools at their feet. 'With what?'

He didn't reply.

She brushed past him in the narrow passage, towards the darkness. It was difficult to do it without pressing up against him.

'Hello?' She called out to no one in particular. The echo suggested the great stretch of tunnel ahead. 'So it's true? This goes all the way to Pyongyang?'

Hyun-min hardly looked up from his concentrated work of filling the sandbag with gravel. Mia couldn't be sure what it was he was doing. He didn't appear to be digging anything in the ground.

'How far are we from the demilitarized zone?'

After a moment's pause, he replied, 'We're right under it. We're in no man's land.'

'So it's true?'

He shot her a look. Then he nodded and shrugged, as if to say that it didn't matter.

'You didn't know about the note?' she asked.

'You think I would have left it lying around for you to find if I did?' He straightened out and stopped what he was doing. 'The son of a bitch. Why would he leave something like this for me? I told him so many times that I didn't want to know what he did, why all those people kept coming to see him. But he kept trying to tell me. It's like he had to share it with somebody. All those times I told him I didn't want to get involved. Now he's got me down here. Now *you* know. Before we know it, there won't be any one who doesn't know about this. I hope he's happy.'

She was confused. 'If you didn't know about the note . . . how did you get here?'

Hyun-min's face grew dark. 'He got me involved in this way before he decided he was a coward. He never looked out for me. He thought he was a saint. He never thought about what he did to me.'

Hyun-min picked up the shovel he had dropped and began to put gravel into a sandbag.

'How did you know?'

'Do you know what it's like for me here? It took me a year, no, longer, to work out why people seemed to know about where I came from. There are no uniforms here, but there's still a code of dress and I wasn't following the rules. I didn't own any Nike sneakers or duck-down jackets. I can't afford it. I would have to pay a fortune just to become invisible. It doesn't matter anyway, because the minute I say something everyone knows I'm not from here. Even the people who are supposed to be sympathetic look at me with pity or as if I'm diseased. Your stepmother – every time she sees me, it's like she's seen a ghost, she can never get that look off her face like she's afraid of me.'

He thought about that for a minute.

'I didn't want to have anything to do with it. I didn't want to know anyone from the North. I didn't want to live with Myung-chul. But I didn't have the money to live anywhere else. He was my only friend. But everyone in the defector community knew about him. Every day people would come to the apartment, bringing envelopes of money, small packages, letters. I pretended that I didn't see. Pretended not to notice when he disappeared for days at a time. I told Myung-chul not to tell me what he was doing. I wouldn't even answer the door. I didn't want to know. It was bad enough that he had this hobby, you know, of taking portraits of defectors who had made up their minds to leave the South. He had this idea that he was going to put an exhibition together one day. Can you believe that? The whole thing made me crazy.'

He was silent for a moment, as if recalling the details. He looked calm. Unlikely to strike out. Was it his intention to harm her? The tunnel was narrow and long, she would not outrun him.

'So what happened? Did he get into some kind of trouble?' she asked, to keep him talking.

'A few months ago, I got called out for a job interview, something about copying DVDs for a guy who would sell them out on the roadside. When I got there, there were three of them. North Koreans. One was a guy people call Scarface, after some Yankee movie. He wanted to know who Myung-chul's broker was. Who was the guy undercutting his business? How could he afford to charge so little for his deliveries? Did I know how much it cost him to run people back and forth across the border through China? If he charged what

Myung-chul charged he wouldn't even be able to make ends meet. He didn't believe anything I told him. Those three guys had fun using my guts as a punching bag. It was only when they got tired that they believed that I didn't know anything. Scarface wanted me to find out. He wanted me to find out as much as I could and report back to him. I went home, furious. I told Myung-chul that he had to stop what he was doing, that I was getting hurt. I told him he had to move out. We couldn't live together anymore. He looked so tired when he told me he was sorry. He would get out of my way soon.'

Hyun-min grew silent.

Mia became aware of the faint smell of gas. She looked about her, trying to find the source of it.

Hyun-min did not seem to notice as he began speaking again. 'Later that night, he left as he usually did. I lay there for a while, thinking about everything. I knew it was only a matter of time before I got picked up by Scarface and his men again. I thought about packing up everything and leaving. I thought about Comrade Park, who I had left behind in the North, and I thought about going back. I had never been able to get rid of my guilt for just leaving the way that I did. Then I got to wondering about whether the rumours were true. Could Myung-chul really have a safe passage back home? I was still angry. I was worried. He was still my friend. The guys who were after him were going to get to him eventually so I decided to follow him. It wasn't long until he figured out I was following him. I mean, it was dark, there was no one around. He was glad. It was like he was relieved just to be able to talk to someone about it. He brought me to this place, told me about the letters and his work. I completely lost it. I said I wished I had never met him. That I shouldn't have come here. Who would want to know about this? We were dead men. I pushed him around, saying that I never wanted to get involved but that there were already people after both of us. Myung-chul didn't say a word. He just stood there listening to me yelling at him. After a while he said that I was right. This was the last delivery that he would do. He asked me if I wanted to join him. I walked out without answering him.'

Mia saw his forehead glistening with sweat. He made no effort to wipe it away. 'What happened then?'

'That was the last time I talked to him. The next time I saw him, he was hanging from the shower railing.'

'You think it's your fault,' Mia said, after a moment.

Hyun-min looked up, as if fighting back tears. 'We're all dead men walking here. Maybe it was a matter of time. But I pushed him. He was the closest thing I had to a friend. I pushed him away even though I understood his loneliness.'

They said nothing for a moment. Putting her torch aside, Mia unzipped her bag and pulled out a cigarette. She put it to her lips, stroked the lighter with the tip of her thumb, when suddenly Hyun-min was on her, swiping the cigarette out of her mouth with his hand.

'What are you doing?' she said, pushing him away.

'Do you want to kill us both?'

Her heart was beating so fast, she could hardly breathe. What was going on here? He had never answered her question. She looked around her. She looked up and saw that he had been drilling in the ceiling of the tunnel. She felt a stab of fear.

'What are you doing?'

He did not answer.

'What are you planning?'

'Keep your voice down.'

'What are you drilling?'

'Myung-chul was wrong. I never would have sold him out. I would never do that. He was stuck. He wasn't here or there –' Hyun-min was talking faster and faster – 'It's worse for people who live between places, you know that? When you can see how both sides live, when you can see the way that people misunderstand each other.

That's the thing that Myung-chul didn't understand. I would never do what he did. Don't you see that the tunnel shouldn't exist?'

'Wait, you mean—'

'Do you know how many people want this tunnel? Scarface knows where I live now. He came to the house. I saw him talking to your stepmother. He's not going to leave me alone. Before I know it, other brokers are going to hear about it. Even the Reverend wanted me to tell him about the tunnel. So that he could use it to send the word of God across the border. He said I didn't have to confirm whether or not it existed, but he tried to give me a letter. As long as it exists, people will try to use me, they'll threaten me, just like they did with Myung-chul. So that's why I have to destroy it.'

She took a step back from him. 'So seal it up, cover up the trail. What do you know about destroying tunnels? You think you can just blow it up?'

'I have to make sure everyone knows that it's over. That there's no tunnel anymore. So long as people think that it exists, they'll come after me. There's a gas pipe that supplies the army barracks up here,' he said, fingering the ceiling of the tunnel. 'It took me months to figure out how to make it work, and then a while to get to it. All it takes is a little leak and this place'll fill up.'

She put her back against the wall to steady the tremble in her legs. She had underestimated him. She said nothing until she could be sure that her voice would be even. 'Do you know what you're saying? You're not sending a message. You'd be starting a war.'

'No.'

'If it's a message you want to send, there are other ways. I won't let you do this. I'm not staying here—' The way he glared at her made her unable to finish the sentence.

'I'm almost finished. All I have to do is puncture the mains. You can try to leave, but if I light this match –' he said, calmly – 'we'll both be dead before you get to the end of the tunnel.'

He sat on the edge of his desk watching the lift doors. It was almost midday and still no word. It was becoming clearer by the hour that Mia was not coming into the office. He accosted staff to determine her whereabouts. Together they pieced together a blank diary. She had no appointments for the day. There was no word from her. Her absence spoke of the extraordinary. Her phone continued to turn him over to voicemail. A deep well of worry began pooling in the pit of his stomach.

Restless, he walked down the corridor. His steps slowed as he came face to face with Charles. He was aware that he should say something conciliatory, but instead asked him if he had seen her.

Charles made no effort to mask his disdain, but answered him quietly. 'Not this morning.'

'She hasn't come in.'

'Awfully concerned about her now, are you?' Charles said, but he began to look worried himself. He lowered his voice and said, 'Do you even have the first clue what you're doing with this audit?'

'I'm sorry I asked—'

'It would help if you spoke a word of Korean.'

He refused to rise the provocation. 'Will you let me know? If you hear from her?' Thomas said, passing him by.

'That's likely,' Charles muttered, as he walked away.

Thomas opened the door, hoping, irrationally, that it would be Mia. Instead there was a young man with an envelope standing at the doorstep.

'Sign here, please,' he said and handed him a thick envelope.

It was from Mr Paik. *Some background notes that might help*, the note attached read. It struck him as odd. Mr Paik had emphasized that they didn't have resources for an investigation of their own and yet their files seemed fairly comprehensive.

He turned on the lamp at his desk. The file that the NIS had given him was filled with birth records. A file from the Holt International Adoption Agency. Medical records. Transcripts. They had been translated badly. There was a litany of facts about her education that meant nothing to him, until he found that she had dropped out of her high school and had studied for, and passed, a university entrance exam. She had been the top of her class, it appeared. It was unclear why she had dropped out of high school, though her medical records showed that she had been hospitalized for several months around the same time. There were surgeons' reports about discussions of plastic surgery for the patchwork scars left on her body. The Holt Adoption Agency files suggested that the girl's mother was English. He resolved to follow up the lead on her mother later. There was something in the files that disturbed him but he couldn't put his finger on it. It hardly mattered. He just had to write the damned thing. He closed the file and typed a few words. There was no record of her birth. She was raised by her father and a stepmother, something that Mia herself had never mentioned. A communist family. It was possible she still held close ties to the North Korean defectors' school. He had followed her there after all. Perhaps the school itself was a sleeper institution, a hotbed of spies. It would seem too obvious, too closely held in scrutiny.

Then it came to him. There was a discrepancy in her address. The report stated that she lived with her father and stepmother. He felt a prickle at the back of his neck. Then whose apartment had they been occupying? He called Mr Paik.

'The address is one of ours. It's a government-owned property. We subsidize the rent for the underprivileged.'

'I'm not sure I know what you mean,' he said.

'You know, the elderly, some defectors.'

'What's the name of the defector who is living there?'

'We have a couple of names.'

Thomas jotted them down and hung up the phone.

He picked up Mia's employee file. All he needed was her home address.

Hyun-min sat on the ground with his head in his hands.

'Myung-chul can't have only told you sad stories. These letters would have also given people hope. You can't ignore that. You'd be destroying that, too,' Mia offered.

He lifted his head and gave her a lopsided, tired smile. 'Hope? That's all just fantasy. It's not real. It gets you thinking stupid, impossible things. Before I came here I had stupid fantasies about this place. If I was hungry, I thought, I'll have all the food I want in Seoul. In the winters, when there wasn't enough firewood to go around and there were boys in my orphanage who froze in their beds, I thought, in Seoul I'll never be cold. Soon I'd built up Seoul to be heaven, everything Chongjin wasn't. I thought I was going to be rich. That because we speak the same language I would belong. But there are things I couldn't have imagined. To suddenly have a choice, to be burdened with responsibility. To be judged. I lived in a place where some people were scared of what other people saw, their neighbours and what they might tell the authorities. People here are watching too. They care about what labels they can brand on you. Where you live, what you wear, which university you go to, and if you aren't in the right place, with the right labels, you're cast off, you're nowhere.'

He paused and gave her a lopsided smile. 'The worst is the guilt.

It's not something I had ever considered. I asked myself why I couldn't hold my head the way others do. At first I thought it was the clothes, my accent, all those things that gave me away to others. Then I realized that it was because I was ashamed. I walk around burning with shame. I walk around feeling filthy. Who could ever love me, when I've abandoned those I loved? I think about Comrade Park, waiting for me to come back across the border. I've abandoned those I loved, and so I don't get a chance again.'

'Don't you see what you could start here? There's no greater guilt than that. Why don't you bury it? Cover up the entrance to this place. You said yourself that no one else knows about it. You could leave. If it's money you need, I can help you—'

'Why is it always about money with you people?' Hyun-min jumped to his feet. 'Do you think that's the answer to everything? You think you can buy solutions to everything? That's how we got in this mess in the first place. People will kill me for this tunnel. Why? Because there are brokers who will profit from it. I have to destroy it and everyone has to know that it's gone.'

She thought for a few moments and studied him carefully. An idea was beginning to form in her mind. 'I've thought a lot of things about you, but I didn't know until now that you're a coward.'

'Think what you want.'

'You're going to destroy all this and let everyone else pick up the pieces? Why not stay and fight?' She drew closer to him.

'You think I haven't thought about this a million times? I don't see any other way out of this.'

He looked tired. His earlier threat reeked of desperation. He didn't really want to do this.

'If it's a message you want to send, there might be another way out of this,' she said.

★

'You're sure this is going to work?' Hyun-min asked.

Mia tried the doorbell again.

'We've been over this. We're just going to have to try,' she said.

Hyun-min stuffed his hands into his pockets. He had said little once they had begun the journey back into the city. She warmed her hands with her breath. The day had turned grey and heavy. A snowstorm approached.

Mia heard the clatter of heels drawing closer. The door swung open. The radio had been turned down low: a drone of crisp words hummed from a room in the back.

'Mia,' Felicity said, unable to keep the surprise from her voice. She looked as though she were trying to recollect whether they had some arrangement. 'Is everything all right? Tom's at the office, I just spoke to him . . .' Her voice drifted off as she laid eyes on Hyun-min.

Mia stepped into the house without being asked in.

'I know,' she said. 'I'm here to see you.'

Their house was exactly as she remembered it. Not even a new speck of dust on the white sofa in the living room. There was no outward evidence of erosion or decay in their marriage. They walked through the intermittent lamplight along the long hallway into the kitchen.

Felicity was saying something, '. . . for the state of the place, I wasn't expecting company . . .'

Mia didn't wait until they were seated in the kitchen before she said, 'I think I may have the story of your career.'

Felicity rose from the table and refilled the kettle. Without turning around, she said, 'Do you trust your companion?'

Mia stole a glance at Hyun-min, who had not taken his eyes off Felicity since they had entered the house. 'I've seen the tunnel, you don't have to worry about that,' Mia replied.

'Well, that's something.' She turned around then. 'But you haven't answered the question. Can you trust *him*? What's his agenda in all this?'

'Taking this to the media is my idea, not his. It's the best way I know to protect . . .' she almost said 'both of us', but instead said, 'him'.

Felicity joined them at the table. Mia caught her studying Hyun-min's dirty hands, as though they were diseased. She could see her performing a complex calculation of trust.

'Does Tom know about this?'

'It's important that he doesn't know.'

'I was afraid you might say that,' she said. 'We need to be absolutely clear about who knows about this and who doesn't. This could land us all in serious trouble,' Felicity said. 'How can you be sure the authorities don't know about any of this?'

'Hyun-min has been down there for weeks and no one has passed through. Myung-chul was the only one who seemed to know. Even if there are others who know about it, the important thing is that the tunnel becomes public knowledge. There'll be less potential for it to be abused.'

Felicity continued to look unconvinced. 'I'm worried about keeping this from Tom. It puts me in a difficult position. We've been here before. Our marriage almost didn't recover . . .'

Mia interrupted. 'North Korean agents are after Hyun-min. He fears that the NIS will try to use him for the same reasons that the North Korean agents are after him – to plant spies. If the tunnel is made public, then the government will have to shut it down, it won't be possible for single-interest groups to manipulate the passage of the tunnel.'

Felicity said nothing.

Mia decided to change tactic. 'Right now, there are only three people in the world who know about this. If you write this story, it'll be all yours. An exclusive . . .'

Mia could see Felicity was tempted by this. Then she felt Felicity watching her. 'Why is it imperative that this is kept from Tom? I have to tread carefully when it comes to matters relating to the Embassy.'

'He's not impartial. He has a different agenda. He'll rush into things, misjudge the situation, he'll get it all wrong.' She could feel her face reddening with anger.

Felicity was silent for a moment, her eyes still on Mia. 'I didn't know you worked with him so closely.'

That caught her off guard. She didn't know what to say to that. 'I guess you could say that.'

Hyun-min looked from Felicity and then back to Mia. 'What is she saying? I don't feel good about this. I should have just done it when I had the chance.' He stood up and paced the kitchen.

Mia shot him a look. 'Will you sit down? We're not finished here.'

'What's she saying? Are you sure we can trust her? How do you know that she's not going to call the police as soon as we leave?'

'The more nervous you get, the more nervous she's going to be. Just let me talk to her.'

Hyun-min sat back down again and looked back and forth between them.

'He's nervous. He wants to know if you'll do the story.'

Felicity looked unsure. 'I hope you can appreciate that I can't take your word for this. I have to see this tunnel myself.'

Mia stole a look at Hyun-min. 'Only if you promise to run with the story.'

'I'll need some time to speak to a few people and do my own research.'

'You can't discuss the tunnel with anyone. That's the condition of us showing it to you.'

'I'd need to see it. And I would need an interview. I would need evidence.'

Mia stole a glance at Hyun-min. 'Of course.'

At the police station, Kyung-ha waited by a rattling electric heater with trembling hands while a policeman interviewed a man who insisted on hiding his face in his sleeve. When Hyun-min hadn't returned from the pharmacy, she knew she had to file a report. She had heard stories of what debt collectors would do. Returning in groups carrying batons, torching everything in sight. She sat fighting the anxiety that threatened to overwhelm her. After all, over the years she had learned that the police could be very efficient at what they did.

By the time the tall officer beckoned her over to the desk, she was filled with doubt. She had made mistakes before.

'Are you here to report a crime?'

Kyung-ha hesitated. 'Not a crime exactly . . .'

The man looked impatient, 'What is it then?'

She didn't know where to start and where to end. Could she mention the debt collector and not the other visitors? The letters?

'I have a boy living with me,' she began. 'He defected from the North some time ago. I think he's in some trouble with a loan shark.'

At the mention of the defection, she saw the officer's expression change. He would not be sympathetic to Hyun-min, no matter what story she told. How quickly they had taken Jun-su away. How quickly people rose to conspiracy and prejudice at the mere mention of the North.

The officer shook his head and looked at her impatiently.

'So what are you reporting exactly? This is the trouble with these defectors. They have no money management skills. They come here and they're lazy. They don't know what it means to work hard at all. That's the problem.'

She could see that the officer wanted something more substantial, an accusation of espionage, perhaps, conspiracy. But she would not do what she had fallen prey to so many years before, when she had gripped the receiver in her hand and made that phone call. She thought of the life that had almost been lost. She picked up her purse from the edge of the desk and stood up.

'I won't waste any more of your time, officer.'

From the police station, Kyung-ha went straight to the alterations shop.

'I'm sorry I'm late,' she said as she came through the door.

On her way there, she resolved to take matters into her own hands. The best way that she could think of to protect them all was to get some money. She thought of the silver hair-pin given to her by her mother. It was the only item she had left that was of any value. She had sold the few items of jewellery she owned during hard times over the years.

She knocked on her boss's office door in the back of the shop.

'I have something to ask you,' she began.

'What is it?' her boss said without looking up from his newspaper.

'I was wondering . . .' It was harder to say than when she had imagined it. 'Could I borrow a little money? Or get a little advance on my pay?'

'*Ahjumma*?'

She didn't understand why he was so angry.

'Do you remember doing this?' The boss handed her a pair of trousers.

Kyung-ha squinted. She had taken the hemline up a few days ago.

'The customer came in here complaining. Can you see that it's not straight?'

Kyung-ha examined it. The hem was uneven, even she could see that. 'I'm sorry. It's just that these days—'

'It's not the first time. I didn't say anything before because I thought it was a one-off. If this keeps happening then I'm going to lose business. What do you think's going to happen when this lady tells her friend to go to the shop next door?'

'It won't happen again.'

He looked away as if she disgusted him. 'I'm sorry to do this, really. How much longer were you thinking of working? You've got a daughter who supports you. You don't need this job.'

Her head shot up. 'My husband's medical bills—'

'You can't work here anymore. That's it.'

Kyung-ha closed her mouth, knowing suddenly that there was nothing more she could do or say.

He handed her an envelope. 'It's not much. Ordinarily I don't even do severance pay but I know you've been here for so many years. It's generous when you think of it like that.'

The door wasn't locked. The church was empty, lit only by the glow of lights from the Christmas tree near the podium. She knelt down, pressed her head against her hands. She prayed to the Lord for an answer. Losing her job, the use of her fingers, was another act of punishment. She had to protect the boy. Not just because she had lost a son. It was because she saw how much her mistake had cost others.

She looked up and saw the collection box. For months congregants had been putting in money for starving North Korean children. Who was a more deserving recipient of that money than Hyun-min?

She opened the box and saw a pile of green notes. She had been many things in her life. Wife of a revolutionary. Breadwinner. Judas.

She stuffed the notes into her bag.

Thief.

He needed to decide what to do. He had not seen Mia since the last time they had met at the apartment. It had been three days. She had called in with an apparent illness and was not answering her phone. After a long day at the Embassy, he had hoped to find distraction in Felicity's company, but he returned to an empty house. He sat in his study, unable to eat anything, looking through Mia's files once again. He thought about getting the NIS's assistance as they had offered it in finding her.

He heard Felicity come in.

'You're late this evening,' Thomas said.

'I could say you're in early. It's been quite a day,' she said, taking off her thick winter coat. She took her boots off at the door. They were muddy and caked with dirt.

He gave her a kiss. Her hair was damp and smelled faintly of petrol. 'Where have you been?'

She hesitated at this. 'Perhaps we can talk about it later. I'm tired.'

He followed her into the bedroom, wanting her to look at him. She turned on the lamp by her dressing table and he turned on the heater by their bed. Outside a light coat of snow covered the garden. Felicity pulled a jumper over her head, then put on some woollen socks.

'Where have you been? Your clothes are filthy.'

She hardly seemed to hear him. He was conscious of her distraction. She was absorbed in thought, as though she were deeply disturbed by something. He put his hands on her shoulders. She tensed a little.

'Is everything all right?'

She said nothing to this.

'Tom,' she said suddenly. She turned to face him.

That's when he caught sight of her camera bag. 'I haven't seen that old thing in quite some time.' He knew what that meant.

Felicity was no longer looking at him. She had the glow of concentration she acquired when she was busy working on a project. He hadn't seen it in her in a long time.

'You've started something, were you going to tell me about it?' he asked, softly, not really wanting to start a fight.

'Tom, will you be honest, just for a moment?' She hesitated. 'Do you think we're happy? Will we be happier than this?'

He was about to answer when she spoke again.

'Is it unfair of me to consider whether this degree of our happiness is worth my throwing away my career?'

They had been stuck like this for too long. He didn't know what to say other than, 'not now, please.'

'Then when, Tom? Can we postpone this for ever?'

'No. Just not tonight.' He decided to make an effort. 'We're not the happiest we've ever been. But we're not the most miserable either. We'll work it out, eventually.'

'So you think, after everything that's happened, that this is worth saving? You don't think we're still here because we both hate to fail?'

He went to her and kissed her. Her hands were icy.

'Of course, I don't.'

Why did he say this? Because it was easier than confronting the truth.

Strangely, he thought she looked a little disappointed by his answer.

The wave of relief she felt at Hyun-min's appearance receded almost immediately. The fact that he had evaded the debt collector until now did little to console her. He could not stay with her. He was not safe in her home.

'Hyun-min ah, sit down, let me talk to you.'

'Not now, *Ahjumma*, I have to get back to this woman . . .'

He wore the distracted weariness of a person who hadn't slept in days. She knew there was no point in asking him where he had been.

Kyung-ha watched him, not sure who he meant. 'It's important. Just sit down for a moment.'

He didn't seem to be listening, lost in a trance of motion towards the living room where he picked up the backpack he kept hidden behind the futon, seemingly looking for something.

'There was someone here asking for you.'

Hyun-min still didn't seem to hear her, his head burrowed inside the backpack.

Kyung-ha took the moment to retreat to her room. Pulling out the Bible from under the bedding on the top shelf of her wardrobe, she removed the envelope of money she had taken from the church. She held the money in her hands, knowing that she could change her mind, that the course of events was still reversible.

In the living room, Hyun-min was putting on his shoes, with the backpack on his shoulders.

'Hyun-min. The man said you owe him.'

Hyun-min looked a little guilty. 'I know. I saw. That's why I didn't come back. I'm sorry.'

'How much money do you owe him? How long have you been in trouble with him?'

Hyun-min's expression grew progressively darker as Kyung-ha recounted her encounter with the man.

'Hyun-min. I don't know how much you owe, this might help you—' she said, pressing the envelope in his hand.

He brushed her off in disgust. 'It's not about money. Money isn't going to solve this!' He grimaced as though he were in pain. 'That man who came here doesn't want money. He wants something more than that. Do you know what he does? He's a broker. He gets people across the border in exchange for money.'

'What would you know about that?' Kyung-ha asked, relieved. It had all been a great misunderstanding.

'He wants to know where the tunnel is,' he said, not looking at her.

Thomas took off his jacket and flattened the map. He had followed the elaborate instructions given to him by the Ambassador's secretary: past the school for the blind, the block of food stalls selling red rice and fish cakes, left where the road forked around an ageing Ginkgo tree. Then he had turned into the steep, narrow alleyway. His knees ached from the climb.

He imagined these houses were built brick by brick with dark-faced labourers carrying heavy weights on their backs up and down the hills. This was a part of Seoul he had never seen before – he realized that beyond the centre there must be many more neighbourhoods just like this one, hidden from view. The single-storey houses were surrounded by water-stained walls. Most of the houses were unmarked. Green sacks hung on the edges of a few gates. He opened one and found a carton of milk. The sack was marked with a few letters and what looked like an address. 57–28. He crumpled the paper in his hand and raised the collar of his coat against the wind and continued walking down the alley, which smelled of boiling meat.

57–42. The two had faded.

Through the gaps in the blue gate, he looked into a courtyard. A haggard, balding man peered from behind a rice-paper door. The two-storey house itself was old, a remnant of the Japanese occupation.

A woman was speaking to a young man in the courtyard. The young man froze at the sight of him.

'Thomas Dalton-Ellis. I work at the Embassy. I'm looking for Mia Kim . . .' he said. He tried to force a hand through the gap in the gate. He felt like a fool. It had been presumptuous of him to assume that the Korean lady spoke English. He should have been better prepared. 'Mia Kim?' he repeated.

She opened the door, reluctantly. He bent his head under the small roof over the gate and walked through. The courtyard was small, but neatly kept, with several snow-covered *kimchi* pots lining the walls.

The young man did not take his eyes off him. He was measuring every move that he made, like a stalked animal, measuring his escape.

'I'm from the Embassy.' He tried to remember the Korean word for diplomat. '*Wei-gyo—gwan.*'

This introduction seemed to have an electric effect on the young man, who began to fire an assault of words to the older woman, while backing into the house, not once turning his back on Thomas. He raised both his hands to convey that he intended no threat, but this seemed to only heighten the panic in the young man, who disappeared out of sight.

'I'm looking for Mia . . .' he began again, in a futile attempt to communicate with the woman, when the young man returned with a can which Thomas could not identify.

The young man threw the backpack off his shoulders as if it were an animal attacking his back. He lifted the lid of an earthenware pot and retrieved a sack. It was only as he began to empty the contents of the can onto the pile that Thomas recognized the smell.

'No!' Thomas said, fearing the man was about to douse himself with the gasoline. But as he rushed towards him, he realized he only intended to soak the backpack, which promptly erupted into an explosion of heat and light.

The woman shouted something at the young man, who, once

satisfied that the damage had been done, darted towards the gate before disappearing. The woman followed closely behind.

Alone, Thomas took it upon himself to attempt to stamp out the fire. He hacked at the flames with a rake that was propped up against the wall. Once the flames had died down, he saw that inside the backpack was a pile of papers.

Thomas stared at the dissipating flames, unsure of what to make of what he had just witnessed, when he realized he was not alone. An old man stared at him from a crack between two rice-paper doors.

'I'm here to see Mia,' he offered, though he assumed that the man did not speak any English. 'Perhaps I could take a look around?'

The man said nothing and offered no objection. He continued to stare at him. Thomas gave him a weak smile. Then he noticed the skew of his shoulder, a continued half-shrug. There was something wrong with him. In the absence of the old woman, he peered into the living room. It was worn and sparsely furnished. The pattern in the linoleum floors had faded in places. The boxy television beside the medicine cabinet reminded him of the televisions of his childhood, the colour of the screen slightly off, a kind of green. There didn't seem to be a place to sit other than the floor. He felt his pocket for the slip of paper with the address on it, wondering if he had found the right place.

Out of politeness, he waited a few more minutes for the woman to return before proceeding to search for Mia's bedroom. Could this really be where she lived? A narrow staircase led to a small landing of two doors. He chose the door on the left and found a washroom with only a washing machine and a sink in the corner. The other door led to a room no larger than a cell. A familiar dark print dress hung from a nail on the wall. He picked up a tiny airplane that was sitting on the wooden desk. A coffee tin held pens and a tiny globe pencil sharpener. There were crumpled pieces of paper with simple linguistic equations on them. A Korean word = affections. In Mia's careful handwriting. Letters perfectly spaced apart. Under sheaves of papers, he found hair clips and odd black and white photographs of villages in what looked like the Cotswolds. Under the desk, he found a Hello Kitty mug full of cigarette butts and a rusty radio.

He opened the narrow wardrobe and saw the dress that she had been wearing at the ball the night he had seen her with another man. It was only then that he allowed himself to believe it. There was an entire world that she had held back from him.

He sat at her desk. Did she sit here every night? He opened the top drawer. A dusty collection of hairpins and an ancient, crusting bottle of maroon nail polish. The next drawer was not as easy to open. A crumpled piece of paper stuck out of it. A note on visa waiver amendments. Dated 1 June. He tugged at the drawer. A telegram he had not sent about his meeting with the finance minister. The pages had been taken at random, though some words had been underlined. *Astonishing. Almost theatrical.* He found a coarse leather notebook, just like the one he had bought in Morocco. On the pages, he saw his own handwriting, his own self-loathing. He flipped back the cover to examine the surface of it.

It was his.

He tried to remember the last time he had seen it. He pulled out all the sheets in the drawer. Most of them were Embassy documents. There didn't seem to be any system of organization. Perhaps the pages were the rejects. The ones that weren't fit for collection or submission or reporting.

But reporting to who?

He sank onto the wooden chair. He had been mistaken. He thought of her attentiveness. The extraordinary coincidence of her being there for him at the moment of his accident. Her resourcefulness. Her willingness to help him. Her elusiveness. A solid lump formed in his throat. Could he have mistaken her affections? He had been a fool for no one. Not like this. A dog yapped continuously in the yard. His head was filled with noise.

He flipped through the stack of papers.

A leak.

There were notes regarding the Finance Minister's visit from London. Sensitive details of correspondence between the Ambassador and himself about details of a recent revision of economic policy. There was no reason for her to have possession of such documents.

Unless he had been wrong about her loyalties.

Hyun-min set the backpack alight.

It was only as she saw the explosion of light that Kyung-ha understood that Hyun-min believed the white man had come for him.

'They must have been working together the whole time. She lied to me. I should have known better. I've seen them together at the apartment. And that reporter – she must be in on it too.'

'What do you mean?' She didn't understand any of it. The white man seemed as surprised as she was at the sight of the fire in the courtyard and had raised both his hands as if he were afraid that the boy would attack him next.

'I have to go,' Hyun-min had said and ran for the gate.

Kyung-ha tried to run after the boy. She didn't get far before the ache in her legs slowed her down. She called out for him until she saw his steps falter and slow.

She began to walk towards him. 'Hyun-min ah, please. Say something that makes sense.'

He had his back turned to her. Even in profile, she could see the anguish on his face. 'How could I let myself trust anyone? I wanted to believe there was another way. I let Mia talk me into it.'

Kyung-ha struggled to put the pieces together. 'What are you talking about?'

'Mia wanted me to talk to this reporter. About all these stories. About the tunnel. The reporter wanted the letters. She must have wanted it as evidence. I shouldn't have . . . I knew it wouldn't come to any good . . . I just wanted to believe,' he said.

He was talking so fast that she could hardly keep up with what he was saying. What did the girl have to do with all of this?

When he looked into Kyung-ha's eyes again, she saw the fear in them. 'You said the broker came here?'

Kyung-ha nodded, still not fully understanding.

'I have to end this. Before the broker comes back.'

He stepped away from her and she gripped his arm. 'End what? What are you going to do?'

'*Ahjumma*, don't worry about me. There's just something I have to do. You're not safe in that house. He'll come back for me. He'll come for you too. You should pack up your things and leave.'

'Where will you go?' she asked him.

'I can't tell you that,' he said, sadly.

Kyung-ha felt something welling up inside her that she had not felt in many years and resisted it, fought it as hard as she could.

She thrust the envelope of money that she still had in her hand onto his chest.

'Take this with you. You'll need it.'

He looked saddened by this gesture. He stroked the edges of the envelope with his fingers. She felt the feeling rising in her and wanted to turn it into anger. Why did he insist on being alone in this? Why wouldn't he let her help him?

It was only when she crossed the threshold back into the ash-scattered courtyard, that she knew what she had been resisting – the certainty of loss, of knowing that she would not see him again.

She could not keep him with her anymore than she could resurrect her son from the dead.

Thomas staggered from the bar onto the street. The sounds and smells of the market were overbearing, the sacks of dried chillies too red and morose, the cuts of meat, the butcher's pedestal which displayed a pig's head. He had been wrong. This was not just another Asian city. Modernity was a farce. This was a nation of savages in disguise. He had misunderstood everything. Here was a leak. She had taken his notes. His journal. What else had she taken from him? She had been to his house without his knowledge. That would have been months before the accident. And it was no coincidence that she happened to be there when he had been most vulnerable. She must have thought that he was an easy target. He felt the betrayal like a gaping hole in his chest. To think that he had almost turned in a blank sheet for her. How had he been such a fool?

He discarded the idea of confronting her as soon as it arose. She lied too well. He had witnessed himself how quickly she could manipulate a story. Had she not seamlessly fixed the problem of his car? Lied to him about the late-night visit to the apartment?

No, he had everything he needed to finish his report. It was his ticket to South America, Europe, Southeast Asia, anywhere he wanted. To confront her would be to be seduced by her version of the truth.

The apartment towered over the market. What was he doing there? Was he still hoping that they might have a life together? He had deceived himself. Convinced himself that he loved her to rid himself of the guilt. Nausea threatened to bring him to his knees.

It was his fault for allowing himself to become a mess. He had to stop drinking. He had to make amends with Felicity. They had to leave this place. They would go away somewhere where they could forget about everything.

He watched the blur of traffic lights from the taxi. All this time he had not allowed himself to believe that she was worthy of suspicion. Despite the evidence. A leak.

He stepped into the sharp cold and walked through a pool of moonlight towards the darkened office. The building security guard looked surprised to see him as he approached the Embassy gates. It took three attempts to tap out the security code, his vision blurred.

Thomas sat down at his desk while waiting for his computer to start. He stared at his keyboard, taking sips of water to coax away the tight fist that had taken hold of his temples.

She had lied to him. That's all there was to it.

He began to type.

Mia Kim has compromised security. Over and above her questionable alliance with the North Korean defectors' school and her history with the communist party is the fact that she is an active leak of confidential Embassy documents. My recommendation is for the termination of her contract and for the NIS to conduct a thorough investigation.

The phone rang.

'Where are you? I must see you,' Thomas said. 'It's urgent.'

Mia stood up from the table. Edged towards the window. The trees in the garden were rake-like, naked in the cold.

'When?' she asked, looking in Felicity's direction who had a look of concentration on her face. They were almost finished.

'How soon can you meet me at the apartment?'

'I don't know,' she said.

There was a long pause. She could hear the static of traffic from the other end of the line.

'There's something I need to tell you. It's important,' he said, his voice almost a whisper. 'Will you come straight here?'

'OK,' she said and hung up.

Meeting him and feigning a story to explain her absence was the best way to buy all of them some time.

All the lights in the apartment were out except for a lamp in the bedroom. A sharp chill greeted her at the door as she slipped off her shoes. A window was open somewhere in the apartment. She heard movement inside and stepped into the living room, sliding the door aside, expecting to see Thomas.

A skeletally thin man sat on the chair by the bookshelf.

'Mia shi?'

He stood up slowly, deliberately, as though he were conscious of a tenderness in his knees. 'Counsellor Dalton-Ellis waited with me for a while but was called to other business.'

She let the sting of it subside before responding. The purplish sagging skin under his eyes made them look swollen, as though he had spent a lifetime weeping. He was wearing a dark suit and a narrow black tie. She had a good idea who he was working for, but felt oddly calm. 'Are you going to tell me who you are?'

'Right. I know so much about you and you have no idea who I am, sorry. Park Hoon-sun. NIS.'

She looked over her shoulder towards the door. She could hear throbbing in her ears. Running would implicate guilt. It was likely that he wasn't alone. She let her bag fall to the ground instead and slumped into a chair, forcing a bright smile. 'You know so much about me? Talk about an introduction. You know how to make me feel nervous and I haven't even done anything. Imagine if I was guilty? Do they offer etiquette classes in the service?'

He seemed to take the question seriously. He surveyed the bare walls of the living room. 'I would compliment you on your modest home, but I don't think, technically, this place is yours.'

'My name isn't on the lease if that's what you mean.'

'You keep very interesting company, Mia shi.' He gave her a long look before smiling a little. 'You don't really seem that surprised to see me.'

'Did you want me to scream?' She shrugged. 'Don't read too much into it.'

'So you'll come willingly to talk to us?'

'About what?' she said evenly.

He gave her a hard look. 'We can talk about it in the car.'

Kyung-ha wasn't sure what it was that woke her. She had been called from a deep sleep, her heart drumming hard in her chest, her breaths rapid in her chest. In the darkness these awakenings felt ominous. The pillow nestling in the hollow of her shoulder felt too soft. Yet as she lay trying to grasp at the last clutches of sleep, she heard a sound she couldn't place. There was something wrong. She sat up. There was a smell in the air that made her grimace.

She pulled back her blanket. Had she left something on the stove?

Opening the door, she immediately jumped back at the sight of thick flames rising from the floor of the living room.

Covering her face against the smoke, she closed her eyes. She had to get to Jun-su's room. Feeling her way against the wall, she backed away from the heart of the fire. A few steps across the living room would allow her to reach him, but the smoke pushed her out into the courtyard. The window to Jun-su's room was broken and seemed to be the place where the fire had originated. It was too high for her to reach. After struggling for several moments, she backed out, feeling desperate and ran onto the street, shouting, 'Is there no one who can help?'

Windows shattered. Neighbours began to appear on the street, sleep still heavy on their faces.

'My husband is in there,' Kyung-ha said, clutching at a man's arm, terrified.

Then suddenly people began to move with more urgency, moving back and forth from the street, gathering buckets of water and tossing it into the living room. Someone grabbed the garden hose and pointed it into the fire. The smell of curling linoleum had everyone coughing. Kyung-ha could hardly breathe. She was breathing too fast and there wasn't enough air. She began to cough, only sucking in more smoke with every gasp. Her legs felt like iron.

She felt someone tugging on her arm, pulling her away and onto the street. Several hands attended to her body. Someone put something over her face. She was dizzy and could only just make out the blur of movement. Yellows and reds. A group of men in uniform had appeared. Her ears had become numb. She realized a paramedic was talking to her, but she couldn't hear him.

'My husband is in there,' she repeated.

He nodded, looking up in the direction of the house.

She followed his gaze and saw movement inside. Figures among the flames. They were pulling something through the clouds of rising ash.

A man on fire.

The windowless room held nothing but a table and a few chairs. The walls were grey, the warm air from the vents, dense. Mia could hardly breathe. She wiped the trickling sweat from her face. Her throat was dry. How would she get out of this? What she needed most urgently was a phone call. She had to speak to Hyun-min, to Felicity. She knocked the walls for padding and checked corners for dried blood. She found nothing. Apparently it was not that kind of interrogation room.

It was impossible to decipher how much they knew. What had Thomas told them? The NIS could draw any number of conclusions from her use of the apartment. Not to mention her relationship with Hyun-min. Was there a chance that they would believe anything that she told them? Even if it was the truth? The more she thought about it, the more unlikely it seemed that they knew about the tunnel. It was best to say nothing at all.

She sat curled up on the hard chair and wrapped her arms around her legs. The best way to survive this was to shut out what might be happening outside. It was all beyond her control. No one knew she had been taken in. She tried not to think about what Hyun-min was thinking, without her constant reassurance. If only he would trust her. She felt torn. If she didn't talk, it would only prolong her arrest.

If she spoke, she would have to keep a firm grip on what she could and couldn't say. It would only become harder the longer they kept her there.

She closed her eyes. Moments later, she heard the door open. A young plainclothes officer came in.

'Your name?'

'I already told you that.'

'It's for our records. Your name?'

They had said this before.

'Mia Kim.'

'Your address?'

She repeated her address, as she had told to several of his colleagues before. It became clear that they were trying to keep her from sleeping. The moment her eyelids grew heavy, someone would come in to ask her menial questions that they had asked her before.

After the officer left, she kicked the table in front of her. Its metal legs shrieked against the concrete floor. When she didn't hear any footsteps, she prodded the table in front of her several times in quick succession so that it squeaked loudly. She hoped that it would get her some attention.

'Can I get a cigarette?' she said to no one in particular, hopeful that they were listening.

She didn't know how much time had passed when a man wearing a grey suit came into the room. He removed a pen from his shirt pocket and wrote something on a small pad. He hardly looked at her. 'How do you know Hyun-min Song?'

She closed her eyes. The repetition of it was torturous. Different interviewers. Each with helpful faces which raised her hopes every time. Then they would ask her the same questions.

'Could I get a cigarette?'

'I don't smoke. You should think about quitting, you know. It's so bad for your health. Not that, it would seem, you're all that worried about that kind of thing.'

She said nothing in reply to this.

'How much contact would you say you have with students at your uncle's defectors' school?'

'I avoid the place.'

'Why?'

'Can I make a phone call?' She needed to talk to Felicity or Hyun-min immediately.

He ignored this and wrote an extensive note for himself, flipped a few sheets of his notebook over and crossed out a few lines. 'Okay. Fine. So you have nothing to do with any of these people and then suddenly you've got this defector living in your house.'

'I told you already. He came to live with us after his roommate died.'

He wrote that down and flipped back a few pages of his notebook. 'That was Myung-chul Lee? How would you describe your relationship with him?'

'I didn't know him.'

'How would you describe your relationship with Hyun-min Song?'

Mia rolled her eyes.

'Are you lovers?'

'How is that relevant?'

He traced some writing on the notepad with a pen. 'Okay. What about all these Embassy documents? What were you doing with those?'

'What Embassy documents?'

'There was a whole handful of them in your drawer. Tell me about them.'

A tight knot formed in her stomach. She crossed her arms. 'I don't know what you're talking about.'

'Interesting,' he said, though he looked vaguely disappointed. He clicked his pen and wrote down a few notes. 'So you don't want to tell us who you're leaking them to?'

She crossed her arms and decided to try a different tactic. 'How about you get me a cigarette, and then we can do this all again?'

'You think you have room to bargain with me here?'

'I've told you everything I have to say.'

'I don't think you have any idea about the gravity of your situation. Why don't I tell you what this looks like? You're stealing Embassy documents on confidential information.'

She shrugged as nonchalantly as she could. They had not yet mentioned the tunnel, but their interpretation of the facts was frightening. If they already believed she was leaking Embassy documents, what would conclusion would the draw if they found out about the tunnel? How would she explain that those documents were simply for Thomas's language alone? That it had nothing to do with the content of what he had written. They would never believe her.

'Suddenly you have nothing to say?' He put one hand on top of the other. 'We could keep you here for as long as we want. Like father, like daughter, is that it?'

'How does that come into it?'

He smiled, as though he had finally got her. 'Come now, don't pretend that you're not aware of your father's career as a communist. He was imprisoned for four years. You can't honestly say you didn't know about that?'

'My father?'

He stood up, suddenly and closed his notebook. 'Fine. Play dumb, but eventually you're going to have to talk because it's not looking good for you. Your uncle runs a school for North Korean defectors.

Your father was well-known for his communist activities in the eighties. You have a defector living in your home and you say you don't know what he's up to.'

'I think you've got the wrong idea about him.'

'Is that right?' He folded his hands over his stomach. He raised his eyebrows. 'Sounds like you know him pretty well.'

'What? It's a conspiracy just because we're dealing with a defector?'

He smiled. 'I'm not oblivious to the fact that your family have a history of communist sympathies.'

'You guys are really boring, do you know that? It sounds like you've already put together your version of the truth. So what I want to know is why the hell you've had me in here for so long?'

'What we want to know is where Hyun-min is now. He could be very useful to us in our investigations.'

'I don't know.'

He was quiet for a moment. 'Do you know about the national security law, Mia-shi?'

'The law you use to arrest anyone who pisses you off?'

'It's specific to your association with communists.' He gave her a half smile. 'We arrested your father under the same legislation.'

He examined his small pad again. 'Would you say it's accurate that your presence at the candlelight protests was related to work you were doing at the Embassy?'

She was taken aback. 'What does that have to do with anything?'

'You were at the candlelight protests, weren't you?' The man flipped open his notebook. 'The tenth of June? That was related to your work at the Embassy? I'd say it's a matter of national security.'

'There were over a hundred thousand people at that protest. Are you interrogating everyone like this?'

'Just the people we think are anti-government.'

'I want someone from the Embassy here. I'm not answering any more questions. You don't think it's a little creepy that you want to arrest me under the same law you used to arrest my father during the dictatorship? This country is going to hell.' She shifted forward in her chair. 'He doesn't talk, you know. My father. What did you guys do to him in there?'

They would not let her accompany him in the ambulance. Instead, Kyung-ha went to the hospital in the back of the police car, but when she arrived, hospital staff had already pronounced Jun-su dead.

Many decades before he had almost died a similarly violent death.

As she stood over the blackened sheet that they had draped over him, she realized the staff were talking to her. Their syllables were soft and indistinct. She felt the hum of their voices but heard nothing except the roar and crackle of the fire. Her eyes stalked the corners of the mortuary floors, looking for edges and surfaces that needed to be scrubbed.

'. . . outside . . .' she heard, '. . . waiting.' Several nurses took turns trying to persuade her, with the tug of an arm, to leave Jun-su's side.

Two men were waiting outside the mortuary, waiting to take her where, many years before, she had once sent Jun-su to die.

The NIS's interrogation room had none of the gore that she imagined to be stained on the walls. When Jun-su had been returned to her broken, she had imagined a very different kind of room: blood stains on the walls, a drain in the floor, white tiles that could be wiped down, dim lights. But the room the police guided her to was clean and empty. She sat facing the two men, blinking against the light.

'Do you know why you're here?'

'If it's about the money, I can—'

The men exchanged looks. 'What money?'

Kyung-ha realized she had made a mistake but it was too late. She would have to tell them.

'We can make sure that they don't press charges, but we'll want information in exchange. What can you tell us about who your daughter is working for?'

'My daughter?'

'We've arrested your daughter and your brother-in-law as part of a larger investigation. Did you know that she's leaking sensitive Embassy information?'

Her head snapped up. 'What?'

'What can you tell us about Hyun-min?'

Kyung-ha hesitated. She hung her head and began to tell them about the letters, the story of the tunnel.

'You're saying you don't know?' the man on the right asked.

'You had those letters in your house?' the man on the left asked.

'Even though this broker came to your house, demanding to know where the tunnel was? You're saying you don't believe it exists?' the man on the right said. Sweat crept from his hairline under the hot light.

'If you didn't know anything about it, why did the broker threaten you? Why did he firebomb your house?' the man on the left said.

'The boy disappeared for days at a time. He never said where he was going,' she replied weakly. She began to fear what would happen if she did not give them the answers that they were looking for.

'You said that the boy came back to you after the broker had come by the house. You must have told him about the broker's visit then. What did he say then?'

'He told me he owed some money,' she said. 'That's all he said and then he was gone again.'

'Where's the tunnel?'

'I told you I don't know.'

'Who are you working for?'

'Me?' She wasn't sure whether she had heard correctly.

'How long have you been working for the other side?'

The men exchanged looks they wanted more.

She trembled. She was becoming increasingly confused. She lost any sense of how long they had kept her. The past and present began to blur. The Lord was finally punishing her as she deserved, showing her what she had done to Jun-su. They had broken a man. It would not take much to break her. She thought of the passage: was it Isaiah or Job? She could no longer remember.

'Let my persecutors be put to shame, but keep me from shame; let them be terrified, but keep me from terror,' she said softly.

She resigned herself to whatever might happen during the interrogations.

She drifted. She thought of the past. She thought of her mother. She remembered the day she had first seen Jun-su among the crowd of students at the university. She remembered his ink-stained hands when he returned in the night. The smell of his women. The light clutch of Mia's hand as a child.

'Hey, stay with us,' a voice said. 'Answer the question. Isn't it true that your family love the commies? Of course you're going to protect him. You lived with a spy for over thirty years, isn't that true?'

Her eyes were half closed; she smiled, sensing that she would be free of the secret at last. 'No, it's not true. You're wrong.'

The interviewers looked bored by this. 'We've got all day . . .'

Kyung-ha paused, not sure how to put into words the secret she had carried with her for so many years.

Her son had lain dying while Jun-su had been grinding against his mistress in an inn with paper-thin walls and rooms for rent by the hour. The illness had come on suddenly. It had been her fault.

She had mourned her only son's death for forty-nine days and forty-nine nights. She didn't say a word to Jun-su while she poured him shots of soju as he wept.

It was not long before Jun-su returned to his routines. His photocopying of Marxist books. On the fortieth day of mourning, she had caught the scents of the white woman on Jun-su's skin again.

She became possessed by a rage that emerged from her body with no arms or legs, only a twisted mouth that screamed as she walked to the nearest phone box on the street. It had been a freezing day in winter. She picked up the receiver and stared at the notice taped to the glass. *Report traitors and spies to this number: 113.* An operator picked up the call right away. Just like that, she gave his name and address, and told the operator that Jun-su had defected from Pyongyang and was working for the government there. She gave the address of the room where they photocopied their Marxist texts.

Kyung-ha looked down at her hands. She could not look at her interrogators.

'I was the one who made the call that night. Just like that. I picked up the phone and I called you people. I lied. I said that he was a spy. I lied because he'd caused me so much heartbreak. I wanted him to be punished. I wanted him locked up. I never imagined the many ways you could break a man. He was so many things. But he was never a spy.'

★

That night Mia woke up screaming in her cell.

And in the morning, to a country ready for war.

She was blindfolded, her arms bound behind her back. As they put her in the van, she could smell the smoke in the air.

The ice water that dripped on her head gave her the sensation that she was shrinking. She would never feel warmth again. Air-raid sirens echoed from a distance. Fighter jets ripped through the sky. They told her very little. She knew what had happened by their change of tactics. The restraints and ice water. The stories told by their repeated questions. What did she know about this act of war? Who was behind the explosion? She had been unable to stop herself shivering. They kept going. How long had she been working for the North Korean government?

They grabbed her hair. Led her to chains. Barbed-wire restraints. She had smiled, almost giddy. If they thought this was how they would break her they had nothing on her. They threw absurd theories around about her father – that he was a communist spy. That her uncle had turned her in. That her stepmother had told them about the tunnel.

They took her to the brink of death and brought her back to life. Broke through scar tissue as they sliced open old wounds. Whose side are you on? they asked repeatedly. They did not trust a person whose loyalties they couldn't discern. They paused to make jokes, trying to make her laugh. She tried to throw them off by laughing at odd moments.

She lost all sense of time, but tried to protect herself by not thinking of the things that hurt most. The tunnel, now apparently destroyed. The border, again drawn rigid.

Mostly, she tried not to think about Hyun-min.

'Your report has been instrumental for us. What we discovered during the interrogations is incredible. We've uncovered substantial information linking Mia Kim and this tunnel. She must have known about it, but she's not talking.'

The NIS had sent three men to the Embassy, all in the same stiff funereal suits and black ties, to consult him about the audit. They sat around him like panelists in the Ambassador's office. Thomas reached for his water glass for the fifth time in a matter of minutes.

'A lot of it checks out, though we're still trying to figure out who was behind this explosion.' The man speaking had a narrow forehead and thick eyebrows. All of them did. Thomas blinked to clear his vision. He kept thinking that he was seeing three of the same man.

He swallowed more water.

'Her uncle has been on our watch list for some time. We started all this because we saw both of them at the protests a couple of months back. We don't like to think of people with those tendencies working in the civil services. It makes us nervous. But we definitely didn't expect this.'

'I believe she was working on a report for us about the FTA agreement,' the Ambassador said.

'That report was for me,' Thomas said, suddenly feeling,

inexplicably, the need to defend her. 'I don't think you should misinterpret her presence at the protests.'

The men exchanged looks. The man on the left of him wrote a note for himself and seemed to decide that the comment would be discarded. 'We'd like a copy of the report.'

This time the Ambassador spoke. 'We can give you what she wrote for us, but not the final report on the matter, that's confidential, I'm afraid.'

'Understood, understood,' the man with the notes said.

The man directly across from Thomas grimaced a little. This brought out the greyish tint to his face, the result, perhaps of too many years of smoking.

'It never hurts to be too sure about these things. Given her family history,' he said. He plucked a piece of tissue from the box on the coffee table and wiped his forehead. 'This whole tunnel business is a mess. The agency is under a lot of pressure. The tunnel ran right under Army barracks. My boss wants to know how we didn't know shit about it. Especially when it seems to be that so many in the defector community did. It makes us look bad. Anyway, we're still trying to find out if she knows anything about this explosion. It's not looking like it. We've been pretty thorough.'

The chill that descended down his back was sharp, electric. He shifted back uncomfortably in his seat. Suddenly he was less sure of what he had seen. The evidence he had found. The men before him had taken things to a sinister level, based on his audit report. He imagined the violence wrought in the word 'thorough'. He had done this. He could hardly hear what the Ambassador was saying.

'Thank you, Ambassador,' the man with the grey face said.

'We hope that was of some help to your investigations,' he said.

'It's just a question of time, Ambassador. I'm going to be honest with you. After all the bad press we've had with these protests, the government wants to consolidate support and war's not a bad way to do it. The last government was too soft on the North Koreans. This government wants to show its strength. Thing is, we've now got delegations from Scandinavia and Switzerland investigating what happened. Before we take any action there needs to be evidence that it was a genuine provocation. We just need to get there first or there'll be heads rolling in our department.'

The Ambassador shut the door to his office and sank into the sofa across from him. The meeting seemed to have revived him, brought some colour into his cheeks. He appeared to be excited by it all. Edging forward, he rubbed his hands.

'We'll have to brief Whitehall on this latest development. They're sending Mark Jenkins over for the official investigation of the incident. Unofficially Jenkins is coming to make the PM's stance on nuclear proliferation clear to all parties involved. He's arriving tomorrow morning. You must brief him first thing. Perhaps you could sit in on some of his meetings.'

The Ambassador rubbed his face. 'And then there's the matter of evacuation of all British nationals and their families. We'll need to move quickly. We need to find out from the consulate how many people have remained in Seoul for Christmas. It looks like things could escalate quite quickly. There's a faction of the government who are gearing up for an air strike and that will not be without retaliation. They want to do this before the investigation is complete. We must be prepared to evacuate, and quickly. We've got some long nights ahead.'

Thomas nodded.

'You must also make preparations. Perhaps Felicity would like to leave as soon as possible.' He paused. 'When all this calms down we can further discuss your future. I gather there are some exciting posts that might be opening in the coming months.'

He made a move for the door and then turned back to the

Ambassador. Then he realized how much it was bothering him. He forced a smile. Understanding the implication. He was being given a significant responsibility. It was over. He would be able to negotiate a substantial position for himself. He felt no excitement or sense of accomplishment. 'Of course, thank you.' He paused. 'You don't think she's been mistreated?' he asked.

'I shouldn't think so,' he said, giving him a look.

He could see that the Ambassador was unconcerned, but this was of little comfort.

Back in his office, he attempted to distract himself by trying to imagine where his next posting might be. He felt no desire to leave, no desire to travel elsewhere. He imagined the foreignness of the places the Ambassador might name and felt exhausted by the newness of them.

No, it was what he wanted. A clean slate. The possibility of a new self in a new place. A desertion of old indulgences.

When she opened her eyes, Charles was beside her in the cell.

'Charles?' She blinked several times to be sure it was him.

'Look at you. They've treated you as though the war's already begun,' he said, looking at her wrists.

'Is it really you?' Her vision was blurred.

'I'm sorry. I should have come sooner, it's taken me a week just to get clearance to see you. You wouldn't believe the red tape I've had to get through to negotiate getting you out.'

She had not even dared to hope for this.

'I thought you'd be long gone by now,' she said. Every bruise and tear on her body came alive as she moved stiffly towards him. 'What happened?'

'There's been an explosion across the border. The South Korean government are saying it's an act of war. The North Koreans are denying any knowledge of it. There are delegations flying in from all over the world to investigate, but the South Koreans are preparing an air strike.'

'Do they know what happened?' she asked, hoping that Charles would contradict what she already knew.

'Apparently there was a tunnel under the border that was exploded. They think it was a gas leak from a mains on the South Korean side, but it doesn't seem to be an accident. They're still trying to work out who did it. The North Koreans deny any involvement. They're going through the rubble now. So far they haven't found anything on this side of the border.'

She didn't want to hear any more.

'Come on, let's get you out of here.'

Charles held her steady as they passed through the lobby. The light hurt her eyes. He seemed older under the fluorescent light. His hair was untamed, greyer than she remembered it. She looked at the marbled floor, the glare of polish from his shoes. Anything so that she didn't have to meet his eyes. They stopped at a vending machine outside and bought some cigarettes. She let him lead her to his car.

Mia propped her head against the window. They stopped at a set of red lights. He glanced in her direction.

'I suppose you were expecting Thomas,' he said. He didn't take his eyes off the road. He turned off the heater.

'I don't want to talk about it,' she replied, turning her face into her shoulder.

'I'm sorry. I know now is not the time.' He paused. 'The involvement you've had with this defector. It doesn't look good. You should consider looking around for other opportunities.'

'Is that why you're here?' she said. 'To fire me?'

There was a long pause. 'I'm sorry. You're a good . . .' he hesitated. 'This isn't easy for me.' He seemed intent on avoiding her eyes. 'They want you to hand in your resignation. It's better for your future prospects and all that.'

She shook her head. 'What about him? What does he get out of it?'

'I don't know the details.'

Her rage had subsided a little.

'I need a favour.'

'What is it?'

'I want to read his report.'

'I don't think that's a—'

'If you can't do it, just say so.'

'I'll see what I can do.'

They sat in the car for a few moments without saying anything. 'There's something else I need to tell you,' he said. 'It seems there was an attack on your house. There was a fire . . .' he hesitated. 'Your stepmother is recovering.'

'A fire?'

'They've found a Molotov cocktail in the wreckage and it doesn't look good. The NIS are piecing all this together. The fire appears to be politically motivated.'

A pause. Mia sensed Charles skirting around a revelation he preferred to avoid. He swallowed several times before speaking. 'There's something else. It's about your father . . .'

Thomas walked down the stairs, two steps at a time. Felicity was waiting for him on the other side of the security doors.

'Tom, I've been trying to reach you all day.'

'I know, I'm sorry, it's madness here. I haven't had a minute to spare. I've gone from one security meeting to another. I don't think I'll get home tonight.'

She was not looking at him. He realized that she was not there out of concern for him.

'There's something I must tell you. It's important. It's about a story—'

He should have known that she would want to write about the conflict. 'Felicity, you can't be serious.'

'Just listen. It's important,' she said. 'I didn't know at first whether I should tell you. Mia Kim. You work with her, don't you? She brought him to me. She and this defector wanted me to write this story.' She sucked in a breath as she saw the look on his face. 'Tom, I'm so sorry, I should have told you. With things the way they were between us I spent too long worrying about what to do and now . . .'

His breath froze in his chest at the mention of Mia's name. He could hardly hear what Felicity was saying. 'Mia? What do you mean?'

'I know I should have told you. Please don't be angry with me now. I need to talk about this; I don't know who else I can tell. Please don't look at me like that, I feel so awful already.'

He couldn't keep the alarm out of his voice. 'What did she say?'

'She came to me and said she had the story of my career. She wanted me to run it, go public with footage of the tunnel. We even went there and I interviewed this defector . . .' She looked distraught.

'You went to the tunnel?' It took him several moments to comprehend the significance of this. 'How could you keep this from me?'

'I know this could escalate to a war. I want to do right by you this time, Tom. They're saying it's an act of war by the North Korean government. But Tom, I don't think that's true. I think this defector did it alone. It's just something he said in the interview. I need to take this to the media, we have to do something, we have to—'

'Interview?' Then he remembered the equipment he had seen in their bedroom.

'He agreed to it. Though he didn't want his face to be shown on camera.'

'You mean you have this recorded?'

She nodded.

'Wait, let's think this through,' he said, shaking his head. He couldn't make sense of it. Why had Mia come to Felicity? What had he missed? The Ambassador would certainly not be happy about Felicity having anything to do with Mia. He would be accused of indiscretion. He needed time to think.

'Perhaps you had better let me talk to Nigel about it. This is delicate,' he said, 'and it's better if I try to explain. It's a matter of national security, after all. It's an Embassy employee who's involved. I'll consult him about how to proceed, whom we approach with this story first.' He paused to search her face, prepared to see her object, but she seemed grateful. He saw how much she believed that he would do as he said.

The clerk opened a fridge door which had Mia's father's name written on it. She saw her own feet reflected in the steel glare of it. The tray was rolled out. The edges of plastic casing had been dirtied with ash. He pulled back the sheet, revealing his toes first, and she turned her face.

His face had the purplish texture of discarded grape skins. He had no eyelashes. His eyes were closed. His mouth hung open a little, his lips invisible. His teeth gleamed, a shock of white among the darkness. It did not seem possible that this was her father. The charred body looked plastic. How long had he been conscious, alight? Had he flung himself on the ground to fight the fire? She had never known him to rage against anything. He had always seemed so peaceful, only ever troubled in his sleep. Had he walked among the flames, stroking his fate? She gripped the edges of the sheet. Why did she have to mourn this man who always eluded her? He who never fought for anything, never resisted.

She tried to remember the last time she had spoken to her father or even acknowledged his presence. Nothing surfaced. The ash version of him would permanently dominate all other versions of him in her memory.

This was all that remained. Hyun-min gone. The tunnel gone. Hundreds of letters between loved ones, lost.

Her father, gone.

She stood before him, suddenly on fire. Unbearably thirsty. She staggered back into the corridor, not caring what she set alight in her path. She could only think of one way to extinguish the burn.

They released Kyung-ha into a changed world. She walked among the commuters, whose faces held purgatory as they waited for the news. The tension in the city was palpable. Long queues formed in stores. Other stores had closed. People fought one another as they bought water, rice, staples. On the bus back to her brother-in-law's house she heard the radio announcer reporting that the won had already devalued in anticipation of the war. They passed groups of people buying large suitcases. Many living in the north of the city had already begun crossing the river before it was too late to do so. Every day the war was postponed the more anxious people became.

Kyung-ha felt no sense of impending loss. But she also did not feel the lightness of confession that she had anticipated either. She had hoped that by telling the NIS what she had done, she would be liberated from the suffocation of her secret at last.

It was two o'clock in the morning when Thomas decided that it was time to go home. He walked out towards the garage, hit by the shock of cold. Checking his watch, he realized that he was due back in only a few hours to meet the delegate who was flying in from England for the investigative commission of the incident. There would be a briefing and then the following day, the meetings would begin. But now all he could think about was the nagging question he had been trying to set aside in his mind all evening. Why had Mia gone to Felicity? What had he missed?

He would have to tell the Ambassador somehow. It was clear that it had to be done. But how would he explain the way that Felicity had come across the evidence? It was delicate. What would they do with it? Take it to the CIA for assessment? The NIS? Back to London? Felicity was eager to hand over the story to the media. Perhaps if they could work together this time. Leak the story after they had had a chance to assess it.

Despite the nagging feeling that gnawed at him, he tried to persuade himself that this could only work in his favour. The evidence could prevent a war. He thought of the statistics he had read. Twenty million people in the greater Seoul area. Calculated casualties of at least half as many. With it being one of the coldest winters in decades, analysts had predicted that many of those who might avoid death in the conflict could freeze to death.

He shivered and picked up his steps. A panel of light flickered over his car so that he did not see the figure at first. It was only as he scratched at the lock with the key that he saw the movement out of the corner of his eye.

He felt drawn to the shadow which hid a silhouette illuminated intermittently by the artificial lightening overhead.

He hardly recognized her at first. The rise of her swollen cheekbones over her thinned face. A vision of the old woman she would one day become.

'Mia?'

'It's impressive, considering what it's been through,' she said, running her hand over the bonnet of the car, hardly looking at him at all.

She kept moving so he could not draw any closer, half concealing her face, so that the full horror of her appearance, coupled with the realization of what he had done, would not haunt him until much later. 'Mia—'

'You'd never guess what it's been through. It really was in a mess.'

'What happen—'

'I guess you think that your report has won you immunity from this?'

'What report?' he said.

'I know about the audit.'

He could think of nothing to say.

'I've known about it for a while.' She paused as if waiting for a response. 'I don't know what you wrote in the report, but I'm sure the Ambassador will be interested in what I have to say.'

'How did you—'

'I'm not here to talk about the audit.' She came towards him.

He didn't move.

She pulled out his mobile from his trouser pocket.

'I don't care about your report. There's only one thing that I want.'

'What is it?'

'Call your wife.'

'What have you told her?'

'Call your wife.' She pressed her weight against him. 'Tell her about me.'

'She told me that you came to her.'

Mia said nothing for several moments.

'Call her or I'll call the Ambassador. He'll want to know about the car, the report, the state of you.'

He hesitated, knowing which was the easier sacrifice to make.

'Call her,' she repeated. 'I want to hear how you describe me.'

He heard the ringtone. The pulsating heartbeat of it. There would be no way to negotiate the situation with the Ambassador, he would not forgive the mistake. Their involvement would arouse suspicion. Would he be accused of being complicit? The NIS would involve him in the investigation.

'Tom? What time is it?' He could tell by Felicity's voice that she had been asleep. 'What is it? What did Nigel say?'

'Felicity . . .'

'What is it?'

He heard her holding her breath. He stole a glance at Mia. She lit a cigarette, her eyes drawn in concentration, almost uninterested.

'Flick . . . ' he said.

'What is it? What did Nigel say?'

'I'm not with Nigel.'

There was a pause.

'There's something I should tell you,' he began. He stole another glance at Mia. She raised her eyebrows, expectant. 'I think I may know why Mia came to you with the story.' He swallowed. 'Nigel asked me to write an audit report. He thought security had been compromised. He suspected her.'

'You mean that you were working—'

'On an investigation.'

There was a pause.

Mia's eyes were venomous – she wanted more.

'I got too involved. What I'm . . . I haven't always been honest. I've been . . .' He paused again. 'I haven't always been faithful.'

There was a long pause. He could hear her breathing on the other end of the line.

'Have you spoken to Nigel?'

'No, I—'

'I should have left you to rot in Phnom Penh,' she said, and hung up.

Mia walked among the ruins. The hole in the roof opened up to a patch of grey sky. Her bedroom had collapsed into the living room. It was as if she were taking a glimpse into the future. There were talks of air strikes. A counter-strike from the North would follow. She walked into what remained of the living room and looked back, half expecting to see her father sitting on the tree stump by the gate. Wood snapped beneath her shoes. Splinters scratched at her ankles. The wreckage was damp and had frozen overnight. What had not been damaged by the fire had been destroyed by water. Mia brushed away a charred sheet of wallpaper.

How strange that she should be here, kicking over remains of broken paintbrushes, the black, frail edges of paper. A door hung on a single set of blackened hinges. She walked through a standing doorframe, to what was left of her father's room. A space that she had once considered so small, so confining, now, in his absence, spread itself large. She had once wanted to be released from this home and now she was searching for something that hadn't been destroyed.

Mia took the lid off a burned box. Inside she found a black-and-white photograph. It was a version of her father that she wished she could remember. It had been recovered from employee records at the University. In his youth he had had a square jaw, a large forehead.

Already then his hairline had begun to recede. These were the things that remained of her father. Was this what was left of people? What would remain of her after death? It was not in places that people left residues of themselves, it was in the way they were remembered by other people.

Had Hyun-min made it to the other side? They had not recovered his body from the rubble. She liked to think that he had made it across. She tried not to think of how he felt about the North and how it had ceased to be home for him. What had he been thinking when he struck the match and set the tunnel alight? Did he believe that she had betrayed him?

She turned back to see that Charles was watching her from the street. 'How long have you been there?' she asked him.

He looked down at his feet, as though he were ashamed. 'I'm very sorry about your father. I lost mine when I was very young. He had been ill for a while. I can't say I know how it feels, given your circumstances.'

She stepped over what was left of the kitchen door, towards him. 'Thanks.'

There seemed little more to say.

'Why are you still here? Shouldn't you be back in Whitehall by now?'

'With things the way they are, they've asked me to stay on a little longer, to see how the situation is going to resolve itself,' Charles said. 'Mia, things are really escalating here. I'm worried about you—'

'I can take care of myself,' she said quickly. She was still clinging to the hope that she had sufficiently provoked Felicity to act.

Charles opened his mouth to say something and then seemed to decide against it. Instead he gave her the large envelope he had been holding in his hands. 'I came to give you the audit report.'

She flipped through the pages and realized that despite his flippant manner, Charles had put himself at considerable risk. She didn't know what to say.

'I could be sacked for this.'

'I know. Thank you,' she said. 'Have you read it?'

He nodded. 'It's fantastical stuff. Perhaps it will break your illusions about the man.'

She nodded, uncertain suddenly of what else Charles was about to say.

'I'm not so bright,' he said. 'Handing it over to you like this. I should be bargaining with you.'

'What do you mean?'

'If the situation continues to escalate there'll be an evacuation at the beginning of next week. I can get you out of here, if you'll say you'll come with me to England.'

'I'm under surveillance, Charles. They're not going to just let me leave the country.'

'If there's a war the NIS will have far more pressing things to worry about. In any case, you don't have to worry about that. If that's your main concern, let me handle it. I can speak to the NIS. We'll call it an exile. It sounds terribly romantic, doesn't it?'

'Leave? To England?' She didn't know what to think. She thought of her uncle. Of Kyung-ha. It wasn't the way she had pictured going to England. In exile.

'Don't answer now. I want you to think about it for a couple of days. But don't wait too long, there are arrangements we'll need to make.'

Kyung-ha came into the living room and found her brother-in-law talking earnestly with Mia, his hand gripping her elbow as if to stop her from turning away from him.

'You should go,' he said.

In the days that had followed their release, the three of them had inhabited her brother-in-law's house in silence, as though the war was something that could be sparked by the sound of their voices. None of them discussed their respective interrogations. They avoided speaking to each other unless it was strictly necessary, wary of each other, as if they were each conscious of having already said too much.

The girl looked ashamed and avoided looking at either of them.

'What's going on? Go where?' Kyung-ha asked.

'Someone from the Embassy has offered to evacuate her with the British nationals when the time comes.'

'It won't . . .' Mia looked stricken. 'No, it can't get to that.'

'Are you watching this news? Do you hear how many helicopters and jets are flying over our heads every night? You think this is just a military exercise?' Han-su's face grew sombre. 'Don't worry about us. You should leave while you have the chance.'

It took Kyung-ha a moment to fully understand the implication of this. When she looked up to see the girl's face, she was shocked to see something she had never seen before. How much the girl resembled her father. She had his jutting ears, the square lines of his face. Suddenly she was flooded with regret. She had never been able to protect the girl. She had never tried, because the girl grew in ways that seemed beyond her control. The girl always landed on her feet. The girl hadn't needed her.

Now she saw for the first time what she had to do.

'You have to go, where you belong,' she said softly. 'We don't owe each other anything. We're not even really family.'

Han-su frowned. 'You've had a shock, with the fire and losing Jun-su like that, but that's too harsh—'

'It's the truth,' she said, calmly. She had to sever the bond between them. Free the girl. She was still young, still unbroken. She could begin anew. 'I did many things to punish myself. I punished myself by taking you in. Every time I saw you I was reminded of that white woman and all of Jun-su's other women. I lost a son and I've been raising a foreigner. Do you know what it's been like to smell that whiteness every day, to see over and over again the selfishness in your blood?'

Then she saw that she had finally broken something in the girl.

'Is that all you can say? After all these years, have you no feeling? No heart? Can you not see me? Can you not see how much I've needed you?' The girl was crying. 'If you could have just reassured me for a moment that I was okay the way I was, but you were always telling me there was something wrong with me, that I was a different breed, that I am like my mother. You know what? I don't even know her. All this hatred and self-loathing I've learned from you.'

Kyung-ha had not expected the turn in conversation.

'If you had just once reassured me, just once been a mother to me. You couldn't even bring yourself to visit me when I was in hospital . . . was I so hard to love? Did I ask for so much? Can't you see that if you asked me to, I would stay, whatever that might mean here?'

Kyung-ha didn't know what to say. She had spent so many years seeing the lightness of the girl's hair, her tall, otherworldly angular frame. She had spent so long focusing on how different the girl was from everything that she had known that she had ended up believing that Mia belonged somewhere else too. She had kept the girl at arm's length for many reasons, not least because she always seemed ready to leave, but also partly because she would not endure any more losses. Kyung-ha had always assumed that the girl's coldness was a feature of her Englishness – something that had been transferred in blood. Yet she began to see how she might have pushed the girl away. But now was not the moment to weaken. She needed to send the girl off.

'You think I cared for your father and you because I'm a good person? I told them and I'll tell you both. I was the one who had your father arrested. I was the one who had him broken. I called the KCIA and told them he was a spy. We'd lost a son and all he cared about were his politics, his women. How could he screw around, when I'd lost everything? I wanted to take it all from him. I did the devil's work, do you understand?'

'What are you talking about?' said the girl, alert.

'That's the kind of woman I am. I break people. So go when you have the chance. There's nothing worth staying here for.'

She could see from the girl's face that finally she been able to reach her. She had said the damaging words at last. Han-su sank into a chair behind him, his hand trembling on his knee.

'Can you still say that you think of me as family? After that?' No one said anything. 'So let's not feel obliged to one another anymore.'

The streets were eerie in their desertion. Filled with the quiet that accompanied snowfall. There were no cars on the roads. The exodus had already begun. Many in the north side of the city had now crossed down to the south. Mia walked around the ghostly city, numbed by the cold, poised to be shattered, but later.

She walked past City Hall and sat on the edge of the road, in front of the statue of General Lee Soon-shin. She removed the audit report that Charles had given her from the envelope and began to read.

When she had finished, she understood something that she had not understood before about Hyun-min. When he walked towards an oasis in a desert only to find it to be an illusion he could no longer trust the very ground he trod on. He had built up the pedestal because he longed to escape and when he realized the destination was a mirage he felt there was nowhere left to go.

'This investigation is redundant if the government is already gearing up for an air strike. The least we could do is be given more time to explore the evidence . . .' Jenkins, the silver-haired delegate from Whitehall, rolled the edges of the paper of the jotting pad in front of him between this thumb and index finger. He sat beside the Ambassador, who passed him a note. Jenkins nodded.

Thomas had been unable to get the Ambassador alone for a moment. He had been inseparable from Jenkins from the moment he had arrived. Thomas had been waiting for the right moment to take the Ambassador aside. He hesitated, in part, because he had been unable to reach Felicity. It would be easier for him to try to coax the evidence from her on his own, rather than to do so with the Ambassador's help. There was, after all, the possibility that she would mention his relationship with Mia.

'Let's not dress this up as something other than what it is. This pre-emptive strike is an opportunistic attempt to wipe out the North Korean regime and reunite the Koreas,' the Russian delegate said.

The Swedish delegate looked appalled. 'A pre-emptive strike is madness. The Chinese wouldn't stand for it. This could evolve into a war of global, thermonuclear proportions. I agree with Mr Jenkins:

we need more time. If war is an inevitability, why do we need to rush this? It's a diplomatic disaster for the South to strike first.'

'The evidence is inconclusive, in any case,' the Australian delegate offered.

'The evidence is pretty self-explanatory,' the American delegate countered.

'We can't rule out the possibility that it was just an accident. A gas leak. Perhaps sparked by an old landmine from the war?'

'The South Korean government seem adamant that that isn't the case.'

'It's not insignificant that the North Koreans have offered their own investigative team. There's no precedent of that in previous conflicts. We should take this seriously,' the Australian delegate said.

'They've ruled out every possibility other than the one of conspiracy to provoke a war of aggression.'

Thomas checked his phone again. Where was Felicity? With every hour that passed, fear grew inside him. He was exactly where he had been before. The Ambassador had warned him there would be no more mistakes. He looked across the room to consider his options. Several beeps echoed throughout the room. Phones began to ring. A clerk rushed into the room, leaned over the Ambassador and whispered in his ear.

Moments later the clerk appeared by his side. 'Mr Dalton-Ellis?'

'Yes?'

'The Ambassador would like to speak to you in the lobby, sir, please come with me.'

As Thomas followed the clerk through the conference room and into the lobby, the television screen caught his eye.

On the screen Felicity stood in front of what appeared to be a cave and then led the camera down a dark passage, all the while explaining that it was a tunnel that connected the two Koreas. In the darkened light, a figure stood against the wall of the tunnel. It was impossible to make out his face.

Thomas heard Felicity's voice again. 'You say no one else knows about this tunnel?'

There was a third voice, an interpreter, who spoke directly to the interviewee. That voice also sounded familiar, but he couldn't quite believe it was Mia's.

'No. No authorities. Only my roommate, my friend Myung-chul, knew about it. He had the burden of being a messenger across the border.'

'What do you mean by "messenger"?'

'He delivered letters for families. Money too.'

'Where is he now?'

'He's dead.' There was a pause. 'He hanged himself.'

Felicity's voice was softer. 'Why do you think he did that?'

'The pressure of it got to him.'

There was a pause.

'I imagine that some would say that it is a privileged position that even money can't buy. To be able to go back and forth between the two countries—'

The interpreter had not yet finished translating when the young man began to speak.

'Next you will say something about the best of both worlds. But that "privilege" comes at a price. It's hardest for those of us who live between nations and who know what it's like on the other side. We suffer the sorrows of each side. We live between loyalties, we are homeless.'

'I'm sure many defectors must think this tunnel is a good thing.' Thomas swallowed hard. The Ambassador would think that he had tipped Felicity off. Would he suspect Thomas of knowing more than he let on? Or would he be viewed with incompetence for not knowing what his wife did? He had been betrayed by everybody.

'. . . I don't think it should exist. If it were up to me, this tunnel wouldn't exist,' the voice in the shadows was saying. 'When things like this are hidden and underground, we create myths about the other side. People are hurt and exploited.'

The announcer returned to the screen. 'This has sparked a new turn in the investigation of the recent explosion at the border, as new evidence suggests that it was the result of the act of a lone individual rather than as a calculated act of war or provocation by the North Korean government.'

'I wouldn't say it's over just yet,' Charles said. 'But it doesn't look like there's going to be a war tomorrow. They're certainly not speaking of going through with the evacuation in any case.'

Mia nodded. On the other side of the road, a bus driver honked and cursed at the traffic. Several school children ran out of a small corner shop holding hands. Slowly, the city had begun breathing again.

'How are things with the NIS?'

'As you can imagine, there are some heads rolling. That report made them look like amateurs. The head of the NIS is furious that some foreigner had evidence that no one internally could get their hands on. Not to mention who it was.'

Mia smiled a little.

'I had hoped you might come with me even if it weren't an evacuation,' Charles said.

She shook her head. 'I can't do that.'

'You'd rather stay, living like this? With spooks watching your every move? Who knows how long you'll be under surveillance? Years? They'll take you in every time there's a crisis and interrogate you for information you won't have.'

Reading the audit report that Charles had given her, it had felt as though she were reading about someone else's life. She read about her father's career as a communist lecturer, about his prison sentence for the conviction of being a North Korean spy and spreading communist propaganda. The report had concluded that it was not yet clear whether he was working for Pyongyang or not. She had tried to remember the last time she had sat with her father and enjoyed his reticence. She had underestimated him. She had interpreted his silence as a state of peace. Now she wondered whether his silence was an inability to translate horror into words.

She had learned that her mother was alive. *Madelaine Carlton is a professor of anthropology at the University of Surrey.* In believing she was dead, Mia had been able to forgive her. But she was alive. She had been shocked to be reading her own history in another's words. The portrait Thomas had composed of her with his prose was ugly. He described her as closed, secretive, a spy across borders without loyalty to anyone and thus dangerous to everyone.

She had taken the report and had lit the corner of it with a lighter. At one time, the answer to the question mark of her past had been what she had wanted more than anything. She had not wanted the narrative that had been written by Thomas.

That was why she had to stay. 'I won't let them bully me.'

Charles looked at her in disbelief. 'What will you do for work?'

'I've decided to work for my uncle.'

Charles let out an exasperated sigh. 'You don't play it safe, do you?'

'It's just something I feel I have to do.' She did not tell him that it had to do with Hyun-min and what she felt she owed him.

'That sounds like a lonely undertaking.'

She could smell his aftershave. Part of her wanted to lean into it, close her eyes and put her head against his shoulder. 'I appreciate everything you've done for me. I do.'

'You'd rather live like this, than to come with me?'

'I didn't know that was your asking price.'

He took hold of her shoulder. 'That's not what I mean.' He shook his head sadly. 'I don't understand.' His expression changed as he looked at her, as though he realized something new. 'If you're worried . . . It's not my presumption that . . .'

She could see his breath in the cold air.

'We wouldn't have to be anything.'

'Wouldn't we?' she asked wearily. 'I don't want to be with you because I feel like I owe you.'

'It wouldn't have to be like that.' Then he seemed to reconsider. 'Couldn't it be some other way?'

She shook her head.

'I still don't understand why you would choose to stay here.'

'I've spent a lifetime wanting to go. Idealizing your country, hoping I might one day be a part of it. I'd love to go with you and pretend I'm one of you and hope that the day doesn't come when I realize that people see me as an exotic conquest that you've brought back with you from your time in Asia.'

'Is that really how you think of me?' His face hardened. 'That's not fair. I'm not Thomas.'

She knew that much was true. She embraced him suddenly. His body tensed in surprise before relaxing against her.

She watched Charles become small against the landscape, the edges of the streets dirtied with old snow. He had the heavy footfall of the defeated. A surrender in the tap of his heel against the slush. He half turned at the end of the road, but did not fully look back to see her still watching his resignation of her.

He woke to the sound of glass being swept from the floor. The bar was empty, the dimmed lights, brightened. He was still gripping a tumbler of whisky in his hand. He tipped the last of it into his mouth and checked his watch. It was three in the morning.

'I'd like another,' he said, to the bartender.

The bartender took the glass from his hand. 'We closed now. Taxi?'

'No. Don't bother.'

He stumbled into the street, feeling the slap of cold air against his face. He crawled into a taxi. The driver waited patiently for him to name a destination. He felt the pull of her across the city. An addict drawn back to old habits.

'*Mapo*,' he said.

He watched the desolate streets pass him. The city never slept, yet it felt empty.

If his report had been a fantasy, who was she? This enigma who had cost him his career. He could not bring himself to consider that he had sent an innocent woman for interrogations. It wasn't as though he had fabricated evidence that simply wasn't there. His conscience stalked his attempt to evade his doubts. That he hadn't been thorough. That he had been a coward. In the end, he returned to the same question: Who was this woman he thought he had fallen in love with? He had held her in his arms and she had dissolved in them.

He crawled out of the taxi, thumbing over more notes to the driver than necessary. The market was packed up for the night. He walked towards the apartment, beneath the hanging neon signs advertising computer rooms, DVD rooms, where others hid from their lives.

The stairwell was damp. Paint came off onto his fingers as he held onto the wall. He knew he would be met with a vacant space but he imagined for a moment that she might be sitting on the windowsill, waiting. He felt his heart lift at the thought.

The door was open. He walked through the police tape into the darkness.

Mia put her hand over his as he reached for the light switch. She had been unmoving, poised, coiled and ready to strike. She wanted him only in the darkness. He would not be studying her this time.

As he turned towards her, she swung her fist and caught his cheek. Falling forward, he had her against the counter. A glass rolled off and shattered near her feet. He held her by the wrists in the same place her interrogators had done. His breath was sour and thickly sweet with the smell of whisky. She would have preferred him sober. She held him back with her forearm against his throat. Thrust him further into the darkness.

She saw his outline, shuffling in the darkness. He wiped something off his jaw and groaned. She swung her fist in his direction, but hit a chair instead. She heard a crack and wasn't immediately sure whether it was her hand or the wood that had broken. He backed away from her, around the futon. They stood frozen for several moments, catching their breaths. Then he came towards her, his hands on her face. She hit him again. There was honesty in it. The flight of a fist, the sting of his skin – none of it tapering the burn. He was not intent on attacking her. He was not defending himself.

He kissed her.

She was slow to resist him.

Then she pushed him to the floor and held him there. She saw even then he was certain that she would not hurt him. He was so assured of his world and the things that he knew. She ripped his shirt out of his trousers; stripped him so that he was naked. All the while he seemed to believe it to be an elaborate opening to the grand finale. She shredded the sheets. Bound his hands together. She felt for his heartbeat in his chest. Clawed his skin. If he was afraid, the only hint of it was in his timid penis, withdrawn in a small curl against his thigh. She lay on him, the full weight of her body against his chest.

'Aren't you afraid of me?' she asked him.

'I suppose I should be. I don't know who you are.'

'I thought you knew all about me. Isn't that what you wrote in the audit report?'

She hit him again. He groaned. She slid back and sat upright, straddling him, her hands around his throat.

'You had all those Embassy documents. What was I supposed to think?'

Her nails dug into his neck. 'All the while, you had no problem fucking me.'

'I didn't know about them then. I was confused by what I was feeling for you, I was falling in love with you.' His face was strained with the tension.

She released him, no longer famished, no longer intent on disassembling him. The idea that he had fallen in love was farcical. How could he love what he did not know? He loved a mirage. He gasped for breath. She saw she had expected too much. She was as bad as he was. All this time she had aspired to have his confidence, to acquire his refinement, but above all to understand the customs and turns of phrases and the world of nouns which had excluded her. She was seeking in him the reasons why even her own mother had abandoned her.

His breaths began to slow and became even. He wrestled against the bondage of his wrists and tried to sit upright. She would not let him get comfortable, would not let him lie down or sit. Instead, she drew closer to him. Put her hand to his cheek, not quite apologetic. Even as she kissed him, she was on the verge of biting him. He was still hungry. Wrapping herself around him, she made him small inside her. She wanted to be satisfied, but felt nothing. She rocked on top of him, trying to find something to ease the dissatisfaction. She forgot him. He had fallen from his pedestal, suddenly disposable. The orgasm was like a knot inside her being tightened and then released. She knew then why she had postponed it. Because of the fall. The hollow that awaited her thereafter.

She sat watching him from the window, smoking to the very tip of her cigarettes. He opened his eyes. It was dawn, the morning light reluctant.

'Where will you go after this? Washington? Paris?'

'Who knows? After all this.'

'How good it must be for you. You can move from place to place, looking down on other ways of life. You've never been rattled in your convictions. You're so sure of your values. Your view of the world is so simple. You see Hyun-min and you think of only the stories that you're told about suffering on your terms. You think of North Korea and you think of war and weapons and cruelty. If you get to thinking about those lives, it's only to measure those them by your standards. You don't imagine the worth of them. Do you know what Hyun-min went through? He was torn between two sides whose flaws he saw equally. All I've wanted was to be sure of your way of life in the way that you're sure of it. I wanted the confidence of your language. That's why I had those reports. Who do you suppose I have loyalties to? Who would I possibly leak those turns of phrase to?'

'You were evasive, you didn't tell me anything.'

'You wouldn't have seen the truth even if I handed it to you.'

He sat up on the futon as she said this and his mouth gaped open as if in protest.

'Let's not talk anymore,' she said. 'When we talk we misunderstand each other.' She was still looking at him, but she was no longer searching.

He came to her by the window, kneeled before her.

'I'm sorry,' he said, simply, dumbly, hesitant to touch her.

She put her fingers in his hair, as if to comfort him.

'We could have a life together,' he said. 'We could leave, go somewhere where we could begin again.'

She wanted to believe him. This was another fantasy, a seduction of words. Even after everything, she knew that betrayals were embedded in the language she knew and he did not. There would always be a part of her that he would not understand and would remain hidden from him. She would read meanings in his words that he did not intend and she would live in disappointment when he did not fully grasp the meaning of hers.

There was just enough light to see his outline, the wilderness of his hair. She didn't recognize him anymore.

Kneeling before her, his eyes fell on her wrists, still raw and bruised from her incarceration. He stared at them for a long time. Then he began to weep.

Like a man who had not wept since his boyhood.

'You should eat something,' her stepmother said, setting a tray down beside her. A cup of steaming black herbal medicine and a bowl of abalone porridge. Luxurious nourishment they could not afford. Since they had been reunited at her father's small funeral, they had forced themselves to talk occasionally, careful not to mention Hyun-min or her father. Some nights they stayed up late and watched dubbed, American television shows where mothers openly wept and hugged their daughters. On others her stepmother would read her passages from the Bible. Mostly, they avoided talking about the future.

Kyung-ha reached for the Bible and held it near her eyes. She read a passage about widows and orphans. Then she fell quiet, but her face was full of things left unsaid. The gestures felt eerie in the apologies they contained. Mia felt them like a blunt knife held against the sinew that kept them together. It was the only reason, aside from the minor annoyance of being under surveillance, that she had given Charles's offer any serious thought. In truth she couldn't imagine leaving. She thought of Hyun-min. Of the fantasies held in crossing borders. The hopes that one pinned on other places. New land brought new struggles. New ambiguities.

Her stepmother had an unfamiliar look on her face.

'You need to eat something. Your face is the size of a pod. I'm not going to let you starve to death, if that's what you're trying.'

'I'm not hungry,' she said.

Yet her stepmother persisted in trying to feed her, though her own hands had become bony, her hair snowy white from the interrogations. A fallen Titan; breakable and no longer immortal.

'I'll leave it here. Try,' her stepmother said, standing up. She opened the door to leave the room. 'Pack a bag. We'll take your father's ashes to the countryside tomorrow.'

They took the bus to Gwangju. The women in the row of seats behind them chattered throughout the journey, sharing clementines and other fruits, while Mia propped her head against the window and pretended to sleep.

They left their bags at the inn and began their hike. They walked through the cold in silence, their footsteps loud in the crunch of fresh snow. They stopped by a naked maple tree, feeling the winds slicing at their faces. From that height they could see nothing but frozen rice paddies and the rugged horizon of snow-capped mountains in the distance.

Mia took the wooden box from her bag. She sat with it on her lap for a few moments before breaking the seal. A breeze lifted ash into the sky. Mia put her hand in the box and released her father's ashes to the wind. She and her stepmother sat against a large boulder and watched the landscape before them.

'Mia-ya,' Kyung-ha began. 'I'm sorry . . .'

Mia said nothing, afraid of what her stepmother would say next.

'I spent so long with my own grief and hate, I don't know what love is anymore.'

She waited for her stepmother to say more, sure that she was about to be abandoned, but she said no more. Several minutes later, her stepmother stood up and they began their descent.

The room they shared at the inn that night had a naked light bulb hanging by a thin wire from the ceiling. Mia rolled out the futons as Kyung-ha turned away from her to change. She left the hemp ribbon of mourning in her hair. They lay under blankets that smelled of raw earth. The scents of the countryside came to them in the slide of wind under the thin door to their room. Kyung-ha lay on her side, her face turned away from Mia in the dark.

'Will you look for your mother when you go to England?' Kyung-ha asked suddenly.

Mia imagined her mother moving through her home, beckoned by the ringing telephone, expecting a colleague or a friend and instead speaking to a voice from a discarded past. She imagined the brief lowering of the receiver, her mother's worried glance towards her family sitting in the other room. Mia stayed awake thinking of the stories her mother might tell to explain her absence. As an anthropologist, perhaps she would speak of spirit possession, which had occurred while she had studied the Korean shamans. Or of a prolonged quarantine following the diagnosis of some exotic, contagious illness. She imagined these alternate histories, though she knew the truth was likely to be much more mundane.

'No,' she said, simply.

'There's something I never told you,' her stepmother began. She turned to lie on her back and Mia could just about make out the outline of her face, the gentle cliff of her nose. 'When you were in hospital, I came to see you every day.'

Mia opened her eyes. The only light came from the soft glow of the lamplight from the street.

'I never made it beyond the door. I lost my son when he was very young. I couldn't put myself through that again.'

She held her breath. She sensed that her stepmother was about to sever the artificial cord that had bound them together. After all, it was as she had said. There was nothing left binding them together.

'I haven't done much for you . . . I know that.'

She could not bring herself to deny it.

'I'm old. You shouldn't feel obliged.'

'Just say what you're going to say,' Mia said, irritated. Her stepmother had never had trouble speaking before.

'You insolent girl, can't you see that's what I'm trying to do? I'm no good with words. Isn't that one of your disappointments with me? That I could never tell you with words what you want to hear? It isn't easy for me.'

Her stepmother's breaths became deep and long. Mia wondered whether she had fallen asleep. It took her a while to realize that Kyung-ha's deep breaths were not signs of slumber, but a suppression of sobs.

'What if you didn't go to England?'

'What are you saying?'

The silence of an entire winter's snow fell between them. After what seemed like hours, her stepmother said: 'I'm asking you to stay.'

Mia thought she had heard incorrectly. There seemed nothing she could say in response to this. She had been so sure that she would be discarded. She had never considered there could be anything more than *jeong* between them. Or, perhaps, she had misunderstood what *jeong* was. Perhaps it was more than an-attachment-whether-you-like-it-or-not and there had been more binding them together all along. Tragedies, she decided, lived in all words, unearthed by interpretations, buried by others; it was only a matter of translation. She imagined how she would translate *jeong* now. A relationship that begins as an obligation, but then becomes love.

She turned to her stepmother in the darkness. They were separated like islands on their respective futons, the distance between them like a river, the distance between them once so great that it seemed insurmountable. She wanted to say that she would stay, but could not. Instead she reached across that divide, reached across those years that had separated them.

She squeezed her stepmother's hand. It was bonier than she expected. It no longer seemed believable that such a small person could have incurred such fear and exerted so much power. Her stepmother was neither unbreakable nor immortal.

She was all the home she had left in the world.

2009

Spring

Thomas splashes his face with water. The basin in the toilet is so small that the act leaves his feet in a tepid pool. It has been months and still he cannot adjust to the African heat. He can never quite get himself clean. He dries his face with a towel and enters the small room.

At the window he looks out over the Embassy compound. Behind him, Felicity's voice is a familiar companion, speaking of the latest civilian casualties in Iraq. He turns off the television and sits in silence. There are no journalists left in Africa. They have all followed the news in the Middle East. He changes into his third shirt of the day and leaves for the hospital, as he does every evening, where he drinks whisky with Seamus, a taciturn doctor who has lived in the town for over twenty years.

He takes his bicycle down the red dirt path, conscious always of his whiteness. A stray dog, dingo-like, greets him at the stairs of the hospital. He enters the ward, where he practises phrases on the patients; mostly it makes them laugh. They think of him a hero because he visibly suffers the humiliations of learning their language, infant-like, looking at the world anew, learning to name things. He does nothing to try to correct them. He tries not to think about the individual purgatory on many of the patients' faces, some of whom have diseases that will be with them all their lives. He is aware of his own fraudulence, the way he does not correct their opinion of him as a generous man, when the real reason he is here is because of the lack of decent bars and decent company in this small city.

He sits and waits for Seamus on a balcony, watching the sun's descent. The unfamiliar terrains of the continent no longer call to him. He has become attached to an enigma that has nothing to do with foreign lands. He feels the loneliness of the only acacia tree in the desert on the horizon. He must keep moving. In these moments of quiet, he becomes conscious of the vast gulf he has to cross to her.

Everywhere he goes, he is haunted by her. This woman he thought he had loved but whom he had never really known.

Mia picks up after her students in the empty classroom and drops the pens and pencils into an old coffee can on her desk. It is the end of another long week extracting reluctant smiles from her pupils. She postpones her journey home; only a quiet dinner awaits her. She pulls out a pack of cigarettes from her worn red handbag and puts one in her mouth, lighting it by the window. Her uncle will scold her for this, but the spring is slow to come and it is still too cold to go outside.

The mess of signs hanging from the buildings advertise English-language schools, a plastic surgeon's private practice and herbal weight-loss clinics. Everyone in the city seems to live on borrowed hopes. In these quiet moments she can hear the echo of Hyun-min's voice in the tunnel. She tries not to see his face among her students as she looks up from the textbook, breaking the chalk in her hand with surprise every time. She tries not to think of him standing in the darkness, a box of matches in his unsteady hands. How long did he stand there before striking that first spark? She imagines the weariness heavy on his shoulders, his exhaustion not from walking so far underground, but because he has run for so long without hope, when all he had wanted was a voice, to be heard, not to have to speak for a nation, but as a boy navigating the unfamiliar terrain of a world beyond his imagination. She longs to be able to look away as she sees, in her mind's eye, over and over again, that sudden brightness, that electric dance of the body set alight.

Does being in one place mean turning your back on the other for ever? Though she does not think of Thomas, she wonders whether someone can ever sever themselves entirely from the past. She does not care to imagine how he lives now, but he has left a spectre that lingers in her present. The past is like a lost limb with phantom itches in the night. Even now her memory betrays her as she reaches for Thomas's shoulder in her sleep.

Outside, a man blows hot breaths into his hands as he sits on a bench by the entrance of the hospital. She has not noticed them stepping on her heels in many months, but suspects that he is one of them. Their surveillance is a game to her. When she notices them, she will enter buildings through service entrances and leave through other exits. Check her watch on street corners with the anguished look of a woman being stood up by a lover. Speak briefly to strangers in busy crowds before resuming her hurried pace away from them.

Tapping out the glow of her cigarette, she packs her bag and switches off the classroom lights. On the street, the cold is a dull ache in her limbs. She steps onto the pavement and heads toward the subway, catching a glimpse of her pursuer in the side mirrors of parked cars. She looks in her bag to see what she can use. An empty envelope. She walks up to a stranger – an elderly man wearing a baseball cap. She puts the envelope in his weathered hands, ignoring his confused protests, and descends underground without looking over her shoulder.

She enjoys wasting their time, confusing those who follow her, those who still believe in borders, those strange lines drawn on maps by men.

Acknowledgements

I would like to thank Jon Riley and Rose Tomaszewska for their great enthusiasm for, and meticulous attention to, this book.

For their encouragement and commitment, I would like to thank David Godwin, Anna Watkins and Jonathan Myerson.

I am indebted to the diplomats who allowed me to interrogate their world and also to the following authors and books: Barbara Demick, *Nothing to Envy*; Carne Ross, *Independent Diplomat*.

I am grateful for, and owe a great deal to, my family – my mother, komo, Woojoo and my father – who have been unwavering in their support since the beginning of the writing process.

Last but not least, huge thanks to my trusted critic and love, Christopher Hallas, without whom this book would not have been written.